MARINE B: SBS

THE AEGEAN CAMPAIGN

MARINE B: SBS

THE AEGEAN CAMPAIGN

Ian Blake

First published in Great Britain 1995
22 Books, Invicta House, Sir Thomas Longley Road,
Rochester, Kent

Copyright © 1995 by 22 Books

The moral right of the author has been asserted

A CIP catalogue record for this book is available from the
British Library

ISBN 1 898125 38 4

10 9 8 7 6 5 4 3 2 1

Typeset by Hewer Text Composition Services, Edinburgh
Printed in Great Britain by Cox and Wyman Limited, Reading

Prelude

August 1943

The British Chiefs of Staff committee listened to the Prime Minister with a mixture of resignation and indignation. After more than three years at the helm the old man was still at it with his impossible schemes. Impossible on this occasion because their great American allies were not interested.

The First Sea Lord reminded the meeting that the navy's strength had been shifted from the eastern Mediterranean for the proposed invasion of the Italian mainland; the Chief of the Imperial General Staff remarked on the burden of the British commitment to the Italian campaign; the Chief of Air Staff just took his pipe from his mouth and shook his head.

Operation Accolade, however many attractions it may have had, was now impossible.

Churchill glared at them through his cigar smoke. The heat of a Canadian summer's day had not improved his temper and the Quebec Conference was turning out to be a wearing, knock-down affair. It had taken much argument before the Americans had finally agreed to increased British participation in the Pacific War and their scepticism of Churchill's policy of bringing Turkey into the conflict and striking at the guts of Germany through the Balkans, had remained undiminished.

The previous day at the conference the British contingent had raised the advantages of snatching the Italian-occupied Dodecanese Islands from under the noses of the Germans in order to encourage Turkish entry into the war. But the Americans had remained adamant: if the British wanted to pursue such a policy they could not stop them. But no help was to be expected from them, and there was to be no draining of resources from the great undertakings the Allies had jointly set in motion elsewhere.

In short, paddle your own canoe up shit creek. It had not been either a friendly or a successful session.

'Come, gentlemen,' said Churchill, 'we must have a special force capability in the Middle East which could move swiftly into these islands until regular troops can be sent to garrison them. The Italians are about to surrender. They are not going to oppose us. I need not remind you how great the rewards will be if Turkey – to whom the islands once belonged – can at last be brought into the war.'

The Chief of the Imperial General Staff reluctantly opened the file in front of him. As always, the brief given to him was meticulous in its detail and range. It covered every possibility, every Churchillian vagary.

'There is, Prime Minister. It is a unit called the Special Boat Squadron.'

There was a satisfied grunt. 'Good!' At last, the Prime Minister felt he was getting somewhere.

'It will need to be Special.' His joke fell flat. 'Who commands this body of men?'

The Chief of the Imperial General Staff glanced

again at his brief. 'An ex-SAS officer, Prime Minister. Named Jarrett.'

Another grunt of satisfaction. As an ex-First Lord of the Admiralty during the First World War as well as the Second, the Prime Minister knew the man's father well. The provenance of a good fighting man was as important as it was for a painting.

'And how do we transport Jarrett and his men?'

The bulldog face now fixed itself on the First Sea Lord, who pressed the tips of his fingers together and pursed his lips. He did not need to open the briefing file in front of him: he knew every word. Nevertheless, he hesitated. Should he argue, or should he not? His duty got the better of his common sense.

'I must protest, Prime Minister. Alone, we simply do not have the resources. The reaction of the Italian garrisons will be unpredictable and they have airfields on Rhodes which the Germans may well seize. They also have others on Crete. Our nearest airfield is on Cyprus. Air and ground reinforcements are easily available to the Germans from Athens and Crete. Most importantly, without air supremacy what naval forces we have will be in jeopardy.'

The other two Chiefs of Staff murmured their agreement. Regrettable as it was, without American support nothing could be done.

Churchill ignored them, and barked: 'What naval forces would be available?'

The First Sea Lord resigned himself. He had done his best. 'Currently perhaps half a dozen destroyers, nothing more.'

'But these could be reinforced when the opportunity arose?'

'Naturally, Prime Minister. But . . .'

3

'And there are coastal forces?'

The First Sea Lord nodded. In this mood he knew there was nothing that would stop Churchill. *He* certainly couldn't.

'Anything else?'

It was like squeezing blood from a stone, but the First Sea Lord said reluctantly: 'The Flag Officer Levant and Eastern Mediterranean informs me that in pursuance of your policy for capturing the Dodecanese – and in particular Rhodes – he has already formed a small naval raiding force. It is similar to one which has been mounting clandestine operations into these islands for some months and is therefore familiar with the area.'

'Its name?'

'It's called the Levant Schooner Flotilla, Prime Minister.'

'And this could transport special troops to the islands at short notice?'

The Admiral's sigh was audible. 'Yes, Prime Minister.'

The cherubic face beamed. 'There we are, then, gentlemen. Accolade can proceed. Another problem solved.'

And a larger one created.

1

The only sound was the slight slap of water on the canvas sides of the cockle as it slid up the dark tunnel of river. The paddles dipped silently. They left – for a second or two – small phosphorescent pools that glittered in the blackness, tell-tale signs for any alert German sentry.

It was like being moved inexorably into a cone of perpetual and impenetrable night. It pressed in on either side, squeezing the cockle forwards into a cul-de-sac, a trap from where it would be impossible to turn back, to even move.

He could feel the tingling sweat on his forehead, and beads of it ran from under his arms down his side. It was not the sweat of exertion but of fear, of knowing what would happen, of knowing there was nothing he could do about it.

Then, on cue, it did. The searchlight, the screaming siren, the shouts of '*Hände hoch! Hände hoch!*' and the high, frantic chatter of a machine-gun. Splinters flew up from the plywood deck of the cockle and he felt one pierce his cheek. Bullets struck the blade of his paddle and spun it out of his hand.

The cockle tilted and as it did so he saw fleetingly, but with awful clarity in the blinding light of the searchlight Matt's blackened face as the force of the bullets twisted his body round towards him: the dead eyes, the open mouth with its shattered teeth, the two small black holes in the forehead already seeping blood.

Then he was in the water under the cockle, and the water and the cockle and the darkness bore down hard on his chest with suffocating force. He thrashed out with his arms, but he seemed paralysed, already dead.

It was cold. Icy cold.

Sergeant Colin 'Tiger' Tiller, Royal Marines, woke, as he always did from this recurring nightmare, to find himself on the floor. He was bathed in sweat. He lay there for a moment, as he always did, taking in the fact that he wasn't dead, that he was lying on a cold stone floor in Eastney Barracks, Portsmouth, very much alive.

But Matt's face was still there in his mind's eye. He cursed silently and wondered if the nightmare would ever stop haunting him, would ever lessen in intensity with time. How could the unconscious retain such details so vividly? He didn't know and the surgeon commander, the only person he had ever told about his recurring nightmare, hadn't known either. The mind, the surgeon commander had said kindly, was still largely an unknown area to medical science. Otherwise, he had said cheerfully, Tiller was in good shape considering the prolonged ordeal he had been through. The nightmare would fade with time, he had said reassuringly. But it hadn't.

Tiller got up from the floor, staggered to the wash-basin, and slopped cold water into his face. Dawn was breaking, but the early-morning light of a late-summer day was only just beginning to show behind the blacked-out barracks window. Tiller shivered and threw a blanket over his bare shoulders, and sat on the bed. Another hour to go before reveille, but he wasn't about to go to sleep again.

He lit a cigarette and inhaled deeply. Slowly the intensity of the dream faded. He wondered if the inner trembling he felt showed outwardly. He held his hands out in front of him and was relieved to see they were as steady as a rock. He showered and dressed, had another cigarette, and walked over to the sergeants' mess for breakfast.

A squad of new recruits was already on the parade ground in front of the officers' mess. They looked a right shower, but he knew that within days they would be marching as one man, and within weeks efficient, self-contained, fighting units. The Corps, as the Royal Marines was called by everyone in it, did that to you. Tiller didn't know quite how it did it, but it did. Perhaps it was a mixture of fostering a man's pride in himself before taking him to what he thought was the limit of his endurance, and then deliberately pushing him beyond it. Whatever it was it worked.

In the sergeants' mess the buff envelope he had been expecting was waiting in his pigeon-hole. He tore it open and read through it as he sipped his tea.

'Movement order?' his mate, Ken 'Curly' Watson, asked.

Tiller nodded. He had been expecting it for days, ever since his CO, Major Henry 'Blondie' Tasler, had called him into his office and had said that Combined Operations had asked for a volunteer from the unit for special duties in the Middle East. The ideal candidate would be a senior NCO, a canoeist with operational experience who was trained in the latest explosives techniques.

'You seem to fit the bill, Tiger,' Major Tasler had said to Tiller. 'That is, if you can tear yourself away from the delights of Pompey,' and he had treated the sergeant to that wry smile of his.

The difference in rank between a major and a sergeant is large at the best of times. In the Marines it was a yawning chasm, but that did not stop the two having a healthy respect for one another based on knowing each other's strengths and weaknesses, and on appreciating the former while making allowances for the latter. They had fought together in that shambles of a campaign in Norway in 1940, where they had come to rely on each another totally, and had taken part together in the raid up the Gironde. So when the Royal Marines Office at the Admiralty had announced that volunteers were wanted for hazardous service, and that men were wanted who were 'eager to engage the enemy' and were 'free of strong family ties', Tiller had guessed that Tasler had been mixed up in it somewhere.

But before Tiller had even had time to respond to the call Tasler had approached him about volunteering. Right up his street, Tasler had assured him, though he couldn't tell him what it was about, of course. Because they knew each other so well Tiller also knew exactly to what – or rather to whom – the major was referring when he had asked his question about Tiller being able to drag himself away. He had been 'free of strong family ties' when he had first joined Tasler's unit, and had been determined to remain so. But somehow, he wasn't sure how, it had become increasingly difficult to stay that way . . .

Nothing, of course, had actually been said. But Tasler had not looked surprised when Tiller had replied immediately that he would go. Nor could the major keep his face entirely straight when Tiller had added fervently: 'Thank you, sir.'

But Tiller now read the movement order again with mixed feelings. Even in wartime, Pompey wasn't a bad place to be and being part of Tasler's secret organization made life more than usually interesting. Besides it was his home town, where he had grown up.

However, the hard fact was that, apart from the raid up the Gironde – the scene of Tiger's persistent nightmare – he had not seen any action since joining Tasler's organization, which had been formed to find different methods of raiding enemy shipping in harbour. There had been no more operations, just constant rumours of them. So the truth was – and he and Tasler both knew it – that, his little local personal difficulties apart, Tiller had been bored out of his frigging mind for some months and had been only too glad to volunteer. It was, after all, pointless knowing everything there was to know about explosives unless you could put that knowledge to good use.

But Athlit in Palestine? And this so-called Special Boat Squadron? What the hell was that? He shrugged. They were flying him out, so it must be operational, must be urgent. He felt a tremor of excitement run through him as he passed the movement order to Curly.

Curly and he had grown up together as kids, had both sat at the feet of Tiger's grandad, who told them tales of the action he had seen with the Marines in Burma and west Africa, and then in the Boer War. Curly knew all about the various special forces units that were fighting their own individual campaigns in the Middle East and the Mediterranean because, for a short while, he had served with the Special Boat Service under its founder, Major Roger Courtney.

'Is this the same outfit?' Tiller asked.

Curly scratched his head and said: 'Don't think so, as a lot of them were wiped out in a raid on Rhodes. We seem to have been trying to lay our hands on that place for most of the war. The rest were absorbed into Colonel Stirling's unit after Major Courtney came back here to form a second section. That's why I left. I like water, not the fucking desert. Remember the old ditty your grandad used to sing to us, Tiger?

> When years ago I listed, lads,
> To serve our gracious Queen,
> The Sergeant made me understand
> I was a Royal Marine.
> He said they sometimes served on ships
> And sometimes served on shore,
> But never said I should wear spurs
> And be in the Camel Corps.'

They both laughed. Tiller's grandad had been quite a character. He liked to entertain visitors by strumming on his banjo and singing various ditties he had picked up. It had been Tiller's grandad who had encouraged them both to join the Corps. Their dads had been pleased enough. But they hadn't shown it, of course – just said: 'You could do worse.'

As the great depression of the 1930s was then at its height – the Jarrow hunger march was splashed across all the newspapers – both young men knew they could have done a lot worse. It was Tiller's grandad who had sneaked them both into the pub to celebrate, though the landlord must have known neither of them was yet eighteen, and, to the embarrassment of the two young men, had entertained the saloon bar with a rendition of a poem by Rudyard Kipling.

'Do you remember when he took us to the local?' Tiller said to Curly. 'Thought I'd sink through the bleeding floor.'

'Two pints of beer, mate, and you were almost stretched out on it,' Curly replied with a chuckle. 'But he was that proud of you, Tiger, and of the Corps. What was that ditty he stood up and quoted about the Corps?'

Tiller knew it by heart, of course, for his grandfather had made him learn it all.

> ''E isn't one o' the reg'lar Line, nor 'e isn't one
> of the crew.
> 'E's a kind of giddy Harumfrodite – soldier an'
> sailor, too!
> For there isn't a job on the top o' the earth the
> beggar don't know,
> For you can leave 'im at night on a bald man's
> 'ead to paddle 'is own canoe –
> 'E's a sort of bloomin' cosmopolouse – soldier
> an' sailor, too.'

'That's the one.' Curly laughed and then indicated the movement order. 'Well, looks like you'll be paddling *your* own canoe again before long, mate.'

Tiller nodded but his mind was still back with his grandad and the time when he had been a raw recruit. His first months in the Corps all seemed a long time ago now, but he remembered how its rituals, its history, its traditions, had swallowed him whole. He had slept, eaten, and drunk it, and had loved every waking moment of it. A King's Badge man – first in his passing-out squad – and a crack shot who had represented the Corps at Bisley, he was, from the start, marked out for promotion.

In any other regiment – and that included those poofters in the Guards – he'd be a sergeant-major by now. But the wheels of the Corps ground slowly. NCOs, the corporals and sergeants, and colour-sergeants, were the backbone of the Corps and the Corps knew it. However good a man was, however thorough his training – and by Christ it was thorough – he still needed time to mature to become the kind of leader the Corps required – no, demanded.

Yes, the wheels ground slowly. And they ground very small. Tiller had never forgotten, as a small boy, the sight of his father on the parade ground, the scarlet sash of a colour-sergeant across his chest, the glitter of his medals and his buttons and his cap badge, the precision with which he had moved, the band thumping out the regimental march of the Corps, 'A Life on the Ocean Wave'.

Tiller knew he was as steeped in the traditions of the Royal Marines as a pickled onion was in vinegar, with their centuries-old connection with the Royal Navy. *Per Mare per Terram* was their motto, 'By land, by sea', and they were, as every recruit had drummed into him, the country's sheet anchor. That was how some admiring monarch – Tiller had forgotten which one – had described them, and they had battle honours that went back to the capture of Gibraltar in 1704.

Some of the young wartime conscripts – the HOs

or 'Hostilities Only' – had thought tradition and discipline, and the spit and polish that went with it, was all so much crap. But Tiller knew better. In battle a man had to rely on others and that reliance came from the parade ground.

'I must say I'd like to know more about this frigging outfit I've volunteered for,' Tiller said, his mind snapping back to the present.

'Can't help you there, Tiger. But I was told by my brother, who was in Cairo earlier this year, that Colonel Stirling's unit – the Special Air Service, it's called, or something like that – was split up after the colonel was captured. Perhaps it's an offshoot of that mob.'

Tiller had vaguely heard of Stirling and his recently formed Special Air Service. The SAS's desert exploits sounded like *Boys' Own Paper* stuff to him – not the kind of fighting the Corps went in for. The Marines had a long tradition of amphibious raiding and a Royal Marine Commando had already been formed, and had taken part in the Dieppe raid the previous year. But a few men dashing around the desert in jeeps fitted neither of these categories and Tiller looked sceptically on anything the Corps wasn't involved in as probably not worth pursuing.

Which was why he had been – he had to admit it now – very doubtful at first about Tasler's organization and schemes, though anything the major normally said or did was all right with Tiller. Indeed he would have followed that resourceful Royal Marines officer to the end of the earth if necessary. Still, he remembered thinking at the time that if the Chief of Combined Operations, Vice-Admiral Lord Louis Mountbatten, had backed Tasler's ideas, then who was he, a mere sergeant, to have his doubts?

'Sally'll take it hard, you know.'

Tiller nodded. 'I know.'

Curly grinned. 'I'll look after her.'

'I bet you bloody will, you randy sod,' said Tiller, who knew Curly to be happily married with two kids and a third on the way. Now that was the perfect example of what was meant by having 'strong family ties' and Tiller was having none of it.

He got up, folded the movement order, and put it in his pocket. 'I'd better get my kit ready and say my farewells to the lads. I'm being picked up first thing tomorrow morning.'

'Rather you than me,' Curly said, but Tiller could detect the envy in his voice.

'Yeah, I suppose so,' he said. 'So long.'

He extended his hand. Curly shook it and said: 'Don't do anything I wouldn't do. The brothels there are notorious for some interesting strains of clap.'

Tiller walked out to the barracks and turned left along the coast road to Southsea. The rest of the mob had local billets since they had the same status as commandos. But Tiller had preferred to sleep at the barracks at Eastney, where he could keep his nightmare to himself.

The unit's training headquarters were two Nissen huts on the sea front. One was used as a lecture room, the other for stores. They were situated right under one of the forts which had been built in Napoleonic times to guard the Solent. Called, for some reason Tiller had never discovered, Lumps Fort, it lay at one end of the six-mile boom which had been erected to protect Portsmouth harbour from torpedo attacks by submarines or from surface attack by small craft. Two other forts had been built in the Solent at around the same time as Lumps. They, too, were now part of Portsmouth's defences, for the boom, which stretched to Seaview on the Isle of Wight, was not only joined to them but they were bristling with anti-aircraft guns.

Behind the Nissen huts was Southsea Corporation's Canoe Lake, which in peacetime had attracted the many day trippers and holidaymakers who came to the seaside resort during the summer months. Tiller remembered splashing around in it as a small kid. Now it was deserted and drained, with only a puddle of rainwater in its middle. One of the concrete sides, Tiller noticed, was badly cracked, perhaps caused by a bomb a 'tip-and-run' German aircraft had dropped nearby a couple of months back.

Tiller skirted it and made for Dolphin Court, a block of flats which overlooked the lake and the Solent. The block had been taken over by the Admiralty. Flat 24 had originally housed the Development Centre of Combined Operations. But the Centre had been absorbed into the Combined Operations Experimental Establishment and its staff relocated to north Devon or somewhere, and Tasler, who had been an early member of the Centre, had requisitioned the flat for his unit.

Tiller showed his pass to the naval sentry and, ignoring the lift, climbed the stairs three at a time. It was all part of the fitness regime Tasler had imposed and which was second nature to Tiller now.

The door of the flat was open but Tiller knocked before entering. A pretty Wren petty officer, the unit's clerk, looked up from her typewriter. 'He's waiting for you, Sergeant.'

'Thank you, Maggie, and how are you this sunny morning?'

'Just fine,' the young woman said, and, fluttering her long eyelashes in mock coquetry, added: 'As if you cared.'

Tiller leant on her desk and looked deep into her amazingly blue eyes. 'Oh, but I do, Maggie, I do.'

But the Wren's pretty face was deliberately expressionless now. She simply nodded towards the inner office. 'You're lucky. He's in a good mood. So you'd better go in before the wind changes.'

Tiller pursed his lips and blew her a kiss. Maggie was a good sort who knew never to take anyone, or anything, too seriously. He turned and strode towards Tasler's inner sanctum while the Wren studied Tiller's straight back and broad shoulders, and renewed her resolve. Men like Tiger, her instincts told her, made wonderful lovers but they were not husband material. And she knew, with more than a twinge of regret, that much as she desired the former her nature and upbringing dictated she acquire a reasonable specimen of the latter.

The door had on it a neat sign reading 'Major H.G. Tasler DSO OBE RM, Commanding Officer, Royal Marines Boom Patrol Detachment'.

'Come,' Tasler called out in response to Tiller's knock. Tiller closed the door behind him, stiffened to attention, and saluted. Even after all these years he still counted to himself 'up, one, two, three, down' as his hand, palm outwards, came up to his beret before snapping down to his side.

Tasler sat at his desk surrounded by trays of paper.

He was a man in his late twenties with red-gold hair, most of which he had lost, and a flowing moustache. He was studying a plan of a small craft which he thrust towards Tiller. 'Morning, Tiger. Beautiful day. What do you think of this?' He handed Tiller the plan. 'We're calling it the Sleeping Beauty.'

'The motor submersible canoe,' Tiller read aloud. 'So here it is at last, sir.'

'The first is just about to be delivered for trials,' said Tasler. 'I'm sorry you won't be here to try it out. I assume your movement order has arrived?'

'Yes, sir. This morning.'

Tasler snorted. 'About time, too. We'd better start the rigmarole for signing you off the unit's strength. But before you go I want to show you something else. Maggie!'

The Wren appeared at the door.

'Sergeant Tiller's leaving us, Maggie, so get the necessary bumf ready for me, will you. I won't be long.'

The Wren's blue eyes rested on Tiller for a moment, but the twinge of regret she felt again did not show in them for an instant.

'The best of luck, Sergeant,' she said. She didn't ask where he was going. No one in the unit was ever asked that.

'Thanks, Maggie,' Tiller said. 'Perhaps you'll stop refusing to come out with me when I come back a hero.'

'I doubt it, Sergeant. I very much doubt it.'

The two men doubled down the stairs and out into the summer sunshine.

'I think that girl's saving herself for her knight in shining armour, sir,' Tiller said.

'I think it's just,' Tasler replied with a grin, 'that at a very young age her mother must have warned her about men like you.'

Half the unit's complement of thirty-four men were attending a navigation lecture in one of the Nissen huts. The other half were training on the beach. The boat-house, where the cockles were kept, was on the road along the sea front. Beyond the road was a sea defence wall with a drop of five feet to the beach. It was another of Tasler's rules that although there were steps down to the beach these were never to be used. Whatever a man was carrying he had to go via the wall not the steps.

As they approached the boat-house Tiller could see that an instructor was supervising a race between three teams of two men each to get their cockle from the boat-house, across the road, down the wall, across the beach and into the sea. The teams then had to paddle round a buoy some three hundred yards from the beach, return, run up the beach with the cockle, heave it over the wall and across the road, and set it back on its cradle in the boat-house. Another three teams were practising how to push their cockles down the beach with their paddles and then into the water, the most effective way, it had been found, of launching a cockle with its crew in rough seas. Others were doing their daily feet-hardening exercises, which entailed running up and down the pebble beach in bare feet or jumping on to the pebbles from the wall. One whole section of ten men would be aboard *Celtic*, an old Thames barge moored in Chichester harbour. Sections were rotated a week at a time to practise, among other routines, shallow-water diving in the DSEA Sladen diving suit and, the most unpopular exercise of all, crawling across the mud-flats at low tide.

But the most effective exercise Tasler had developed was for his canoeists to sneak up on, and board, the official boom patrol boats before their crews were aware what was happening. It was like a game of grandmother's footsteps at sea and some of the canoeists had become very good at it. Favourite targets were the patrol boats which were dispatched to keep the Solent clear while the anti-aircraft batteries on shore and on the forts practised shooting. These patrol boats were sometimes manned by Wrens and in the summer, when they thought they were safe from prying eyes, they were often tempted to strip to their undies and sunbathe.

Tiller had met Sally that way. She had been lying on her back on the deck when he had silently levered himself aboard. She had been modestly attired in nothing more than a small towel draped across her middle. Her scream must have been heard in Southampton.

Tiller smiled to himself now when he remembered the heated conversation that had followed. Perhaps it was the manner of their first meeting that had persuaded her to try and make an honest man of him.

Yes, it was time to move on.

'They all look ready for action, sir,' said Tiller.

A shadow passed over Tasler's face. 'So am I, Tiger, so am I. But whatever plans we put up, there seems to be a good reason for not going ahead with them. As you know, we were going to have a crack at going up the Gironde again, but in the end the good and the great decided against it. I certainly wouldn't let you be leaving us if there had been any chance of us being able to have another go. That is, presuming you would have wanted to have another try?'

Tasler looked at Tiller enquiringly.

'I'm sure I would have, sir,' Tiller replied. Like falling off a horse, he knew the best possible way of combating fear was to remount as quickly as possible. Now he would have to find another way of eradicating his nightmare.

'Well, "if ifs and ands were pots and pans",' Tasler quoted cheerfully. 'It didn't happen so we must get on and hope something else crops up.'

As they walked back past the two Nissen huts the major said: 'This is what I wanted to show you.'

They entered the store hut and walked to the back of it. Tasler threw back a canvas cover and displayed the captured Italian explosive motor boat.

'The Eyeties officially call them *Motoscafi di Turismo modifacti*, or MTMs,' said Tasler, 'though the pilot who we captured said they were generally known as *barchini esplosivi* or *barchini* for short.'

Tiller whistled. 'So that's what it looks like. It's bigger than I had imagined.'

'Eighteen feet. Vosper's have finished with it as ours is now well developed, so I am sending it to *Celtic* for the lads to practise on.'

So this, Tiller thought, was what the unit's secret weapon was being modelled on; the weapon which had always been referred to as a boom patrol boat to cover up its real identity. It had been the hub of Tasler's activities, the original reason for the formation of his unit. Yet no one had yet had a chance to see even the Italian version of it.

'It looks fast, sir.'

'It's powered by an Alfa Romeo engine which can crank out 120hp. Vosper's got over thirty-five knots out of it.'

Tiller studied the craft intently, astonished by its compactness and the audacity of those who had operated it. He touched a hinged rectangle of wood attached to the boat's counter right behind where the driver sat, and looked quizzically at Tasler.

'That's the flutterboard,' said Tasler. 'It's attached by a line to the driver's wrist. When he wants to bale out he pulls this lever here and the flutterboard drops into the water. The driver can climb on to it to escape the concussion of the explosion when the boat hits its target. It can also be used as a surfboard.'

'Ingenious.'

'Very. The Italians aren't half as daft as some people make out.'

'And this is the detonating device?' Tiller pointed to the bumper-car rim around the bows of the boat.

'That's it. This one had 500lb of TNT in its bows. It was meant to be detonated by a hydrostatic fuse, but something went wrong with it and it ran up on to the beach with the driver. Suda Bay in Crete that was, in April '41. But others managed to cripple a tanker and damage the cruiser *York*. Gave everyone a nasty shock, I can tell you.'

'Is that how we're going to use them?'

Tasler shook his head. 'We're going to drop them by parachute near their targets, complete with driver.'

Tiller whistled quietly again. So that was why they had all been put through a parachute course earlier that year.

The two men walked out into the sunshine and back

to Dolphin Court, where Tasler shook Tiller's hand. 'Good luck.'

'I reckon I'm leaving just when things are beginning to happen, sir.'

'Let's hope so,' Tasler replied, but he sounded doubtful. 'Anyway, I look upon you as the unit's standard-bearer in the eastern Mediterranean. Not enough of the high-ups know what we're about or what we're capable of. Show 'em what we can do, Tiger. I'm relying on you.'

2

The roar of the Halifax bomber's engines made it impossible to hear anything, and the fuselage vibrated and bucked. The dispatchman touched the shoulder of the young army officer sitting nonchalantly on the bench reading a book. For the first time the dispatchman noticed the officer's sand-coloured beret with its unusual winged badge. He had no idea what it signified, and it was now too late to find out. Anyway, on this type of mission it was better not to ask too many questions.

The officer looked up and the dispatchman gestured to the officer's beret and then to the pudding-basin-shaped paratroop helmet lying next to him. The officer nodded and smiled, and reached for the helmet. He took off his beret and tucked it under the epaulette of his left shoulder, which had a single crown stitched to it.

Christ, thought the dispatchman, if majors are *that* young nowadays the British Army must have suffered heavy losses among its officers. Or perhaps, he corrected himself, this chap's just brilliant. He looked the studious type. The dispatchman glanced at the dog-eared service-issue paperback the major was reading, its cheap paper already greying and frayed. *The Aeneid*, it was called. The title meant nothing to the dispatchman.

He held up five fingers.

The major buckled the chin strap of the parachute helmet, and nodded.

Five minutes, the dispatchman mouthed, just to make sure.

The major nodded again, moved his beret from his shoulder to a pocket of his battledress trousers and buttoned it up. Then he leant across to the two figures lying on the floor of the Halifax, and shook each in turn.

One was the major's wireless operator, a sergeant, the other his Italian interpreter, an elderly English captain. Both buckled on their gear and donned their helmets. The sergeant put his helmet on with practised ease, but the captain initially put his on back to front. The major grinned at him encouragingly. The captain smiled grimly and allowed the major to adjust his chin strap.

'It's easy!' the major shouted above the roar of the engines, but the captain shook his head, not in disagreement but because he couldn't hear.

The dispatchman was back now. He held up two fingers and indicated that they should attach their static lines to the wire running along the bomber's roof.

Parachutists dropped from Halifax bombers usually had to exit from a hole in the fuselage floor. But this one, part of a Special Duties squadron based in the Middle East, had been specially converted by having a door cut into its side. But it did not run to such refinements as red and green lights to indicate when the parachutist had to jump.

The dispatchman opened the door and it swung inwards and clipped itself open. The rush of night air and the increased noise made all three men gasp and lower their heads.

Below them the major could see flickers of light and it took him a few moments to realize they were being fired on from the ground.

The dispatchman had decided the wireless operator should jump first, then the elderly captain, and finally the major. That way the captain would be able to see the sergeant jumping and his parachute opening. This would encourage him to follow. If it didn't, then the captain knew he had the major behind him, which should be encouragement enough to jump. In parachuting, pride usually conquered fear.

Thirty seconds, the dispatchman mouthed, and the wireless operator, his set strapped to his back, took his position by the door, gripping each side of the opening. The dispatchman banged the operator's shoulder and the operator was gone, and seconds later the captain saw the operator's parachute bloom. It did nothing to alleviate the dryness of his mouth or the thought that he must have been stark raving mad to volunteer for such a mission.

He gripped the sides of the door as he had seen the operator do. He had seen the signal the operator had been given to jump, and expected the same slap on the shoulder. But the dispatchman knew his job and wasn't taking any risks. With just the right amount of force he ejected the captain by pushing him between the shoulders and watched until his parachute opened. Poor bugger, he thought, he was much too old to be jumping.

The dispatchman saw the young major watching him with a grin on his face. The dispatchman grinned back and gestured him forward, waited the obligatory amount of time, then raised his hand.

But the major was gone. Even above the roar of the engines and the rush of air the dispatchman was sure he heard the major whoop with joy as he jumped. Well, it took all sorts. He unclipped the door and swung it closed.

'Chums away, sir,' he told the pilot through the intercom. The crew of aircraft on Special Operations always called their human cargo 'chums'.

Without replying, the pilot put the Halifax into a steep, climbing turn. Whoever was firing at him must be pissed as a newt, but he wasn't taking any chances.

The major had indeed whooped, but with relief not joy. The spread wings on his battledress showed that he had passed the parachute course, but he never much liked the sensation of jumping into space. But doing so from an aircraft was infinitely easier than from a balloon, which was what the first training jump was usually from. That was gut-wrenching. And once the parachute was open after jumping from an aircraft there was that blissful, transient feeling of being suspended in time as well as space.

The major looked down and saw that the sporadic flashes, now accompanied by a high-pitched crackle, were still coming from the ground. At first they seemed to be firing at the diminishing sound of the Halifax grinding its way back to Cyprus and he thought what silly sods they were wasting their ammunition like that. Then he realized they were firing at him too, and the tracer bullets were arching into the sky either side of him. He searched for any sign of the ground and as he did so remembered how he had last visited Rhodes. It had been by boat from Brindisi. He'd been an archaeology student then. It was only five years ago but it seemed a lifetime away. Perhaps the Italian professor of archaeology who had so courteously taken him under his wing on Rhodes was now in charge of those taking a pot-shot at him as he swung helplessly above them.

He suddenly saw the ground appear out of the dark. It seemed to be coming up towards him at an alarming rate. It always did. He flexed his legs. There was no time to pick a landing place. It looked horribly rocky. The shock of landing jarred right through him, even though he rolled as he had been taught. A rock hit him under the ribs and knocked the wind out of him. A gust caught his parachute and pulled him like an express train through some gorse. He struggled to release it and just managed to do so before it threatened to throw him against a rocky outcrop. The parachute collapsed and the major staggered to his feet and began winding it rapidly towards him. It was only then that he realized that it was blowing half a gale. The met people had got it wrong. Again. There was little chance they had landed in the right place in such a wind.

The major finished winding in the parachute, took off his helmet, put the helmet into the parachute and pushed the bundle out of sight under a gorse bush. He put on his beret and then checked his equipment: water bottle, commando knife, silenced Sten gun with extra 9mm ammunition, pistol, rucksack with rations, night binoculars, and lastly the letter. Nothing missing.

A gust of wind brought with it the staccato sound of semi-automatic weapons. What the hell were they firing at now? He tried to identify the sound: German Schmeisser or Italian Breda, but it was too indistinct and sporadic to be certain. The major decided they – whoever they were – must be firing at his two companions. But it was also possible, perhaps more likely, that they were firing at each other. He had been warned that the Germans and Italians might clash when the surrender of Italy became known.

He began making his way cautiously towards the sound of the battle. The ground was very broken and steep. Twice he stumbled and fell. After ten minutes or so he came to a crest. He flung himself down and crawled cautiously up to it so that he was not silhouetted against the night sky. Now he could see tracer flying in all directions and a flare spluttered upwards, burst, and lit the ground with an eerie light before extinguishing itself. Someone seemed to be putting up a hell of a fight. He started to shift forward when his ankle was gripped in a vice. His hand went for his knife but then relaxed when a voice hissed urgently: 'Major Jarrett, sir. It's me. Kesterton.'

'What the hell's going on?' Jarrett whispered to his wireless operator. Whoever was firing was obviously not doing so at Kesterton. 'Are they firing at Dolby?'

'I don't know, sir. If they're Eyeties they're probably firing at one another. Regular Guy Fawkes night, it is.'

As the major's eyes became accustomed to scanning the area he could see figures moving. They seemed to be approaching the ridge where the two men were lying. Jarrett knew there were only about 10,000 Germans on Rhodes while the Italians had a garrison of 35,000. Perhaps the Italians had decided to make a pre-emptive strike at their former allies.

He trained his binoculars on the moving figures but they were still too far away. He passed them to Kesterton. 'Krauts?'

Kesterton peered through the glasses. 'I don't know, sir,' he said doubtfully. 'Could be. It's mostly rifle fire now, though they were firing something much heavier earlier on.'

It mattered to Jarrett who it was. It mattered a lot. He fingered the letter in his pocket. It was addressed to Admiral Campioni, the Italian governor of the Dodecanese, who was based on Rhodes, and was signed by General Maitland Wilson, Commander-in-Chief Middle East. It was couched in diplomatic terms and expressed the wish of the British for the Italian garrison to co-operate with incoming British forces. It flattered Admiral Campioni no end. It was not the kind of document Jarrett would like the Germans to find on him, especially if there happened to be any Gestapo on the island. The Gestapo shot parachutists out of hand and probably had a more lingering and painful death in store for those who were trying to suborn the Führer's former allies.

But what really mattered was that, once the Germans got a whiff of what the British were planning to do, they could decide to take over the islands themselves, and Jarrett's orders were precisely to prevent that happening. Campioni would have to do without his letter. He explained the situation briefly to Kesterton and could hear the surprise in the operator's voice.

'You're going to eat it, sir?'

'Well, I can't burn it, can I?' Jarrett said irritably. 'And there's nowhere to hide it.'

But it was the Italians who found them an hour later. By then Jarrett had laboriously swallowed the letter and was badly in need of the Chianti bottle that an unshaven but friendly *carabinieri* corporal offered him.

Admiral Campioni surveyed his visitors cautiously. If they were who they said they were things might be looking up. The one now lying on a stretcher with a broken leg spoke good Italian and certainly knew more about the surrender of Italy than he did. Campioni had only been told about the armistice the previous day – by the wife of a German officer who had just happened to be passing by – and this information had been followed by an agreement with the commander of Sturmdivision Rhodos, General Klemann, that both commanders would not move their troops.

The agreement had suited Campioni as he had no transport. But the Germans had then promptly broken it by sending patrols to take over the three Italian airfields at Marizza, Calato and Cattavia. It was, Campioni thought gloomily, typical of how his country – of which he was inordinately fond – had fought and lost the war. No proper communications, treacherous allies, and a lot of promises, all broken.

He wiped his heavily gold-braided sleeve across his brow and began reading the teleprinter message his aide had brought. It came from Cairo and was in Italian, and confirmed the names and ranks of the three Englishmen, and the purpose of their visit. Campioni smiled. Major the Earl Jarrett. If the

British were prepared to risk an English milord –
and one whose father Campioni had much admired
– on such a mission then they must be serious. Things
were definitely looking up.

'Of course,' Campioni said to Dolby. 'If we were
to be supported by a British armoured division and if
an airborne brigade were to be dropped within, say,
the next twenty-four hours on the airfields then we
would be in a position to go on the offensive against
the Germans.'

Campioni's staff officers clustered around him and
nodded their agreement. Jarrett looked quizzically at
Dolby. 'Well?'

'He wants the whole damned 8th Army air-dropped
here this evening,' the interpreter said wearily. 'And I
daresay he's going to want Monty in command of it.
Under him, of course.'

Despite the morphine injection the Italian doctor
had given him, Dolby's leg hurt abominably. But he
felt the shock he was suffering was more from being
within an ace of being shot by the *carabiniere* who had
found him. Only some quick talking had saved him.

'You're joking,' said Jarrett.

'Am I? You had better believe it, George,' Dolby
said, then turned to Campioni. 'You have many
more troops than the Germans. Are such strong
reinforcements necessary?'

Dolby hoped he was implying that the reinforcements were all lined up, ready to go if Campioni
really needed them. So far as he knew there was half
a battalion of the Buffs on Cyprus, and most of them
were on leave.

'Oh, but certainly. And we would also, of course,
need strong logistical support and good air cover.

Then we have a famous victory. We would wipe those damned Germans right off the island.'

The Admiral's staff looked as if they were about to applaud his brave speech.

'He does want the 8th Army,' Dolby told Jarrett. '*And* he wants the bloody Desert Air Force as well.'

'To avoid the – ah, unfortunate – reception you received this morning,' Campioni said to Dolby. 'I would like to inform our batteries as to when and where these reinforcements are arriving. Will it be at dawn or afterwards?'

'What's more, he seems to think they're already on their way.'

Jarrett's face was a mask. 'What can we tell him?' he asked Dolby.

A spasm of pain crossed the interpreter's face. 'How many men do we have available, George?' he asked curiously.

'About fifty,' said Jarrett.

'Well, I won't tell him that,' said Dolby firmly. 'I'll let him down as gently as possible.'

Jarrett did not try to follow the rapid flow of Italian that passed between the two men but the result was obvious. Campioni's expression changed from amiability to irritation to petulance. Watching the Italian admiral reminded Jarrett of the story that had lately been circulating in Cairo. When Stalin was told by Churchill during a conference in Moscow that the Pope would not approve of some action the Allies were about to embark upon the great leader of the Soviet people had leant forward and asked: 'And how many divisions does the Pope have?'

Jarrett did not have any divisions either – just a wireless operator, an elderly captain with a broken leg, and a lot of promises. His knew his advance party of fifty men would have already left their base and would at this moment be landing on Castelrosso, a small Italian-held island between Cyprus and Rhodes which was to be their base for operations in the rest of the Dodecanese. An infantry battalion on Malta was being readied to follow but that could not arrive for another six days.

'Remind him that his king has ordered all Italian commanders to defend Italian land.'

Dolby did so but it did not go down well. Campioni simply shrugged and spread his hands open; his staff looked glum. In his mind Jarrett dwelt fleetingly, and adversely, on the fighting qualities of Italian troops generally and of Italian admirals in particular.

Beads of sweat glinted on Campioni's forehead. His fingers picked at the resplendent gold braid on his sleeve. An awkward silence descended which was broken only by yet another member of the Admiral's staff who entered the room and whispered in his ear. Campioni produced a handkerchief so seeped in eau-de-Cologne that Jarrett caught a whiff of it ten feet away. He dabbed his forehead and spoke imploringly to Dolby. It was a long, involved explanation.

'He says General Klemann wants to confer with him,' Dolby explained when the tirade had ceased. 'As soon as possible. We have to go. He'll fly me out in a seaplane immediately, while it's still dark. He'll arrange for you and Kesterton to be taken off by torpedo boat this evening. In the meantime you must put on civilian clothes and keep out of the way while this is being arranged. Under no circumstances must the Germans know we've been here.'

Dolby waited for Jarrett to absorb this information, before adding needlessly: 'He's running scared.'

3

'We don't stand on ceremony in the SBS,' said Captain Magnus Larssen of L Detachment, SBS. 'The chaps just call me skipper.'

Tiller studied Larssen discreetly. He was fresh-faced, fair-haired and looked appallingly young. But Tiller discerned there was something razor-sharp about him, too. Touch him and you'd cut your finger.

Tiller's salute snapped up and down. He registered Larssen's Scandinavian accent, the absence of any badges of rank on his blue shirt, the fact that his feet, clad in disgracefully dirty desert boots, were propped on the ramshackle table which he presumably used as his desk.

'Yes*sir*,' Tiller replied loudly. Marines didn't call officers by their nicknames. Especially scruffy army officers without pips on their shoulders, especially foreign-sounding officers, especially ones who had crossbows hanging on their walls. What was he, frigging William Tell or something?

Larssen's eyes, a piercing, very pale blue, caught Tiller's and bored into him. Tiller grinned lamely.

'Good,' said Larssen briskly, leaning forward to shake his hand. It was, Tiller couldn't help noticing, like shaking a piece of particularly tough leather and the grip was vice-like.

'So that's settled, then. Sit down, Sergeant. Let's have a gossip.'

Gossip? Tiller gingerly lowered his six-foot frame on to the edge of a rather rickety chair.

'So,' Larssen said softly. 'You are Sergeant Tiller. I call you Tiger, is that right?'

Tiller nodded. He stifled the 'yessir' that was on his tongue, but he couldn't bring himself to call this extraordinary individual 'skipper'. He had too many other unusual things to get used to.

Tiller took off his beret and wiped his face. The tiny island of Castelrosso seemed hotter than Hades, hotter even than Athlit had been, and the crumbling house that Larssen had requisitioned as headquarters for L Detachment was like an oven.

'I'm glad you catch up with us at last,' said Larssen. 'We were ordered to move quickly.'

Tiller had been travelling non-stop for five days. It felt like five years. At Athlit no one appeared to know where his detachment had vanished to, so they had sent him to the 'Killer School' for a refresher course while they tried to find out. The school was in the old police station in Jerusalem and was run by a major who wore two pearl-handled revolvers. Until he had shot the ace of diamonds out of a playing card at twenty paces with one of them Tiller had thought him a bit of a comedian.

When they still hadn't been able to find his detachment they had sent him to Haifa on an aircraft identification course – why he never knew – but before he had had time to savour the delights of the city he had been bundled on to a plane bound for Akrotiri airbase in Cyprus, so he hadn't even had time to collect all his new kit.

His one evening in Limassol had proved entertaining but abortive as, for some reason, the Turkish belly dancer had proved unresponsive to his approaches. Perhaps he was losing his touch. Then at dawn he had been flown to Castelrosso by a jovial RAF type in a captured Italian Cato floatplane which, with its load of ammunition and food supplies for the SBS, had seemed inordinately reluctant to become unstuck from the waters of Limassol harbour.

'Underpowered,' the RAF pilot had shouted cheerfully at him as they had bucked across the waves. 'Bloody useless, really. Like everything Italian. Still, it's better than warming a chair in some Cairo office.'

Tiller, who would not have minded being in Cairo at that particular moment, had shut his eyes. A fortune-teller Sally had taken him to had predicted he would have a watery grave, but he had never supposed his coffin would be a clapped-out Italian seaplane. He had never been more glad to step on to terra firma after the two-hour flight, even if it was a bare, hot, miserable rock like Castelrosso.

'You know anything about the SBS, Tiger?'

'Not much, sir. You were part of the SAS at one time?'

The forbidden sin had slipped out. Larssen scowled but let it pass. 'That's right. We were D Squadron SAS. In April, after Colonel Stirling was captured, we became SBS – Special Boat Squadron. Full establishment is three detachments each of seventy men and seven officers, but we are still recruiting. We're part of what is known as Raiding Forces, controlled operationally by GHQ, Cairo. A few of the men served with Courtney in the Special

Boat Service, but they've spent a couple of years attacking Kraut airfields in the desert, and have probably forgotten everything they learned. Anyway, techniques and equipment have changed. You will have to instruct Corporal Barnesworth, the man we have given you as your swimmer.'

'Here?' Tiller asked. He had already met Billy Barnesworth and had taken an immediate liking to the lugubrious, powerfully built guardsman.

'Yes, here. We are ready to move but the navy takes a little longer to get ready. We'll be here for a couple of days at least.'

A couple of days! He hoped Billy was a quick learner. To help him get the picture of how he might be used he asked what the SBS did exactly.

'We were formed for raiding operations in the eastern Mediterranean. Quick in-and-out affairs to harass the enemy. Blow up a few ammunition dumps, cut a few throats. What Mr Churchill calls a "butcher and bolt" policy. You get the idea?'

A jolt of excitement ran through Tiller. 'Sure,' he said.

'So we've been training in Palestine for the past few months to mount that sort of operation. But instead of jeeps taking us to our targets, as the Long Range Desert Group took the SAS, we have caiques of the Levant Schooner Flotilla doing the same job.'

Larssen pronounced the word 'kayik'. Tiller shifted uncomfortably in his seat. He felt he was getting out of his depth, but Larssen quickly came to the rescue. 'Caiques are the locally built sailing vessels for fishing and inter-island trade. They vary in size but the Flotilla's are mostly between ten and thirty tons. They're armed and have engines, but to the

Krauts and Eyeties they look Greek or Turkish. Very useful.'

'Useful?' Tiller queried.

'They just run up a Greek or Turkish flag. Then they are left alone. Very useful.'

And illegal, Tiller guessed.

'You look doubtful, Tiger?'

'Is that allowed?' Tiller asked uncomfortably. Tasler had made his men learn all about the Hague Convention, which laid down the rules of warfare, in the hope that if they were captured they could argue their case with their captors. A fat lot of good it had done Dick and Terry: the Germans had shot them out of hand.

Larssen's eyes opened wide and then he burst out laughing. 'No, of course it's not. The caiques also hide out along the Turkish mainland when necessary. That's illegal, too, as Turkey is neutral. Does that worry you?'

Tiller shook his head. It didn't worry him at all, but it confirmed his opinion that he had joined an unusual unit.

Larssen looked at the latest addition to his detachment with approval. He liked Tiller's open face, his determined jaw, his movements, deft for such a large man. He could be a very useful addition. But Larssen wondered if Tiller would fit into the Special Boat Squadron, whose unofficial motto 'Sink or swim' reflected not only the operational medium in which they were going to work but the individual nature of the way the unit operated. There was no one to tell an SBS man what to do. It was up to him. Individual initiative, it was called, and if he was unlucky, well, he sank alone.

Tiller, with his dark, short-cropped hair and immaculate uniform, looked to Larssen like one of the thin red line the British Army was so proud of. Brave, no doubt, and superbly trained to obey orders unquestioningly, but did he have the ability to act and think on his own? Larssen knew the task of the SBS wasn't going to be about charging the enemy trenches with bayonets fixed, of bravery over and above the course of duty in the face of the enemy. On the contrary the SBS had to make sure the enemy was facing the other way so that they could be outmanoeuvred, bypassed, or simply stabbed in the back. The SBS was all about silent infiltration of the enemy's position, not of storming it with banners flying, amid blood and guts.

How was he, Larssen, going to convey such a concept to this immaculately turned-out Marine who had obviously had centuries of tradition and discipline drummed into him?

'I'd remove all that shiny brass if I were you,' Larssen said in a friendly way. 'We don't have the spit and polish in this detachment.'

Tiller looked awkwardly down at the glistening globe and laurel badge in his blue beret, the gleaming brass of his belt, and the brilliant shine on his boots.

'At Athlit there was only sand,' Larssen explained. 'Can't parade on sand. So we didn't try.'

He leant forward. 'The first thing we always ask volunteers is whether they will jump. But I see you have already jumped.'

'Jumped?'

'A parachute course.'

Tiller grinned. 'Oh, yes, that. I did it at Ringway.'

He now saw that Larssen wore the spread wings of a parachutist over his left breast pocket.

Larssen grinned back at him. 'It's a good way of sorting out the sheep from the goats. If anyone refuses we RTU them immediately. Not, I suspect, that we're going to be doing any parachuting for the time being.'

'So we're here to raid?' Tiller asked.

'Castelrosso is our forward base,' Larssen said. 'But God knows what we're doing here.' He glanced at his watch. 'The boss will tell us soon enough. Any other questions?'

Tiller hesitated. 'Yes. What's the crossbow for?'

Larssen glanced up at the wall behind him. 'You have never used one? It is a wonderful weapon. Accurate, without noise, kills a man instantly if you hit him in the right spot.'

Tiller was intrigued. 'You've used it in action?'

Larssen just grinned.

'If it's so effective, why aren't all the special forces issued with them?'

Larssen sighed. 'Ah, rules and regulations. Nothing but damned rules and regulations. They were used by the Carlists in the Spanish Civil War, you know. They killed quite a few Republicans on night raids using bows and arrows. I recommended to the bigwigs in London that they were used. You know what they told me? I couldn't use it because it was an inhuman weapon.'

He bent forward again and his voice suddenly changed from being light-hearted, flippant, to one of great intensity. His blue eyes were like ice. 'I tell you, Tiger, me, I have only one rule of warfare. You kill the other man before he kills you. You have killed a man, yes?'

Tiller shook his head. Larssen said softly. 'But you know all the different ways because you went to the Killer School. But did they tell you where not to knife a German?'

'No. I wasn't there long.'

'I tell you. With the German army uniform the water bottle is worn so that it protects the kidneys. Also, the braces, where they cross over, they protect the vulnerable part of the spine. So don't try either place. Go for the subclavian artery. Here.'

Larssen pointed to his collar-bone. 'You pull the man's chin sideways and put the knife in here. He is unconscious in three seconds, dead in four. Silently. He drowns in his own blood. So when I can I use my knife. It's quick and silent – and not classed as an inhuman weapon.' He laughed lightly. 'Tell me, what is a human weapon?'

He did not seem to expect an answer to that conundrum. Instead, he swung his feet from the table and stood up with a speed that surprised Tiller. 'Come, I show you around before the boss's briefing.'

'Right, gentlemen.' The thickset, donnish figure rapped the stick he was going to use as a map pointer lightly on the table before him. 'I've not had time to meet any newcomers yet, so I'd better introduce myself. I'm your CO. Jarrett's the name.'

Corporal Billy Barnesworth leant over and whispered in Tiller's ear: 'Major the Earl of, Sarge. Just in case you didn't know.'

Tiller didn't, but he was already sure he had joined a unit unlike any other. He was far from certain he was going to enjoy it. Captain Larssen's appearance and demeanour had rather shaken him. His detachment officer had looked and talked – and no doubt behaved – more like a brigand than an officer of His Majesty's armed forces. Billy was one of the few survivors in the Middle East of the Special Boat Service. He had informed Tiller he had been a professional swimmer before the war, but it hadn't been Billy who had told Tiller that the guardsman was so at home in the water that he could eat bananas and drink beer while submerged. Quite how he managed this Tiller had yet to find out.

It was Billy who had also told him about Larssen, that he was a Danish merchant seaman who had escaped from his country to fight the Germans. 'Don't ask him why he hates the Germans so much,' Barnesworth had advised him. 'Otherwise he'll give you a twenty-minute lecture on how the Danes lost Schleswig-Holstein to Germany in the Middle Ages. Just take it from me that he does.'

Barnesworth had added that, because of his knowledge of the sea, Larssen had somehow become involved in the pinprick cross-Channel raids during the early years of the war. He had been picked to ferry ashore members of the Small Scale Raiding Force on a Channel Islands raid in 1941 and had distinguished himself by covering the raiders as they had re-embarked. He had been commissioned more or less on the spot and had been in the special forces ever since. A good man, Barnesworth had said, but a bit of a head case. 'He's had no military training whatsoever.'

Tiller had looked dumbfounded. 'None?'

'None. He couldn't march to save his life. But he knows more about weapons than anyone I've ever

43

known. He's apparently killed more Germans than the rest of us put together.'

'Never been on a parade ground?'

'Never. But he's already got the Military Cross and bar. Not bad, eh, for someone who doesn't know what "port arms" means?'

Tiller had looked surprised. 'But he wasn't wearing any ribbons.'

'Nah,' Billy had replied casually. 'Our Magnus doesn't bother about things like that.'

Jarrett tapped the map. 'Here's our objective. Or rather, here they are: the Dodecanese islands. Not far from the Turkish coast, as you can see. The population's nearly all Greek, but the Italians were given the islands in 1919 after the Great War and they garrison them. However, Jerry has also set up shop on some of the strategically more important ones.'

He paused and a voice interjected from his audience: 'We can take care of them, sir. No problem.'

Jarrett smiled. 'Possibly. But as there are only about fifty of us at the moment I don't propose a confrontation. No, our task is to secure the other islands and to persuade the Italians to help us defend them. We also have to mount reconnaissance patrols and set up a communications network to prepare the way for army units who will be sent in as proper garrisons. We'll be ferried around by courtesy of the Levant Schooner Flotilla. Since they brought you here, they don't need any further introduction from me. If the Italians co-operate I'm sure we can thwart any attempt by Jerry to take over the islands should he try to do so.'

'But why should the Eyeties help us, sir?' asked a voice from the audience.

'We don't want them on *our* side, for Gawd's sake,' said another man. 'They're much more useful to us fighting with the Germans.'

There was ribald laughter. Jarrett smiled and raised his pointer, but silence had fallen before it ever touched the table. 'Anyone heard of the 10th Light Flotilla?'

No one had.

'An Italian unit. Its men blew holes in our only two battleships in the Mediterranean a couple of years ago. Right under our noses in Alexandria harbour. It was the Italians who invented – and used – midget submarines in the Great War. And it was an Italian who first sunk a warship with explosives by swimming into the harbour where it was anchored. Don't knock them. They can be as brave – and as foolhardy – as any of you lot. We are going to need them to secure these islands against the Krauts.'

There was a murmur of appreciation as this sank in. Jarrett decided not to dwell on the cowardice of Admiral Campioni, who earlier that morning had surrendered his 35,000 men to 10,000 Germans without firing a shot. Instead he just said briskly: 'The bad news is that my mission to Rhodes failed. We have just heard that the island is now in German hands. This means that unless we can retake it quickly they will have three airfields at their disposal, though I doubt if they have either the aircraft or the fuel to make maximum use of them immediately.'

Jarrett paused while this piece of unpleasant news was digested. It was received in glum silence. Raiding airfields in enemy territory was what those present knew and did best, but obviously that was not what their CO had in mind now.

'We have every reason to believe the Germans may try and seize the other islands, too, if they think they can get away with it,' Jarrett continued. 'So the good news is that my orders still stand. I therefore propose to send out preliminary patrols of three or four men to find out the disposition of the Italian garrisons. I shall be going to Leros in the north. We will land a couple of you on Stampalia, the most westerly of the group, to act as an observation post, and Captain Larssen will go to Simi, in the south. He will support any of the nearby islands which may have Italian garrisons on them. These patrols will sail tonight at dusk. The remainder of you will stand by to be ferried wherever you're needed. You'll be reinforced by some members of the Greek Sacred Squadron, who should arrive tonight.'

Tiller glanced at Barnesworth, who whispered: 'Fancy name for a handful of Greek bandits Colonel Stirling picked up somewhere. They're part of Raiding Forces now.'

'Those of you who were with us in the desert will also be pleased to hear that our friends from the Long Range Desert Group, fresh from their Mountain Warfare course in the Lebanon, will also be joining us,' Jarrett announced. 'They will be working in the more northerly of the Dodecanese. Oh, yes, there's just one more thing I should mention. Just to complicate things the Greeks, as you probably know, have several different guerrilla organizations. Andartes, we call them. The two main ones are ELAS – pro-Communist, anti-royalist – and EDES, which is apparently working with the objective of restoring the King of the Hellenes to his throne. The Allies have been trying to work with both, but they're at each other's throats as much as they are at those of the occupying forces. We have no idea which group might be working in the Dodecanese, or even if there are any there at all. Now, any questions?'

'What's the chance of a good scrap, sir?' a voice asked from the back.

Jarrett smiled. 'Pretty high, I'd say. Though quite who we'll be fighting is another matter.'

4

They spent several more days hanging around waiting for their final orders. The time dragged and Tiller remembered the saying that war was ninety-nine per cent boredom and one per cent sheer terror.

The island was a miserably poor place, its inhabitants thin and ragged and dirty. The children, especially, were pathetic to look at, their stomachs distended by starvation. It seemed to Tiller that even at the best of times the island's occupants must have had great difficulty scraping an existence from the rocky ground. Most of the buildings clustered around the harbour were in a terrible state of repair and some seemed little better than ruins. Only the church on the hillside, newly painted, looked untouched by the war and the poverty.

The Italian garrison of thirty or so members of the *Fascisti*, who had surrendered after firing a few desultory shots, had made themselves scarce. The Greek inhabitants hated these blackshirts, that much was obvious, and already one of them had been found in an alley with his throat cut.

The detachment's orders eventually came late on the third day and the word was passed round for the patrols to muster on the harbour quay. To pass the time, and because it came to him automatically, Tiller was cleaning his gear when Barnesworth came to tell

him that at last they were on the move. He watched
Tiller with amusement.

'I'm a guardsman, Tiger, but I've learnt there are
better things to do in life.'

Tiller breathed heavily on his cap badge and buffed
it vigorously. 'Just habit, I suppose.'

When they arrived at the quay the rest of the detachment was viewing the motley collection of vessels tied
up along the harbour quay with misgiving.

'Jesus!' one of the men exploded, running his eye
over them. 'What's this, the local fishing fleet?'

Tiller's only experience of serving with the Royal
Navy afloat had been a pre-war two-year stint aboard
the battleship HMS *Ramilles*, and the submarine
which had taken him to the mouth of the Gironde.
On the battleship he had served as part of the gunnery
team for X turret, the traditional one reserved for the
Royal Marine detachment aboard a warship. It was
this time that had started his interest in explosives,
but it had left him with no abiding love of the senior
service or of life afloat.

The submariners, on the other hand, had been a
friendly lot and he had had nothing but admiration
for the way they taken the raiders to the correct
release point in as accurate a piece of dead reckoning
as he had ever witnessed. And they had stayed on the
surface, refusing to panic when the steady throb of
an E-boat had been heard in the distance. As cool as
cucumbers they had been. He had appreciated that,
had known then that they would be waiting for him
when he returned. He often wondered how long they
had waited. He bet it was longer than their orders had
stipulated.

He strolled over to a leading seaman who had a

sheaf of papers in his hand and was obviously going to help organize the embarkation.

'What's this lot, then, Killick? The Dunkirk Veterans' Association?'

The man grinned and said: 'I suppose you're used to serving aboard nothing smaller than a battleship, Sarge? This is the cream of His Majesty's Mediterranean Fleet. As fine a squadron as ever flew the white ensign.'

'Spare me the Nelson touch,' Tiller groaned. 'What the hell are they?'

'That's an ML, a Fairmile Motor Launch. A hundred and twelve foot long. They can do about sixteen knots in a seaway, so they are nothing like as fast as MTBs. Silent engines, they've got some of them.'

'What are they?' Tiller queried.

'The engines' exhaust pipes are below the water, not above it. Now, those two are Motor Torpedo Boats, one's a Thornycroft, the other a Vosper. The Vosper's got three Packard engines that give her a speed of thirty-four knots or more, but the Thornycroft . . .'

Tiller interrupted him firmly. 'I meant those.'

He pointed at half a dozen or so curious wooden vessels, some with one mast, others with two. They lay tied-up neatly alongside each other and moved in unison in the gentle swell caused by the arrival of an RAF high-speed launch. At a convenient extremity each flew a white ensign which flapped sporadically in the light evening breeze.

'Oh, those,' said the seaman offhandedly. 'They're the Levant Schooner Flotilla. Powered with Matilda tank engines and whatever sail they can hoist, and armed with anything the crews have been able to lay their hands on.'

'Rather them than me,' said Tiller, who didn't immediately associate this tatty collection with Larssen's more romantic description of the Flotilla's vessels. 'I wouldn't fancy sailing in a beer puddle aboard any of that lot.'

'Don't malign them, Sarge. They're your principal means of transport from now on.'

'Good grief,' muttered Barnesworth, who was standing beside Tiller.

'So *that's* a caique,' said Tiller. 'I didn't know they'd be quite so small. They all look different, too.'

'Each island that builds them has its own design,' the leading seaman said. 'They're constructed to ride out the *meltemi*, so they must be seaworthy.'

'*Meltemi*?' said Barnesworth.

The leading seaman looked at the two SBS men with amusement. 'Well, if you two gents haven't heard of the *meltemi* I won't spoil your holiday cruise. Now, if I could have your names, I'll tell you which of these luxury vessels you're sailing in.'

When they told him he looked down his list and then assigned them to LS8, the most outboard of the group which were tied up alongside each other. From the quay it also looked one of the smallest. They picked their way gingerly across the decks of the other caiques, stepping between piles of stores, ammunition boxes, and the usual clutter found aboard a sailing vessel. When they eventually arrived they found Larssen already aboard, smoking a pipe and gazing up at the hills behind the port, which were etched out by the last rays of the setting sun. He pointed to the ruins of an ancient fortress on one of the summits. 'A Crusader castle,' he said. 'The Knights of St John held this island until 1440.'

Tiller and Barnesworth glanced at each other. 'Is that right, skipper?' they replied in unison. They had quickly learnt during the course of the last few days that when their detachment commander was spouting history it was best to sound interested, but not to prolong the conversation by asking questions they didn't want to know the answer to.

LS8 still smelt of fish but her captain, wearing a bushy black beard which hid his schoolboy face, showed them over her with ill-concealed pride. He introduced himself as Andrew Maygan. The two interlinked wavy gold stripes on the epaulettes of his service shirt showed him to be a lieutenant in the Royal Naval Volunteer Reserve, the 'Wavy Navy' as it was called.

'Either of you know anything about sailing?' he asked.

They said they didn't.

'You'll soon pick it up,' Maygan said cheerfully. 'Just keep your heads out of the way of the boom – this chunk of wood here that the mainsail's attached to – because it will crack them open if you don't.'

Tiller knew that many RNVR officers were drawn from the ranks of knowledgeable amateur yachtsmen and this gave him some cause for comfort. LS8 might be flying the white ensign but she was more like a yacht than a warship. She certainly wasn't like anything Tiller had come across in his days with the Royal Navy where quarterdecks were scrubbed white and brass glistened like gold. He reckoned no regular naval officer would be seen dead aboard this crate. Which was just as well. What was that jibe about the three most useless things to have aboard a sailing boat? Oh, yes: an umbrella, a cuckoo clock and a naval officer.

'Bit cramped, I'm afraid,' Maygan said, 'but you'll only be aboard overnight. We want to get to Simi before dawn.'

The two SBS men peered into the caique's small hold, which was filled with jerrycans, food cartons, ammunition boxes and assorted weaponry. Tiller checked that his crate of plastic explosive and limpet mines was among them and noted the wireless set screwed to the bulkhead. No doubt its aerial ran up inside the mast.

'I haven't seen a set like that before,' he said to Maygan.

'The Kittyhawk fighter-bombers they were fitted in have been re-equipped with the latest VHF sets, so we managed to scrounge them from the Yanks. Ideal for what we want.'

The deck was equally cramped. The sail, rolled loosely around its boom, took up a good deal of room. There were two small anchors lashed astern of the small cockpit and two larger ones in the bows, their warps coiled neatly on the deck. 'You've got enough anchors,' Tiller remarked.

'Our engine's got no reverse,' Maygan said cheerfully. 'We've got to stop somehow.'

In front of the mast, shrouded, was a gun set on a bipod. Maygan lifted its cover and Tiller noticed that, unlike any British weapon, its magazine was mounted on the left side. He had never seen anything quite like it.

'A Solothurn,' Maygan explained. 'Swiss-made 20mm semi-automatic anti-tank rifle. The Eyeties used them against our tanks in the desert. Against any armour except sardine tins it's pretty useless, but it would give most things afloat around here a fright.'

The Matilda engine started with a roar that sent a belch of black smoke from the exhaust in the stern.

'What *are* we likely to meet?' Billy asked.

'Nothing, I hope, now that the Eyeties have surrendered. But they have a number of MAS boats – small torpedo boats – which Jerry may well have purloined. The Germans have several armed schooners for supplying their outlying garrisons and a Siebel ferry or two. They're nothing more than floating platforms really,' he added when the SBS men looked blank. 'But they're heavily armed with AA weapons. Their main armaments are two 105mm guns which could blast us out of the water in thirty seconds flat. L-boats we call them and I don't go anywhere near them. Anyway, we're not here to sink the opposition. Our job's to keep out of sight – or be sufficiently well disguised to pass as a local caique – so that we can land you blokes and take you off again, if necessary, without Jerry knowing what we're up to until it's too late.'

The seaman deck-hand and the caique's engineer, who had been introduced to them as Sandy Griffiths and Jock Bryson, started casting off from the caique LS8 was moored alongside. Then Maygan took the tiller to steer LS8 out of harbour.

'We avoid open water if we can,' he said, 'so we'll be going into Turkish waters and following the coast.'

Once out of the harbour he held the tiller between his knees, opened a chart he had under his arm, and showed the SBS team where he proposed to go by tracing the Turkish coastline with his finger.

'It's here, where we have to leave the coastline to cross to Simi, that it could be a bit dodgy. Jerry may have air patrols out now that he has control of the Rhodes airfields. But hopefully we'll be crossing while it's still dark.'

Griffiths appeared from the hold and the SBS men noticed that he and Bryson were now wearing civilian clothing: old caps, baggy trousers and threadbare jackets.

'Hoist the Turkish ensign, sir?' said Griffiths.

Maygan nodded and they watched the white ensign being hauled down and be replaced by a red Turkish flag with its crescent and star.

'We call ourselves filibusters,' Maygan said. 'Now you know why.'

'Filibusters?'

'Irregulars. Pirates, really. If their lordships at the Admiralty knew we were sailing in neutral waters under a foreign flag – especially a neutral one – we'd be hung, drawn and quartered.'

Out of the shelter of the harbour the caique bucked and rolled and its hull and rigging creaked under the strain of being pushed through the waves at eight knots. The Matilda engine, Bryson explained, was far too powerful for the size of the caique, but at least it was quiet because it was running at quarter throttle.

Maygan steered LS8 north-east towards the nearby Turkish mainland and then turned north-west to clear the headland that protected the harbour. Once past it they saw the sun dip into the sea on their port side. Ahead lay what, to them, seemed to be pitch-darkness, but as their eyes slowly adjusted to it they could see the first stars pricking the sky and could just make out the outline of a headland. Even at this distance it looked high and forbidding.

The hump of Castelrosso dropped quickly astern and gradually merged with the sea. The caique jerked and plunged and a cascade of spray swept over them. The helmsman swore loudly as some of it hit him.

'Quite a swell on,' said Maygan.

'What's the *meltemi*?' Barnesworth asked Griffiths.

'No need to worry about that tonight,' Griffiths replied. 'I'd get your heads down while you can.'

'Where?' Tiller asked.

Griffiths pointed to the rolled sail. 'It's as dry a place as anywhere.'

The sail smelt of tar and canvas, and was, after they had managed to wedge themselves between the boom and the cockle that had been brought aboard, surprisingly comfortable. Tiller stretched out, his unloaded Sten gun cradled in his arm, his beret a thin pillow between his head and the fish-impregnated deck.

LS8 rose and fell beneath them and the Matilda engine thumped away comfortingly in their ears.

The nightmare was taking a slightly different form when Tiller was suddenly awake, instantly alert. He sat up and slid the magazine into the Sten. It was an automatic reaction to an unknown situation but he could not instantly discern what was the matter, only that something was. Then he realized it was the silence that had woken him. The caique's movement had changed. With the engine stopped it was wallowing motionless in the sea.

Tiller levered himself out of the sail and on to his feet, and walked aft. Maygan, now also dressed in civilian clothes, was handing an adjustable spanner to Bryson, who was crouched over the engine, which lay below the cockpit floor. Larssen was holding a shaded torch.

'You know anything about engines?' Maygan asked him. Tiller shook his head.

Larssen chuckled. 'Tiger doesn't mend them. He blows them up, don't you, Tiger?'

'I wish someone had blown up the tank this fucking engine was in,' Bryson grumbled into the engine space. 'It's always been dodgy. I told them so in Beirut.'

Maygan glanced anxiously at his watch. Its luminous dial showed it was 0230. The cliffs of the Turkish coast looked close, very close. For a quarter of an hour Bryson laboured in silence except for the occasional expletive.

Then Maygan said: 'I think we'd better hoist the sail. At least we'll be able to stand off from the shore and not get taken too far off our course by the current.'

Tiller hadn't been aware of any breeze but once the mainsail and foresail were hoisted they filled at once and the caique stopped wallowing. It surged forward and the motion, Tiller noticed, was quite different under sail than it had been under power. Instead of punching into the waves the caique moved over them with an easy, rhythmic motion.

Maygan and Larssen spread the chart across their knees and studied it with the torch. 'There's a Turkish coastguard station on Cape Alupo,' said Maygan. 'I had hoped to get past there while it was still dark.'

'Trouble?' Larssen enquired.

'You never know. Nine times out of ten they'd never look at you twice. Nothing we can do about it anyway, except keep you lot in the hold. Might make sense to lie up in the daytime somewhere in the Gulf of Doris and cross to Simi tonight. We've got camouflage nets. No one would spot us, not even from the air.'

'My orders are Simi today, Andrew,' Larssen said. 'We've got to get to the Italian garrison before Jerry does.'

'Well, I'm game if you are,' said Maygan.

An hour later the engine broke into a healthy roar and Cape Alupo was passed just as the sun had begun to burn the night mist off the sea. The ensign was dipped to the coastguard station but there was no reply and half an hour later they changed course for Simi and the island's main port, where the Italian commandant had his headquarters.

Tea had just been brewed and some bread and jam distributed when Griffiths, who had been acting as lookout, shouted: 'Aircraft, port quarter, sir. Looks like a flying boat.'

Maygan threw his tea into the sea and snapped: 'I want all SBS below. Now.'

'Shall I man the gun, sir?' Griffiths asked.

'No, just make sure it's covered with the foresail. And make sure that canoe's out of sight under the mainsail.'

'Aye, aye, sir.'

'Jock, can we increase speed without shaking the hull to bits?'

'I doubt it, sir.'

'Well, try.'

'Aye, aye, sir.'

The orders had been issued crisply and were being obeyed with an easy assurance. As he crouched in the tiny hold Tiller decided that perhaps the three men on deck did know about white-honed decks and shining brass, after all.

'Put those binoculars away, Griffiths,' he heard Maygan tell the deck-hand. 'If the sun catches the lenses it'll be an open invitation for him to blast us out of the water. The wages of Turkish fishermen don't run to binoculars.'

They could all hear the aircraft now. It seemed to be moving very slowly and quite high. Every now and again it dipped its wings as if the pilot wanted to have a better look at what was below him. It moved north of LS8, circled and came lazily back to them.

'Wave!' Maygan ordered his crew as the aircraft passed astern of them. The aircraft, its Luftwaffe crosses plainly visible on its wings and fuselage, wiggled its wings in acknowledgement.

It flew south and then banked and headed back towards them. 'Never seen one like that before,' Maygan said. 'Any of you know anything about German aircraft?' he shouted down into the hold.

'A bit,' said Tiller.

'Be careful, but poke your head out and see if you can recognize it.'

Tiller stuck his head out and saw the aircraft approaching from astern. He shaded his eyes from the sun. 'Your beret, man!' Maygan shouted. 'Take your beret off.'

Larssen, standing behind Tiller, grabbed it from his head as the aircraft passed overhead. It was much lower this time. Then it swung round and came at them at masthead height. Its engines thundered and they could see the pilot leaning out to have a closer look. This time he didn't wave back.

Tiller poked his head up after it had passed and said: 'A Blohm and Voss, would be my guess.'

They waited for it to turn and come back again. If it did they knew the pilot would be making up his mind what to do. It was probably a forbidden area for

Turkish fishermen or the pilot had divined the caique was not all that it appeared to be. He was probably radioing his base for instructions before returning to rake them with his machine-guns.

'There's a Bren down there somewhere,' Maygan shouted into the hold. 'Get it ready. We may need it.'

The aircraft banked and flew off at a right angle. It was worse for those below because they could not see what was happening – just hear the dwindling sound of the engines.

'Is it going?' Larssen asked.

'He'll be back,' said Maygan grimly. 'He's turning now.'

This time, when he turned the pilot dived steeply and came straight at them towards their port side. Now he was flying below the height of the mast.

'Bloody show-off,' Maygan shouted.

The noise of the engines increased as Barnesworth passed up the Bren light machine-gun to Larssen, who sat crouched in the entrance to the hold. He covered the weapon with the corner of a tarpaulin and brought its muzzle level with the approaching aircraft.

'I reckon I could take him, Andrew,' he yelled.

'No! Hold your fire!' Maygan shouted. 'Wave, for Christ's sake, wave.'

He took off his ancient cloth cap, stood on the caique's counter, and waved his cap above his head. When the German opened fire he knew he would be the first to be hit. But then he could have overruled Larssen. LS8 was his command and now he was going to lose her. At that moment he was more angry than afraid. The sound of the German's engines filled the caique's small hold.

'What's he going to do?' Barnesworth snarled. 'Sink us by ramming us?'

But at the last split second the pilot drew back his joystick and missed the mast by a matter of feet. The whole hull of the caique shuddered.

'Fucking hell!' shouted Maygan. He was frightened now. The shock wave of the passing aircraft had nearly thrown him into the water. 'Fucking silly bugger!'

The aircraft was already half a mile away and was beginning to climb. They all knew that if he came back again it would be to sink them. The aircraft began to bank.

'Here he comes again!' Maygan shouted. 'Flat on the deck this time, lads. And I want Lanchester up here too.'

But then the aircraft straightened out and headed off in the direction of Rhodes. It steadily dwindled into the distance and soon all that was left was a dot in the sky and the faint vibrations of its engines in the early-morning air.

'Christ,' said Maygan. 'I have a feeling that was a bloody close call.'

Larssen handed Tiller back his beret and pointed at the badge. 'The sun must have caught this. Now you know why no spit and polish, Tiger. You can have my spare beret. And I have an SAS badge somewhere. All cloth, no brass. But you bloody sew it on yourself.'

Tiller grinned and retrieved his headgear. He removed the gleaming badge of the globe and laurel and put it in his pocket. This simple action seemed to him an acceptance of this strange new life.

Larssen slapped him on the back. 'That's a start,

Tiger. But it's up here,' he said, pointing to his head with a forefinger. 'That's where it really counts. But it's a start.'

Maygan had his log open on his knees. He licked the end of his pencil. 'How do you spell Blohm and Voss?' he asked.

Maygan would have liked to hug the eastern shore of Simi until they had reached the far end, where the port of Simi lay in the deep natural harbour of Yalo Bay. He knew the garrison was a small one, perhaps no more than fifty Italians, but Jarrett had told him there was no knowing how they would react. And somewhere – no one quite knew where – there was at least one gun battery. Having nearly lost his command already once that day Maygan explained that he wanted to keep out of the range of any guns for as long as possible, or at least not sail up their muzzles.

He spread out the chart and showed Larssen his proposed course. 'We could put into Marathonda or Nano Bay, but I wouldn't like to approach the shore any further north as at least one of the batteries is bound to be sited close to Simi.'

'What is the safest from your point of view?' Larssen asked.

'Put into Marathonda Bay.'

'And how do we get to the port?'

Maygan shrugged. 'Hijack some donkeys, I suppose. It's about five or six miles as the crow flies across the hills. Probably twice that if you find and follow the track which connects Panormiti Bay with the port.'

'And the quickest way?' asked Larssen.

'Sail into Simi flying the white ensign and our best uniforms, and hope for the best.'

'I prefer the quickest,' Larssen said immediately. 'Are you game?'

Maygan hesitated. 'I'll keep offshore until we reach the port and then sail straight in. That way we won't suddenly appear, which might make them shoot first and ask questions afterwards.'

'They'll be trigger-happy, that's certain,' said Larssen.

The caique worked its way steadily up the island's coast, but no one aboard saw any sign of life on the rocky shore. Behind the arid littoral the mountainous interior looked bare of vegetation. The heat shimmered on the water and contorted the rugged coastline. They passed Pethi Bay and turned north-westwards towards the tiny island of Nimos, which lay just beyond Simi. Gradually the large expanse of Yalo Bay opened up before them.

'I can see the port, sir,' Griffiths, who had the binoculars, shouted from the bows.

'We'll stand on for another ten minutes,' Maygan called out, 'and then head inshore. Hoist the white ensign.'

Maygan tossed his cloth cap into the cockpit and donned his service one. Off came the baggy trousers and on went the regulation navy shorts. Off came the seaman's vest and on went the regulation white naval shirt with the lieutenant's ranks in gold braid on the epaulettes. Both officers also buckled on their holsters. Pistols would be of little use in the situation they now found themselves in, but they were a kind of symbol of authority.

After ten minutes Maygan turned the caique into the bay and headed for the port. He cut the engine right back, and then put it in neutral so that LS8 was just moving gently through the calm water.

'Any shipping?' Maygan called out to Griffiths.

'Nothing that I can see, sir.'

'Keep a sharp lookout.'

'Aye, aye, sir.'

They left behind the headlands that protected the bay and could soon discern with the naked eye the buildings clustered around the port. Rows of multi-coloured houses were built on the steep hillsides that surrounded the port, which was dominated by an old castle. Atop this flew a very large but indistinguishable flag which flapped lazily in the light breeze.

They strained their eyes and ears, looking for movement or for the sound of the alarm being raised. But all they could hear was the chuckle of water under the caique's bows.

'Do you know, I think we've made it, gentlemen,' Maygan said. 'They're going to welcome us with open arms.'

As he spoke there was a large splash a long way astern of them and then they all heard the dull crack of a distant gun.

Maygan swore loudly.

The second shot was close enough for them to hear the curious whirr the shell made as it passed over them.

'Where is it, Griffiths?' Maygan shouted.

The deck-hand pointed and said: 'On that point there, sir.'

Sure enough, with the third shot they saw the flash.

'That's incredibly bad shooting,' said Larssen cool-ly.

'Perhaps they don't want to hit us?' Maygan suggested. 'Perhaps they're just firing warning shots across our bows to make us stop.'

'Then why are the shells all falling astern?' Larssen replied scornfully.

'Well, they're wasting valuable ammunition we might want,' Maygan argued. 'We might as well stop and see what happens.'

He put the engine in neutral and the caique slowly lost way and came to a halt. It bobbed up and down in the flat calm water. There was hardly any wind now and Maygan had the ensign hauled down and draped over the side where those manning the battery could see it. The battery fell silent, and they waited for the Italians' next move.

This came quite quickly, for they saw a motor launch leave the port and make its way towards them. It circled them warily and then came to a halt about 300 yards from them. In the bows a naval rating manned a machine-gun, which he pointed straight at them, and flying from the stern was a disproportionately large Italian flag with the emblem of the Italian royal house at its centre.

But what drew the immediate attention of the men aboard the caique was the figure seated in the centre of the launch. He was dressed from top to toe in pure white. A cascade of gold-braided tassels flowed from one shoulder and a parasol of delicate hue protected him from the sun.

'Cor,' said Barnesworth in mock awe. 'King Kong himself.'

A more modestly dressed officer stood up and bellowed through a loud-hailer: 'You spik English?'

'We are English,' Maygan shouted back. He pointed

at the white ensign. 'Royal Navy. Special Operations.'

'What you want?'

'We have come to talk with your commandant. We come as allies.'

The two figures conversed, then the man with the loud-hailer called out: 'Please. Follow us.'

Those in the launch obviously weren't completely convinced of the caique's identity for the machine-gunner was ordered to move with his weapon to the stern, where, to the amusement of those aboard the caique, the large flag kept winding itself around his head.

'Should I man the Solothurn, sir?' Griffiths asked. 'I can load it, but keep it under the foresail.'

Maygan nodded, and said: 'And let's have the Bren where we can get at it quickly.'

Larssen also slid up a Lanchester carbine he had found in the hold. He pushed it into a position where the folded mainsail prevented it being seen from the launch. He sighted down the barrel carefully.

'If you keep them slightly on your starboard bow as you're doing now I can take the machine-gunner,' he said to Maygan quietly. 'Then I'll puncture the elegant bastard under the umbrella.'

'Good. If it's a trap we can always turn and make a run for it. That battery couldn't hit a battleship at a hundred yards.'

'Oh, no, Andrew,' Larssen said softly. 'I think we run nowhere. Look at that.'

From behind the stone pier of the inner harbour a low, grey silhouette slid into view. It turned towards them and they could hear the powerful grumble of its engines as it picked up speed.

'Shit, eh,' Larssen whistled admiringly. 'That's some boat. What is it?'

'A *Motoscafo Anti-sommergibile* or MAS boat,' said Maygan, who had been chosen for the mission because of his smattering of Italian. 'A smaller equivalent of our MTBs.'

'We captured one earlier this summer,' Bryson said. 'They've got three Isotta-Fraschini engines and go like greased lightning, but are hopeless in any sort of a sea.'

They watched the MAS boat approach. It had a very low freeboard and seemed excessively narrow for its length, but it looked fast. Very fast. It had two torpedo tubes which were positioned either side of its bows and between them was mounted a dual-purpose machine-gun. Two members of the crew stood by it.

'Boy,' Larssen breathed, watching the white feather of water growing under the MAS boat's curved bows. That's a forty-knot boat, I reckon.'

'Nearer fifty actually,' Maygan corrected him. 'At least that's their design speed.'

The MAS boat surged forward effortlessly and circled astern of them. Maygan saw with some relief that the two-man crew of its main armament, twin 20mm Bredas positioned aft of its bridge, kept their weapon trained fore and aft. But the trap, if it was a trap, was now closed.

But, having shown its turn of speed, the MAS boat turned back and came alongside the caique. Abruptly, its engines were cut and the sleek grey hull stalled in the water. It had an open, streamlined, aluminium bridge on which a naval officer was sitting on a stool. He wore not a cap but a leather helmet rather like those worn by racing drivers of the day.

He stepped down from the stool, took off his helmet, and came down on to the deck. He leant on the rails of his elegant craft and called across to the caique. 'British navy?'

'That's right,' Maygan shouted back.

'Your ship's name?'

'LS8 of Levant Schooner Flotilla. Special Operations. *Buon giorno.*'

'*Buon giorno, Capitano.*' The officer smiled broadly as he snapped to attention and saluted. 'Welcome to Simi.'

Maygan returned the salute. 'Thank you. *Grazie.*'

'When you get into harbour you come aboard, *sì*? I want to welcome you.' The officer made the gesture of lifting a glass to his lips.

'Thank you,' said Maygan with more feeling.

'Pink gin. It's good?'

'That'll do nicely,' said Maygan.

'*Arrivederci.*'

The officer saluted again, returned to his bridge and his stool, and the MAS boat surged forward.

'He seems friendly enough,' said Maygan. 'I wonder how he knows about pink gin.'

Larssen grunted. Jarrett had told him how complicated the situation was, how nothing would be what it seemed, and he remained sceptical. Put in its simplest terms, Jarrett had explained, the Italian *Fascisti* still supported the Germans, whereas the non-fascist Italians certainly didn't. The non-fascists loathed the Germans and Mussolini's jackbooted supporters in equal measure, but were scared of both. Most Greeks loathed all Italians and all Germans and were scared of neither, but only the Andartes had arms. And then there were the fascist Greeks, the collaborators. Who were on which islands and in what strength remained a mystery, as did the allegiance of the various groups to the Allied cause. It was, Jarrett had told Larssen, a bit of a hornets' nest.

He could say that again.

A group of civilians had gathered at the end of the breakwater as they passed into the inner harbour.

'*Yasus!*' Larssen called out, using the only word of Greek he knew.

The civilians waved frantically. '*Yasus! Anglika! Yasus!*'

They waved and called, thin, ragged figures alive with delight. They ran along the breakwater, ignoring the MAS boat, which was returning to its berth there. They waved and shouted as they went, and then the crew of the caique saw that small groups of other locals were beginning to gather on the quay that ran the length of the tiny port.

'Unload the Solothurn, Griffiths,' Maygan ordered. 'Make sure it's covered up.'

'Aye, aye, sir.'

'All other arms in the hold. If it's a trap, there's nothing we can do about it now. I'm not going to risk hurting the locals in a running gun battle.'

They watched the launch go alongside the quay and tie up. The elegant figure in white stepped out from under the parasol and on to the quay. They could see him flicking dust off his uniform and pulling his skin-tight jacket straight.

'What the hell's he got on his head, sir?' Bryson asked.

'Looks like ostrich plumes to me,' said Maygan.

'Jesus,' Bryson said quietly.

The other officer aboard the launch jumped ashore

and indicated to those aboard the caique that they should berth alongside the quay next to the launch.

'Here we go, lads. Mooring warps ready fore and aft.'

Tiller watched with admiration as Maygan manoeuvred the clumsy vessel. It came alongside with hardly a bump.

'Cut the engine, Bryson.'

The crowd surged forward and began to clap and call out their welcome.

Many eager hands grabbed the mooring warps and stretched out to greet the caique's crew. Thin, lined faces, nut-brown from the sun and wreathed in smiles, clustered round. A bunch of green grapes and a bottle was handed through the crowd and passed to those on deck.

'Drink, drink, drink,' the crowd demanded.

Maygan raised the bottle and drank deeply. It was retsina, very harsh and dry but welcome nonetheless. Everyone in turn on the caique took a swig and each time the crowd cheered its approval. The babble was tremendous but then half a dozen soldiers wearing the curious cocked hats of the Italian *carabinieri* pushed their way through the crowd to make a path for the two officers in their white uniforms. The crowd muttered among themselves and stepped back reluctantly. One or two even resisted the soldiers' advance but were shoved aside by their rifle butts.

The soldiers looked nervous, the Italian officers even more so. They approached the caique and halted, then both gave the fascist salute, the right arm outstretched at forty-five degrees, the open palm of the hand held outwards.

No one on the caique moved. The muttering in the

crowd stopped. The silence was broken when one old man at the front hawked noisily and then spat into the water. Another copied him but he spat on the ground. Maygan could see that some of the saliva had splashed on to the shiny black knee-boots of one of the officers, who pretended not to notice. The tension between the two groups was unmistakable.

'There's going to be trouble,' Maygan said to Larssen quietly. 'I think we've got to do something. Quickly.'

Larssen swung himself up on to the bulwarks and grabbed the rigging to steady himself.

'Does anyone here speak English?' he addressed the crowd. A tough-looking man with greying hair and a lined face burnt almost black with the sun pushed forward. He wore a large knife on his belt and his right hand lay loosely on its hilt as he spoke. 'My name is Christophou, Angelios Christophou. My family are fishermen. We have lived here many generations. The British navy is welcome.'

They shook hands and the crowd murmured appreciatively. It had not gone unnoticed that the British visitors had refused to acknowledge the Italians' salute.

Larssen quickly explained that they were the advance guard of a larger British force, that the British were old friends and allies of the Greeks, that he understood how the local people felt, but that there must be no trouble, and that they must all disperse to their homes.

'Tonight we celebrate,' he ended. 'But now we have business to discuss.'

He gestured towards the Italian officers. The fisherman nodded and turned and addressed the crowd.

When he had finished someone shouted something from the back. The crowd tittered and the fisherman grinned. 'He wants to know if you have come to hang all the Italians. He will help you. He has some good strong rope.'

Larssen thought of telling them that the Italians had to be their allies if the islands were to be kept free of Germans. But he looked at their faces and thought better of it. That would have to wait.

'No hanging, no shooting, no fighting,' Larssen announced firmly and loudly. 'Any of you making trouble will be answerable to me.'

Larssen pointed his finger at random into the crowd and then at his chest. He saw that they knew what he meant before Christophou had even translated his words, and that they didn't like it. They had scores to settle and the sooner they started settling them the happier they would be.

It looked like being an impasse. But then in one of those gestures that only a natural diplomat can plan Larssen took a small Greek flag out of his pocket, knotted it to a halyard, and hoisted it to the masthead. They went wild with delight, shouting at Christophou to translate their demands. Christophou grabbed his arm.

'They do what you say. But tonight you come to the taverna. Tonight at nine o'clock. We celebrate. They want your promise.'

Larssen pointed to his watch and then to the taverna, and then lifted an imaginary glass to his lips. They cheered.

'Nine o'clock,' he shouted, and they cheered some more when they knew they had his promise. But it was not quite over yet, for each of the male inhabitants insisted on hugging each of the crew and pumping his hand before they would leave. Even so, within twenty minutes the quay was deserted except for the *carabinieri* leaning on their rifles and the two dejected officers wilting in the heat.

'And who,' said Larssen pointing at them, 'exactly are you two comedians?'

5

'*Prego*? Comedians?' The more plainly dressed of the two Italian army officers looked perplexed; his elegant companion impatient.

An hour previously the SBS patrol had received a hostile reception from the Italian garrison. Now the SBS men realized that their erstwhile enemies were in more imminent danger than they were. If the nearby Germans didn't get them the local Greeks certainly would. And if the two standing before them were typical examples of those defending the Dodecanese, there didn't seem much hope of keeping the Germans at bay if they chose to come.

'*Prego*?' the Italian officer said again.

'Who are you?' Larssen repeated.

The officer drew himself up and his chest swelled beneath his exquisitely cut uniform. He was a young man with an oversized moustache the ends of which he tended to bite when he was nervous. 'I am Giuseppe Antonio Giuliano Perquesta, lieutenant in the army of His Majesty King Victor Emmanuel, and until recently a troop commander in the Cavour armoured division. Now I am the interpreter on the staff of His Excellency Colonel Ardetti, the island's commandant. At your service, *signore*.'

'And him?'

'The colonel's aide-de-camp, *signore*. Captain Salvini.'

At the sound of his name the captain bowed stiffly. His ostrich feathers made his head look top-heavy. He was dark and swarthy, with narrow eyes and twitchy hands. Larssen didn't like the look of him at all.

'Look Giuseppe,' Larssen said firmly. 'Firstly, no more of this.' Larssen waved his arm above his head in a parody of a fascist salute. 'Understood?'

The lieutenant nodded and grinned his agreement, but Salvini looked glum.

'Secondly, we come as friends and liberators, not as conquerors. That applies to you as much as to the islanders. We come as advisers. You understand me?'

'*Sì, capisco, signore.* I quite understand.'

'My first piece of advice is don't annoy the locals. Your men should keep out of their way.'

'I understand, *signore*. But of course that is a matter for the commandant. He sends you his friendly greetings.'

'He has a damned funny way of doing it,' Maygan interrupted crossly. 'It's bloody lucky your gunners can't shoot straight.'

Perquesta smoothed his moustache in embarrassment. '*Scusi, signore.* It was a mistake. Everyone is – how do you say? – very nervous. At any moment we expect the Germans. They demand we still fight on their side. The commandant has already had a radio message from General Klemann on Rhodes. The general is a hard man.'

It dawned on Larssen as he watched Salvini's expression that it had not been a mistake at all. If the Italian garrison resisted any English intrusion the Germans could hardly accuse them of treachery. On the other hand the Italians would not want to damage, much less sink, a Royal Navy ship in case the British appeared in force. Which was why the battery had made quite sure it had not hit the caique. And doubtless there were warring factions among the Italians themselves – probably represented by the two men standing in front of him.

Perquesta could see Larssen disbelieved him. He tugged nervously at the scarlet cravat around his neck. 'The commandant would like to meet you to hear what the British propose. May I take you to him?'

Larssen told him to stay where he was and took Tiller and Barnesworth to the other side of the caique.

'We've got to do some swift talking,' he said. 'We'll go armed to show we mean business, and we're going to have to smarten ourselves up.' He rubbed his chin. 'I'd better shave.'

'I could put on my cap badge again, skipper,' Tiller said with a grin. He had found that Larssen's nickname came easily to him now.

'Good idea,' said Larssen seriously. 'Clandestine warfare is one thing, diplomacy quite another. We're going to have to get used to wearing several hats.'

'I volunteered for the SBS to fight, skipper, not pander to a lot of comic-opera characters,' Barnesworth grumbled.

'You'll get your fighting, Billy,' Larssen promised. 'I'll see to that. Now let's get this ship looking like a fishing boat. That damned Jerry plane might still be nosing around.'

The commandant's headquarters was in the Crusaders' castle that was perched above the port. It took them some time to climb the steep track to it but, as Perquesta explained apologetically, the garrison had no transport. The commandant's office was like a hothouse. A dowdy grey-haired figure, Colonel Ardetti stood up behind his desk and pumped their hands while Salvini, bareheaded now, stood silently and moodily behind him. The colonel talked in rapid Italian which was accompanied by expressive gestures with his hands.

His duty, he said through Perquesta, was to defend Italian soil. If the British would help him, so much the better. The aide-de-camp bent and whispered something in his ear. The colonel's face darkened, but he nodded his agreement. However, he continued, it was not as simple as that. The armistice was by no means clear. The loyalty of the armed forces was divided. There were other ways of defending the integrity of Italian territory besides fighting over it.

He shrugged apologetically, spread his hands out, and then shrugged again. What can I do? his expression said; my hands are tied.

'But the commandant does agree that the garrison must not clash with the civilian population,' Perquesta said. 'His excellency says it is a delicate situation. But he will give orders at once for all patrols to be withdrawn and for his troops to be confined to their barracks. Maintaining law and order on the island is now in British hands. Once that has been established, gentlemen, perhaps you would care to have further discussions early tomorrow?'

'First round to Salvini,' Larssen muttered to Tiller as they left. 'He's a Fascist if ever I saw one. I think we must knock the colonel off the fence he's sitting on.'

'And how do we do that, skipper?' Barnesworth asked.

'We visit our Italian naval friend. He might be prepared to declare his hand.'

They returned to the caique, which now had a large fishing net 'drying' halfway up its mast, collected Maygan and then walked along to the stone pier where the MAS boat was moored. The sentry at the gangplank saluted smartly and her captain appeared at the rails.

'Welcome, welcome,' he called down. 'Come aboard.'

He took them below to the tiny ward-room under the bridge and mixed the two officers a pink gin each, expertly swirling the Angostura bitters around the glass before adding a generous measure of gin and a touch of bottled water. Tiller and Barnesworth opted for the local ouzo.

The Italian then introduced himself as Lieutenant Commander Balbao. 'Cheers, as you say. The British Navy's favourite drink, eh?'

'You speak good English,' Larssen said.

'I attended a staff course at your Royal Naval College at Greenwich before the war. What a place, eh? That painted hall. Never shall I forget those guest dinners.'

He stood up and raised his glass in imitation of the senior naval officer who presided on such occasions. 'I give you the toast, gentlemen: Admiral Nelson.' He sat down, happy that he had remembered the occasion so well. 'And I found the sweetest girl, a real English rose.' He kissed his fingers.

'We need help, Commander,' Larssen said.

'Then you come to the right place,' said Balbao, suddenly serious. 'You have already talked to the commandant here, yes?'

Larssen nodded cautiously. Balbao twiddled his

glass, drained it, mixed himself another pink gin, and glanced at each of them in turn. Then he seemed to make up his mind. 'What can I do for you?'

'You are under the commandant's orders?'

Balbao shook his head. 'My superior is Admiral Maschinni on Leros. I answer to him and him only. But naturally my task is to liaise with the army garrisons.'

'And where do you stand, Commander?' Larssen asked quietly. Balbao knew exactly what he meant.

'I hate fascism. I hope that someone strings up that jackal Mussolini. But I am proud of my country, gentlemen. Italy will rise again.'

'You are on our side, then?'

'Of course.'

'And you'll fight alongside us if necessary?'

'Admiral Maschinni has already given orders to defend Italian territory,' Balbao said cautiously.

It was the reply of a diplomat. Balbao knew it and the tone of his voice changed to one of anger. 'I have no love of the Germans. But what is more important to me is the honour of the Italian Navy. We are an honourable service with a brave past. But never were we allowed to fight. We were always told to avoid it. Run here, run there. Always away from your navy. You understand?'

Larssen and Maygan nodded in agreement.

'I have no respect for those who commanded our navy. You know what our great poet D'Annunzio said that MAS stood for? For *Memento Audare Semper* – Remember always to dare. But never, never were we allowed to dare.'

Maygan and Larssen listened respectfully and later Larssen was to say that the Italian had 'a buzz in his bonnet, yes?' Then they led him to the problem in hand by asking how they could best get the commandant on to the British side.

Balbao sighed. 'That is another matter. Ardetti, you understand, is not a young man. He wants to get home alive to his wife and children in Genoa. He is much swayed by possible retaliation from the Germans and there are committed Fascists among his staff.'

'Salvini, for instance?'

The Italian nodded, and added: 'And some of the men. They are not to be trusted. If I were you I'd lock them up.'

'But we can trust the local people?' Larssen asked.

The Italian shrugged. 'At a time like this, who can tell? Why do you ask?'

'We must visit the smaller islands around here,' Larssen explained. 'We therefore need someone with local knowledge. Unless of course . . .'

He looked at Balbao hopefully, but the Italian shook his head ruefully. 'I would like to help but it is not possible. I do not have the fuel. I left harbour today because I, too, must be seen to be supporting the commandant. Every move I make is noted.'

'There is no fuel on the island?' Maygan said in astonishment.

'There is some fuel, but it is under the commandant's control. I only have what is in my tanks. Enough to get us back to Leros. No more.'

'Ammunition?' Larssen asked.

'Plenty of ammunition. Plenty of food.' Balbao lifted his glass and grinned. 'Plenty of drink. But no fuel.'

'Well, it won't run on gin, I can tell you that,'

Maygan said to Larssen as the captain ushered the SBS party back on deck.

'It needs high-octane petrol. Aviation fuel,' Balbao said. 'If you can find me fuel, I can help you.'

The local taverna, a crumbling building on the quay, was packed when the SBS party arrived, and a small crowd had also gathered outside it. A path to the bar was cleared for them and they were slapped heartily on the back as they walked along it. Inside the bare wooden tables were packed with locals.

'*Yasus! Yasus!*' they called out, lifting their glasses. 'You are welcome here.'

Angelios Christophou stepped forward from the crowd of men at the bar and gripped their hands. It reminded Tiller of when, as a small boy, he had got his fingers caught in his mother's wringer. A table was dragged out from the back for them and a bottle of retsina and some glasses placed on it. An ancient radio on a shelf behind the bar blared out martial music. Christophou gestured to it in disgust. 'Music, music, but they tell us nothing. What is happening, my friends? Italy has surrendered, but no one knows anything else.'

He poured out the retsina and pushed the glasses brimming with the clear liquid towards his guests. 'We drink to the Allies, and to give thanks for the defeat of the Italian fascist scum.'

Larssen glanced at Maygan and knew they were both thinking the same thing: it was going to be difficult to persuade the islanders that Italy was no longer the enemy.

'We know no more than you do,' Maygan said. 'Except that the Germans may want these islands. Once they have had time to organize themselves they might try and occupy them. They have already taken over from the Italians on Rhodes. We have come to stop them if they try.'

Christophou was instantly alert. 'The Germans?' He uttered the word 'Germans' with unmistakable venom. 'Why should they come here?'

Larssen pointed in the direction of the mainland. 'Turkey. They want her to stay out of the war.'

Christophou spat on the floor. 'Bah! the Turks.'

'He doesn't seem to like anyone very much,' Tiller murmured to Barnesworth.

'I'm glad he's on our side,' Barnesworth replied softly. 'I wonder if there are any more like him.'

Both SBS men had already glanced around the taverna to see what local manpower might be available to help defend the island, and had come to the same conclusion that there would be none. There were no young men in the taverna, nor any women come to that, though they had seen plenty of children around the port, thin and in tattered clothing.

All the men they had seen looked over fifty, and many appeared much older. Grand-looking fellows, some of them were, with their long moustaches and dark, piercing eyes. But many appeared to be victims of the islanders' traditional method of making a living, sponge-diving, for both SBS men recognized the symptoms of diver's palsy among some of them and noticed in others the swollen joints caused by nitrogen saturation.

'They must be keeping the womenfolk out of sight,' said Barnesworth, nudging Tiller. 'They saw you coming, Tiger.'

The more they looked around them the more obvious it was that the islanders were living on the brink of starvation. Compared with the smooth, well-fed faces of the Italian garrison, the islanders were in a pitiful state.

'We eat,' Christophou announced. 'Then we drink some more.'

He clapped his hands. Tiller made as if to protest, but Larssen shook his head at him. 'You don't refuse a Greek's hospitality even if you know what he is offering you has meant sending his children to bed supperless.'

The first woman that they saw now appeared from behind a black curtain at the back of the taverna. Her tray was loaded with bread and olives and a plate of cheese. Behind her a girl, her eyes cast down in embarrassment, brought a large plate of salted fish.

'My mother,' Christophou announced proudly. The old woman nodded and smiled, and shook each hand in turn, but her eyes were sad and cast down.

'And this is my daughter, Angelika. My mother speaks no English but Angelika speaks it well. She is clever, aren't you, Angelika?'

The girl looked as if she wished the floor would swallow her up. Tiller caught her eye and smiled encouragingly. 'This food' – he gestured at the table – 'you are very kind.'

She recognized at once that he was trying to make it easier for her and he was rewarded with a quick glance of gratitude.

'It is nothing,' she said softly in clear English. 'You must excuse me', and before her father could stop her she had slipped away behind the curtain.

Christophou growled in disgust. 'Clever she may be, but stubborn, too. That is what is wrong with giving women education. It gives them minds of their own.

She would not stay in Athens when the war started. She insisted she came here, and I must say she has been very useful. She is strong and without the young men we need every pair of hands we can find aboard the fishing boat.'

'Where are your young men?' Tiller asked.

'Many were drafted into the Italian army or navy,' Christophou answered, 'but those who escaped are in the mountains.'

'Here?'

Christophou shook his head. 'On the bigger islands. That is the trouble. We can't stop the Germans from coming to Simi or prevent the Italians from staying.'

Larssen leant forward and said: 'We can't stop the Italians from staying either, Angelios. That is something that will be settled when the war is over. But we can stop the Germans coming. To do it we need the Italians to help us, at least until we can bring our own troops to the islands.'

Christophou absorbed this information without changing his expression and Tiller realized that he had underestimated the Greek, that Christophou had already arrived at that equation himself.

'And us?' he asked. 'You mean you want no trouble between us and the Italian pigs?'

'Exactly.'

Christophou stroked the stubble on his chin. 'That is a hard thing to ask. We are Greeks. The Italians have no right to be here. For most of my life they have suppressed us. They have starved us. Many of us have been beaten by them.' He shook his head angrily, remembering the injustices. 'How can I tell the people here not to take revenge? Many are already sharpening their knives.'

'We understand,' said Larssen. 'But that has to be settled after the war.'

Christophou thought for a moment and then shouted across the taverna to a tall, swarthy Greek, who stood up and joined them. He solemnly shook hands all round, and accepted a glass of retsina but refused the food. Christophou talked rapidly to him in Greek. The man argued, then shrugged his shoulders, and eventually nodded.

'Dimitri is the mayor here. He will see there is no trouble. But can you get us food? Our children are hungry.'

'In the morning I am seeing Colonel Ardetti,' said Larssen. The Dane had seen the condition of the children on Castelrosso and on Simi, and it angered him. 'I promise you that he will release some food.'

Dimitri shot a sentence in Greek at Christophou and lifted his glass in turn to the SBS men, who reciprocated. 'He says we help the English by not cutting any Italian throats. But is there no other way we can help?'

Larssen hesitated. He was reluctant to involve the islanders, but their local knowledge was needed if he was to fulfil his mission. 'There is. Tomorrow more of my men will come. Not many, but enough. They will stay and organize the island's defences while we visit the other islands around here. Piscopi, Calchi, then Alemnia. To do that we need the help of a pilot – someone who knows the area well.'

Christophou translated rapidly into Greek. Dimitri nodded, and pointed to Christophou, who spread out his hands in a gesture of modesty which he obviously did not feel. 'Dimitri says I am the right man.'

'You agree to go?' Larssen asked. 'It could be dangerous.'

'Dangerous? Bah! You know the old way we use here to get to the sponges? Just as we did in the time of the ancient Greeks. A rope is attached to us and we sink to the bottom by holding a heavy stone. Like this.' He clasped an imaginary rock to his chest. 'We had . . .'

He gestured to show his eyes were covered.

'Face masks.'

'Yes. Nothing more. Then we use – how do you say? – a kind of fork to take the sponge from the bottom. As a boy that was how we did it. Don't talk to me about danger.'

'Shit,' Barnesworth said admiringly under his breath.

Tiller's professional interest was aroused. 'But you've got diving equipment now?'

'Of course. Diving suits and boats with air pumps. Off the North African coast that is the only way because the sponges are in very deep water. Now that can be dangerous, yes?'

Tiller remembered a time, in Chichester harbour, when the Davis submarine escape apparatus he was testing malfunctioned. They had got him up just in time. He nodded sympathetically.

'But we sail in my boat, not yours. Many Turkish caiques visit Simi, but not so many sail west of here. Everyone knows my boat. No one will be suspicious.'

Larssen nodded. 'That makes sense. Agreed, Andrew?'

Maygan nodded. The arrangement suited him well. He didn't fancy putting his caique in the hands of a pilot of unknown skill. Anyway, Bryson needed time to strip the Matilda engine to find the cause of the trouble that had been plaguing it.

They agreed that only one guard was needed. Tiller took the first watch. He sat next to the covered Solothurn, his back propped against the mast, his Sten across his knees. The taverna shut soon after they left and the few flickering oil lamps in the houses around the quay were extinguished one by one. A dog howled in the distance. The night was moonless but the glittering stars seemed to illuminate the quay with a pale light. The water slapped lazily against the side of the caique, which moved uneasily when the wind gusted in occasionally from the sea. Tiller saw a cat move swiftly between two houses, but no other movement.

His thoughts strayed to Angelika. Had that look contained anything except polite gratitude? He guessed not but the two hours' watch was passed pleasantly enough speculating about the shy Greek girl and the nature of her stubbornness.

When his watch was up he leant over and shook Griffiths awake, handed him the Sten gun, pulled part of the mainsail over him, and slept without the nightmare recurring. He was woken at first light when Bryson prodded him with the butt of the Lanchester. 'Tea's brewed, Sarge. Captain Larssen says he wants to go to the castle in ten minutes.'

As soon as they were ushered into Colonel Ardetti's presence it became apparent that the Italians had had at least a partial change of heart. Perquesta told them that Admiral Maschinni had radioed the previous evening to say that Jarrett and his party had arrived on Leros, and had told Ardetti he was to co-operate with the SBS.

The SBS men sat down with the Italians, who showed them the plans of the island's defences. On paper these appeared adequate but on closer questioning Ardetti admitted he was short of ammunition and that not all the gun positions were manned. The ground, he said, was too rocky to dig slit trenches, so stone sangars had been built instead. These overlooked likely landing places, but they provided inadequate protection against anything except small-arms fire and virtually none against air attack.

There were no landlines between the outposts on the island and no central reserve force to reinforce any of them. Even if there had been there was no method of transporting them as Simi had no roads.

Larssen then inspected the outposts on the island's only vehicle, a tractor. At the end of it he advised the colonel to withdraw all his troops from the other parts of the island and concentrate them around the port. 'And make them dig slit trenches,' he added. 'The ground's not too rocky. They just need to expend a bit of sweat.'

Many of the garrison, Larssen had noticed, were fat, others were well past their prime. Their morale was suspect – some saluted Ardetti half-heartedly, others ignored him – and their weapons were hopelessly antiquated. They were all equipped with the outdated 6mm Mannlicher-Carcano rifle, which had remained practically unchanged from when it had been first manufactured in 1889 as a copy of the bolt-action Mauser.

Even the garrison's light machine-guns were the 1930 model 6.5mm air-cooled Breda, which had all sorts of design problems. Larssen remembered the comments of his instructor on the foreign weapons training course he had attended outside Haifa. If something looked right it generally was right: the Breda looked wrong, was wrong, and invariably went wrong.

The two coastal batteries were in no better shape than the garrison's personal weapons. Both had been sited incorrectly and were short of ammunition. The one that had fired at the caique had just half a dozen rounds of 75mm ammunition left. Most seriously, there were no anti-aircraft guns. If the Germans came Larssen knew it would only be the bravery of the garrison that stopped them, not the weight of the defenders' fire-power.

Ardetti, who looked pale and rather shaken by his excursion round the island, turned even paler when Larssen told him, through Perquesta, what he expected from the garrison.

'Naturally, we will support the British force here,' Ardetti replied. 'But as you can see my garrison cannot prevent the Germans from taking the island if they want to. We shall need a brigade of good troops here, supported by artillery, of course. When can we expect such a force?'

'Some reinforcements will be arriving this evening, after dark,' Larssen told him.

Ardetti's face lit up when Perquesta translated this. 'Good, good. A battalion perhaps?'

Larssen looked at him. 'No. Four of my men.'

Perquesta's jaw dropped. 'Four?'

'Four,' Larssen repeated, and held up four fingers.

Perquesta wrung his hands as he translated. The colonel just shook his head. Salvini smirked. 'They don't seem to have much faith in us, skipper,' Tiller remarked.

'I'll boot their arses from here to Cairo,' Larssen said in a sudden flash of temper. 'They'll fight whether they want to or not. I'll see to that. You make your colonel understand that,' he snarled at Perquesta.

The Italian lieutenant bit the edges of his moustache and nodded, but Larssen had now worked himself up into a fury.

'I want work on the trenches started now and I shall inspect them this evening. I want them manned at all times. I want flour and pasta released to the local population. Now. And I want fuel for cooking and for the MAS boat.'

Ardetti's Italian was so rapid when Perquesta told him this that Perquesta had trouble in translating the torrent. 'He says the garrison is short of food. They now only have one cooked meal a day. The other two meals are cold. The fuel they need for cooking and for refrigeration and . . .'

'And for what?' Larssen snarled.

Perquesta hesitated. 'For heating, *signore*. The colonel says the castle is damp. It has to be dried out as he suffers from rheumatism.'

'Then the colonel is relieved of his duties and is, as of now, officially on sick leave,' Larssen snapped. 'You, Perquesta, will take immediate command.'

'But *signore*,' Perquesta protested. 'Captain Salvini is of senior rank to me.'

Larssen turned to Salvini, who flinched under the Dane's hostile stare. 'Tell our friend here that I don't like his politics or his face. So I do not propose to put the garrison under his command. However, I won't lock him up so long as he behaves himself. I want

90

from him a complete list of stores and fuel held by the garrison to be delivered to me on the caique immediately. Is that understood?'

Salvini, who obviously understood some English, nodded before Perquesta had finished translating. He looked glummer than ever.

'I shall be assigning one of my men to conduct a daily routine of physical exercises for the garrison which will include all officers,' Larssen added. 'The first of these will be held in exactly two hours. Captain Salvini is personally answerable to me that these orders are carried out. You, Lieutenant Perquesta, can get on and lick this garrison into some sort of shape. We may not have much time.'

'You can't do that, skipper,' Tiller said admiringly as the SBS party descended the hill to the quay, 'you don't have the authority.'

'Just watch me, Tiger,' Larssen retorted. 'Just watch me. Our job is to keep the Krauts out and that's exactly what we're going to do.'

Salvini, realizing Larssen meant business, had a list of stores and fuel brought to the caique within the hour and an hour after that Barnesworth was putting the garrison through a series of physical jerks and making them negotiate an improvised assault course.

As soon as it was dark Christophou's caique came alongside LS8, and arms and ammunition and equipment were passed over. Tiller felt a flicker of disappointment when he realized that Angelika was not aboard. Instead there was a slip of a youth whom Christophou introduced to them as Giorgiou. The youngster smiled shyly, and did what Christophou required of him with a practised ease that came with utter familiarity, but uttered not a word to anyone.

The Italians, Christophou explained, had taken away both Giorgiou's parents to the mainland. They had been betrayed by a collaborator on another island who had accused them of being Andartes. Since then Giorgiou had said very little. In his few unoccupied moments aboard the caique he sharpened his knife on a whetstone and tested its sharpness with his thumb.

Soon after midnight another caique from the flotilla came alongside, having lain up under camouflage nets on the Turkish coast during the day. It offloaded Corporal Ted Warrington, two other SBS men, and a member of the Greek Sacred Squadron, and then set sail for Kos, where it was to meet up with Jarrett.

Larssen briefed the SBS men to help the Italians organize the garrison's defences along the lines he had recommended, and ensure his orders regarding the food and fuel were carried out. He then assigned the Greek Sacred Squadron officer, a young lieutenant called Kristos, to the job of making sure the local population kept the peace.

Before dawn broke, borne on a light wind that eddied off the hills, Christophou's caique left the port with Larssen, Tiller, and Barnesworth aboard. Their first stop was at Piscopi, south-west of Simi. Piscopi, Christophou told them, meant 'lookout', as men in olden times had been sent there from Rhodes to watch for Turkish shipping. It was about the same size as Simi – some eight miles long – and was well named, for the high ground dominated the surrounding waters. But it was not as strategically placed, for it did not bar the passage of shipping southwards along the Turkish coast, as Simi did. The Italians had therefore only garrisoned it with a dozen *carabinieri*, who seemed to have become quite accepted by the population. One had even married a local girl.

A local Greek spoke a smattering of Italian and through him Larssen impressed the corporal in charge with the importance of radioing Simi if the Germans arrived. The caique then sailed south-east under a clear blue sky and reached Calchi that evening. As they were uncertain whether the Germans had already occupied the island from Rhodes – only a few miles to the south-east – Christophou landed the SBS men outside the port.

This proved to be a wise precaution for they were soon met by a young Greek who had obviously run from a nearby lookout to greet them. Breathlessly he introduced himself as Demetrios and in broken English explained that ten Germans had arrived in a motor launch from Rhodes earlier in the day and had requisitioned a house near the quay. Soon afterwards, the boy had gone on to explain contemptuously, the small Italian garrison had melted into the hills without firing a shot. After patrolling through the port the Germans had retired to the house with food and wine they had demanded from the locals.

Larssen sat Demetrios down and had him sketch out on the ground the exact location of the house the Germans had commandeered, and where they had moored their launch. The boy told them there was a sentry outside the house and they had also put one to guard the boat.

With a twig the boy then traced in the dust a route the SBS patrol could take that would bring them to the back of the house without being seen. Larssen pointed to Demetrios and then to the route. The boy grinned and nodded.

'Good, we have a guide,' said Larssen. 'What do you think, boys?'

'I could take the sentry guarding the launch, skipper,' Tiller volunteered, 'while you and Billy knock off the one outside the house. Then you can both get into position at the front and back of the house while I'll chuck in one of those Eyetie grenades you're so fond of, skipper. They'll come out like scalded cats and you can finish them off.'

At Simi they had found a box of Italian grenades, and Larssen, who had used them before, had brought them along.

'No. I don't want too much shooting in the streets. Locals might get hurt.'

'Set the house alight,' Barnesworth suggested. 'Burn the buggers.'

'And probably half the port,' said Larssen. 'It would also almost certainly alert the Krauts on Rhodes and we want to be well clear before they send anyone to investigate what's happened to their patrol. No, that's not the answer. I think we dispose of the launch's sentry first, then kill the other sentry, and then finish off the others inside the house. That way there'll be not much noise.'

The other two nodded. It made sense.

Demetrios led them at a brisk pace until they arrived at a high wall that ran alongside the quay. The boy signalled to them that the sentry guarding the launch was on the other side of the wall, and that further along there was a break in it. They moved forward cautiously on their rubber-soled commando boots, stopping to listen every few yards. Soon they heard the sentry's boots scraping on the stone quay. Then a match was scratched and the faint flare as it lit showed that the German was some thirty feet from them on the other side of the wall.

Larssen took out from his holster the special .22-calibre pistol all SBS men were issued with, screwed on the silencer, and tapped Tiller on the arm to show he was ready. Tiller and Barnesworth moved silently along the wall until they came to the break that Demetrios had indicated. They went through it and crouched by an upturned boat.

At first they could only see the glow of the sentry's cigarette, but then they saw his silhouette. Tiller was relieved to see he was wearing a desert-type forage cap. It would have been more difficult to break his neck if he had been wearing a helmet. They waited what seemed an age. Then they saw the glow of the sentry's cigarette butt as it arced through the air into the harbour, heard the clatter as he picked up his weapon and the bright ring of his boots on the stone as he approached them.

The SBS men shrank back behind the counter of the upturned boat until the sentry was just beyond them. Tiller made no sound and the sentry neither saw nor heard anything until Tiller's forearm tightened around his windpipe and turned his brief cry to a subdued gurgle. But then the German twisted round with a desperation born of terror and for a heart-stopping second Tiller realized that his grip had slipped and that he was not going to be able to break the man's neck cleanly.

Suddenly the sentry went limp and Tiller lowered him gently to the ground.

'A strong fellow,' Barnesworth whispered. 'But not strong enough.'

He wiped his knife clean on the German's uniform before sheathing it. 'Shove him under the boat.'

'Thanks, Billy.'

'Think nothing of it, mate. Now where's this fucking launch?'

They found it further down the quay, a wooden motor boat painted white with a swastika flag fluttering at its stern. Tiller lowered himself into it and opened the seacocks, then climbed back on to the quay. He watched the water rising rapidly up to and then over the thwarts, and then severed its mooring lines. It sank quickly and quietly. If the Germans wanted it they would have to send a diver down to get it.

They rejoined Larssen and Demetrios, and gave Larssen the thumbs up. Larssen indicated to Demetrios to lead the way to the house. It was a small, two-storey villa, somebody's holiday home in peacetime. Larssen moved quietly around it while the others waited nearby in the shadows. He returned with a grin on his face, the cheese wire with its wooden handles at either end still dangling from his hand.

'The sentry was sitting near the back door,' he whispered. 'Very easy. Let's go. I take the first floor. You two clear the ground floor. You' – he pointed at Demetrios – 'wait here.'

The sentry lay where he had dropped. Even in the half light Tiller could see his face was puffy and black. His eyeballs were almost out of their sockets and his tongue stuck out. There must be more pleasant ways of dying, Tiller decided, than being garrotted.

The back door was unlocked. They eased their way

in and found themselves in a passage that led straight through the house to the front door. On either side were two rooms, their doors shut. Larssen indicated that Tiller take one and Barnesworth the other, then pointed upstairs and held up his hand with the fingers spread apart, and then bunched them three times.

Tiller and Barnesworth nodded. They'd give him fifteen seconds after he had reached the first floor before opening fire.

They watched Larssen move silently down the corridor and listened for any sounds. Through the doors they heard snoring but otherwise the house was as silent as a tomb.

As Larssen reached the stairs Tiller took one of the scarlet-painted grenades from his pocket. Larssen had told him they were only made of tin, and were nothing like as lethal as a British No. 36 grenade, the so-called Mills bomb. But they made a hell of a bang and, unlike the British grenade, you could follow up behind it immediately without worrying about being hit by fragments. He just hoped Larssen was right.

Fifteen ... ten ... five ... Tiller pulled the pin from the grenade, kicked the door in, tossed the grenade into the room, and followed in behind the explosion.

There was a scream and a guttural curse, but at first Tiller could see little through the smoke. Then he saw something move in the far corner and remembered the advice of the instructor at the Killer School: 'Shoot the man who moves first, as he's the one who's recovered first', and gave the lurching figure a short, measured burst. The man jerked and then slid gently down the wall as the Sten's 9mm bullets thudded home.

Then Tiller turned and shot a man who was still

on the floor groping for his rifle. The third one had received the full force of the grenade and wasn't moving.

It was over in seconds. Tiller cautiously inspected the three bodies by kicking them over on to their backs. They were all dead. The room stank of vomit. Obviously the soldiers, confident that they were safe, had drunk their fill of the local ouzo.

Next door Barnesworth had killed four others with his grenade and precise, conservative bursts from his Sten. That left one upstairs somewhere.

The two men took the stairs in quick bounds and found Larssen on the landing.

'No one up here,' he hissed. 'Were they all downstairs?'

Tiller shook his head. 'Only seven.'

'Shit!'

They stood stock-still alert for any movement in the house. They could not hear anything, but Larssen's instincts told him the German was there. Somewhere.

'The lavatory,' Barnesworth suddenly whispered. 'It must be downstairs.'

He thrust his Sten at Tiller, drew his pistol, and in two quick movements jumped down the stairs and vaulted the banisters. He landed in the correct crouching position in the passage below, his pistol held out in front of him in both hands.

Bending double saved him as the first burst from the German's Schmeisser almost took off his beret.

The German was a big fellow. His bulk filled the passage, blocking out the little light that there was. He was stark naked, and he came at Barnesworth at full tilt, screaming obscenities.

Barnesworth rolled sideways just before the second burst from the Schmeisser ripped by him, and then carefully and clinically shot the German through the head. Barnesworth had never believed the cliché of a single bullet stopping a man dead in his tracks, but then he had never shot anyone at quite such short range.

The German's head went back, his knees buckled, and down he came, his forward momentum reversed by the impact of the bullet.

'Timberrr!' Tiller called softly from the stairs as the man pitched forward.

'Christ,' said Barnesworth with feeling. 'I know how those big-game hunters feel now. That was close.'

'Well-trained bugger, wasn't he?' said Larssen admiringly. 'Taking his gun with him to have a pee. But next time shoot for the middle, Billy. The head is too small a target.'

6

They left it to Demetrios, to whom they awarded the German rations they found in the house, to explain to the locals what had happened. To avoid any possible reprisals, they were to clean up the house, dispose of the bodies, and to tell any other Germans who might appear that the first patrol had moved inland to find the Italian garrison. A battalion of men could vanish without trace in such wild country.

Before leaving they threw all the Germans' weapons into the harbour. To leave them would be too great a temptation for the locals, whose hatred of the Germans, so Demetrios told them, was matched only by their wholehearted contempt for the Italians. In the early-morning light they also looked to see if the launch was visible, but it lay safely out of sight in ten fathoms of murky water.

The sun was well up as they got back to the bay. In their absence Christophou had moored the caique by a stern warp to a tree. Its bows were held from swinging on to the rocky shore by an anchor whose warp was strained and taut. Demetrios bade them an emotional farewell.

The wind had freshened in the night and was now blowing strongly from the north-west and the water, even in the sheltered bay, was flecked with white.

Christophou, who had always been quite imperturbable, seemed agitated. 'This is a dangerous place when the *meltemi* blows. We must leave at once. There is a good anchorage at Alemnia for sheltering from a northerly gale.'

Tiller listened to the wind as it shrieked through the rigging and watched the waves pounding the shore.

'So this is the *meltemi*,' he said to Barnesworth. 'No wonder they didn't want to tell us about it.'

It seemed inconceivable to him that there could be gales in such tranquil waters, and when the sky was such a vivid blue, but there was a faint chill in the air and the boat moved uneasily under their feet. Giorgiou released the stern rope while Tiller hauled in on the anchor warp and Larssen and Barnesworth hoisted the sails. The mainsail canvas cracked noisily as it ran up the mast and the foresail slammed to and fro until its sheets were hauled tight and it filled with wind.

Outside the bay the waves had begun to build. They ran with white crests off which the wind whipped spray that stung the eyes of those aboard the caique and soaked their clothing. The caique's timbers groaned as it forged through the water and every now and again water slopped over the bows and ran down the scuppers.

'Should we reef?' Larssen asked.

Christophou shook his head and pointed ahead. 'Once we get beyond that headland we will be more sheltered.'

He grinned at Barnesworth, who had gone very pale. 'If you want to be sick, my friend, be sick over that side. Otherwise it all blows back into your face.'

'I know how to be fucking sick on a fucking boat,' said Barnesworth, and was.

'I didn't know you suffered from *mal de mer*, Billy,' said Larssen with mock horror. 'You should have stayed in the Guards.'

'I like being in or under the bleeding water,' said Barnesworth, 'not on it. At least not in a tub like this.'

The wind continued to rise, but once beyond the headland the caique moved more easily through the choppy water and, with the wind now on its quarter, it sailed close to its maximum speed of six or seven knots.

Alemnia, at first an indistinct hump on the horizon, grew rapidly bigger and an hour after leaving Calchi they were entering the tiny island's one good natural harbour. There were a scattering of cottages at the inner extreme of the large inlet, two churches, and a castle ruin atop a hill, but no sign of life.

The beach shelved so steeply that Christophou was able to throw out a stern anchor and run the caique gently on to the sand. The SBS patrol, their Stens at the ready, jumped off the caique's bow and looked around them. The door of one of the cottages banged in the wind. Nearby was a flag-pole with a tattered Italian flag fluttering halfway up it.

They searched the houses. They were all empty except for one whose occupants lay dead on the earth floor. A horde of flies buzzed over the bodies. There was only one man – the rest were women or children. Larssen slammed the door shut, his face aflame with anger.

Behind the last house was a crude stone wall, perhaps the beginning of some unfinished building. By it lay five bodies dressed in Italian army uniform. Their hands were tied behind their backs with wire. Larssen turned them face up with the toe of his boot.

'Executed,' he said. 'They must have been propped against the wall and shot.'

When they returned to the beach Christophou was talking to an old priest whose grey beard reached to his chest.

'Does he know what happened?' Larssen asked.

'The Germans came,' Christophou said with a shrug. Whatever the Germans did came as no surprise to him. 'He hid in a tomb. He heard firing. The Germans searched the church but didn't find him. He saw them go.'

'How did they go?' Larssen asked, his fury unabated. 'What were they in? How many of them were there?'

It took time for Christophou to extract the answers from the old priest, who was still visibly upset, but eventually Christophou was able to say: 'He thinks there were ten of them. In a white launch. It had a flag at the back.'

'If I'd known about this,' said Barnesworth. 'I'd have shot that bastard a lot lower down than his head.'

'Tell the priest that justice has been done,' Larssen told Christophou. 'That they are all dead.'

They found spades and a pickaxe and dug eleven graves by the beach. The two babies they laid to rest with their mothers. The priest said a few words over each of the graves and they found some driftwood and made crosses for each mound of earth.

When they had finished they searched the area for arms or supplies. They found some Chianti, which they drank, but the Germans had destroyed or taken everything else. The priest wrung their hands and blessed them as they climbed aboard the caique from the beach. As they hauled in on the stern anchor and the caique's bow slid off the sand he called out to them.

'What'd he say?' Tiller asked.

'He says war is a terrible thing,' said Christophou. 'But you have behaved honourably. He says: God speed.'

It was open water between Alemnia and Simi and Christophou took the precaution of reefing, but even with its sail area reduced the caique seemed to be more under the water than riding on it. The wind continued to rise and it chopped up the sea into vicious steep-sided waves that threatened to sweep the deck from stern to stem. Each time this looked inevitable the caique's counter managed to lift itself above the foaming water at the last moment, the bow would dip, the old sail would shake itself like a dog, and the caique would plunge forward, spray cascading over the deck.

Barnesworth retched occasionally over the side, and looked miserable. Giorgiou, impervious to the water cascading over him, sat propped against the mast, ready to lower the sail if necessary. He stropped his knife with quiet intensity. Larssen, brought up on the waters of the Skaggerak, was in his element.

Tiller, experiencing the power of the wind and the sea at close quarters for the first time, was surprised at the noise the storm generated. The wind shrieked through the rigging, a loose halyard banged with fearful force against the mast, the hull shuddered and groaned like a dying man, and below in the hold something rolled and clanged. How everything held together was a miracle, but Christophou, who was having to use all his strength to control the caique with the long, curved tiller, seemed quite unconcerned.

'The *meltemi* comes out of a clear sky,' he shouted at the SBS men above the racket. 'Brrm, just like that. This one is not too bad. By this evening it will be flat calm.'

'Is there no warning?'

'None. It blows from between north-east and north-west during the summer months. August is the worst month. If you are in harbour and it starts to blow hard you must stay there. If you are at sea run for shelter quickly. If there is no shelter make for open water, drop your sails, and run before the wind. If the storm is very bad you throw out warps to slow you down. I have known boats to be blown halfway to Cyprus by the *meltemi*.'

Larssen noted this information; there might be a time when he would need it.

As if on cue, the wind began to die as they approached Simi and its last puff bore them into the port as the sun dipped behind the mountainous interior.

Warrington, like Barnesworth, a Special Boat Service survivor from the days of Roger Courtney and Stirling's D Squadron, was on the quay to greet them.

'The major was on the blower earlier today, skipper,' he said to Larssen. 'He asked that you stand by the set at 2000 hours.'

'Thanks, Ted. All quiet here?'

'Lieutenant Kristos has the locals under his thumb, but the Eyeties seem to blow hot and cold. No sign of any Krauts yet.'

The garrison had begun to dig slit trenches and some food had been delivered to the village from the castle. But no fuel had been sent to the MAS boat, which was still moored at the far end of the quay.

The radio in LS8 came to life at exactly 2000. 'Sunray calling LS8. How do you hear me? Over.'

'Strength 8, Sunray. Loud and clear,' Griffiths replied and handed Larssen the microphone.

'Sunray minor here. Over.'

'I am on Epsilon, repeat Epsilon.' Larssen glanced at the code-book on his knees which the SBS patrols had devised for communicating unimportant tactical information to one another. Alpha was Simi, Omega was Rhodes, Epsilon was Samos, north of the Dodecanese. What the hell was Jarrett doing there?

'Roger, Sunray. Over.'

'Beta, Gamma and Delta all secured, and will be replaced shortly. I am still negotiating here. Accolade going to plan, especially on Beta. Over.'

That meant SBS patrols had established control on Kos, Kalimnos and Leros, and that they would be relieved by army units, probably the battalion of the Durham Light Infantry that had been dispatched from Malta. It also meant that the single airfield on Kos was fit to receive the seven South African Air Force Spitfires earmarked for the islands. That was a big bonus. Without any air cover the whole enterprise was in jeopardy.

'Good going, Sunray. But why Epsilon?'

'Our friends require our presence. We have reasons to believe that Epsilon may receive visitors. Any sign of them around you?'

Larssen briefed Jarrett on the situation on Piscopi, Calchi and Alemnia, and expressed his doubts about the garrison on Simi. Jarrett advised further pressure on the Italians as 'visitors' had to be expected eventually.

'Intelligence sources indicate preparations around Athens and on Crete. You can take it our friends will arrive. So you have my authority to use whatever persuasion you think best on our friends. Alpha is essential as a base for you. But minimum force. We have enough problems without creating more. Is that understood? Over.'

Jarrett then said his operator was going to send a coded message by the one-time pad method, and Larssen handed the microphone back to Griffiths. Decipherment was Griffiths's business, not his.

Jarrett's operator gave Griffiths the number of the top sheet of the one-time pad and then switched to Morse code. Griffiths took down the encoded message – a string of meaningless letters and numbers – and then translated these from the top sheet of the one-time pad. Then he ripped off the sheet from the pad and put a match to it before dropping the charred remains overboard. The one-time pad was the most secure method of transmitting signals in code. It was also very slow and laborious.

Larssen waited with ill-disguised impatience while Griffiths went methodically about his task of decipherment. Eventually Griffiths handed Larssen the message on a piece of signals paper and logged that he had received it in his book. Jarrett's message said that he had been ordered to send a patrol to Rhodes as quickly as possible to find out if the Germans were reinforcing the island. A co-ordinate was given where the patrol should land to reconnoitre Marizza airfield in the north-west corner, and the following evening the patrol would be met there by Andartes, who would hand over what they knew about German reinforcements elsewhere on the island.

Larssen swore under his breath as he read the signal. He could hardly ask Christophou to go on such a potentially dangerous mission, the MAS boat still had no fuel, and the engine of LS8 was spread out on its deck.

But then he read: 'T-class submarine will be with you by midnight tomorrow. Acknowledge. Jarrett.' Well, that settled who the patrol would consist of: it was a job for the cockle and its crew.

Larssen decided that Jarrett's orders gave him a free hand with the garrison. 'Minimum force' was, in the circumstances, a conveniently vague phrase. It was time to get some action from the Italians. But when Tiller and Barnesworth went with him next morning to confront them Larssen sensed that Salvini knew the Germans were going to try and pre-empt British occupation of the Dodecanese, for he was wary and certainly in no mood to be helpful. He said, through Perquesta, that the garrison had spared as much food as it could for the local population.

'Crap,' Larssen snapped. 'There wasn't even enough for the kids.'

Salvini shrugged as Perquesta translated and Larssen's quick temper nearly got the better of him. Instead he pointed at Salvini's prominent stomach and said to Perquesta in as level a voice as he could manage: 'Tell the captain that being so overweight is unhealthy. I am recommending a diet for him.'

Perquesta nibbled at his moustache. 'A diet, *signore*?'

'That's right. I shall make sure he eats only what the children eat.'

'But how? . . .'

'An enforced diet, if necessary. Do I make myself clear?'

He did, and Salvini was quick to take the hint.

'The captain says that the food that was delivered was only a first consignment. Naturally, more is being sent today.'

'Naturally. Please congratulate the captain on his generosity and common sense. Now there is the little matter of fuel for the MAS boat.'

Salvini appeared to consider himself on firmer ground with the fuel. It was, he said, regrettable that none had yet been delivered to the MAS boat but he had to have the permission of his superiors on Leros and so far he had been unable to contact them by radio.

'So how long will it be?' Larssen snapped.

Not long, Salvini promised.

'What do you reckon Salvini's word is worth, skipper?' Tiller asked as they made a quick tour of the garrison's new defences with Perquesta.

'Not a row of beans,' said Larssen. 'But I want food for those kids first. We don't know for sure if Balbao will help us. We know the locals will. Remember the garrison outnumbers us by ten to one.'

'Make it fifty to one and I'd still fancy our chances,' said Barnesworth, looking at the men who were manning the slit trenches. He turned to Perquesta. 'When did these men last see any action?'

'Some fought in Abyssinia,' Perquesta said.

'Abyssinia!' Larssen exploded. 'Christ, that was eight years ago.'

'They are middle-aged,' Perquesta admitted, 'and the fire has gone from their bellies. They are confused, too. Whose side are they meant to be on? They are in no man's land and they are afraid they will be shot at from both sides. When are your reinforcements coming, Captain? What is needed is a show of strength.'

'Soon,' said Larssen. 'In the meantime the garrison has an obligation to defend Italian soil. They must understand that.'

Perquesta shook his head. 'They know it. They also know – because the population never lets them forget it – that these islands are not Italian.'

The transport turned out to be one of the T-class submarines the British had handed over to the Royal Hellenic Navy. The *Papankolis* had been diverted at the last minute while on passage from Alexandria to its operational area off Salonika. Its recognition signal had been radioed to the SBS men an hour before it arrived and the Italians were warned of its arrival.

Few submariners, Larssen knew from experience, liked being involved in clandestine operations. These were risky enough for those going on them, but they were even more risky for the submarine and its crew. Submarines needed deep water for safety, and depth was not to be had near any coastline. Caught on the surface, a submarine had little chance against air attack and was horribly vulnerable to fast surface forces. Coldly calculated, it meant risking a highly trained crew and a vessel worth God knows what to get two men ashore in a flimsy canvas contraption on a mission that could be, and often was, a wild-goose chase.

Commanders-in-chief valued their submarines, and did not risk them lightly. When an admiral reluctantly agreed – and it was always reluctantly – to assign one to a clandestine mission his staff tended to choose one that had some connection with the operation it had been ordered to mount.

However, the Greek CO of the *Papankolis* saw no connection at all. As far as he was concerned he was wasting valuable time and valuable fuel which he could have spent sinking German shipping off Salonika.

He told Tiller and Barnesworth all this in no uncertain terms after they had paddled the cockle out to the submarine to where it lay off the port. They must understand, he said, that if they did not return to the rendezvous on time the following night he could not wait for them.

They supervised the stowing of the cockle, watching to make sure the fragile craft was not damaged in any way. The sixteen-foot cockle they had brought with them from Castelrosso was of the collapsible kind, an improved version of the Mark II that Tiller had used on the Gironde raid the previous year. It had a plywood deck and bottom but canvas sides and by hinging forward the struts that kept the deck in place they were able to concertina the whole structure to a compact depth which enabled it to fit down the torpedo hatch.

The submarine submerged and ran at periscope depth.

In Christophou's caique the voyage of twenty miles or so had taken much of the day. In the submarine it took under two hours. When it surfaced they could see from its bridge the hump of Alemnia on the horizon on their starboard side.

The white-flecked waves had gone now, for the *meltemi* had long since blown itself out and had been replaced by a gentle offshore breeze which hardly ruffled the water. The captain of the *Papankolis* kept the profile of his submarine as low as possible and its decks were almost awash as the crew opened the torpedo hatch to bring out the cockle.

The north-west coast of Rhodes, where the Marizza airfield lay, loomed straight ahead in the darkness. Tiller remembered the massacre on Alemnia and regretted he was only on a reconnaissance patrol. He was itching to use his explosives, but Larssen had expressly forbidden any attacks on the airfield. Information was what was needed. Any attack would lessen the chances of the two men returning with it and could jeopardize the safety of the submarine when it returned to pick them up the following night.

'Are you going to use RG equipment?' the captain asked, referring to the infrared lamps with their invisible beams of light which canoeists sometimes used to rendezvous with a submarine.

Tiller shook his head. 'No. We now use what we call the bongle', and he explained how it worked.

'Good. The Mountain will come to Mahomet, then. Make sure you're at least three miles offshore. Good luck.'

The cockle was carefully extracted from the hatch by two of the submarine's crew and laid on the deck. Their faces blacked with camouflage cream, and dressed from head to foot in their rubberized paddler's suits with rope-soled boots, the two SBS men carefully checked for a final time that everything was in place.

They moved the cockle under the barrel of the submarine's four-inch gun. Beneath the barrel was clamped a steel girder, rather as a bayonet was to a rifle. They placed the craft gently into a specially designed sling and attached it to a rope tackle which hung down from the end of the steel girder. Then they climbed carefully into the two circular cockpits, Tiller in front, Barnesworth behind him, and two members of the submarine's crew then hauled in on the tackle and lifted the cockle from the deck. The gun was elevated slightly, and then swivelled sideways before the craft was lowered carefully into the water so that it floated alongside the slowly moving submarine.

'Don't keep the warps too taut,' Tiller called up to the crew. In the choppy water this could have caused the cockle to hit the sides of the submarine and capsize. They unshipped their double paddles, ensured they were properly locked in the middle so that the blades at either end were at right angles to each other, and then with fierce, quick strokes moved the cockle away.

Dispatching the SBS team was a vulnerable moment for everyone involved. Tiller knew this and he had been trained to leave the submarine's side with the utmost speed. He was pleased to see how quickly Barnesworth acted, too.

The submarine, which had remained with its deck nearly awash throughout the launching, now began sliding silently into the depths. The water boiled for a moment around the top of its conning tower and then it was gone.

The submarine had submerged slowly but its bulk created a wash that made the cockle yaw violently. Tiller flicked his paddle expertly into the water to steady it while Barnesworth took a bearing with the hand compass on a prominent headland off the port bow and then on Alemnia, now hardly visible on the horizon on the starboard side. He jotted the two bearings on a slate and then tapped Tiller twice on the shoulder to indicate that he was ready.

Tiller adjusted the grid of the P8 compass – which was fixed to the cockle in front of Tiller – to 160 degrees and then propelled the cockle forward with steady, powerful strokes. By locking the blades of the paddles at right angles the two men were able to 'feather' the blade that was in the air. This kept down wind resistance and gave the craft a lower silhouette.

If the submarine had dropped them in the right place this would bring them to a beach just three miles from Marizza airfield. It was always a big 'if'. After an hour they stopped for a few minutes to take new bearings and to rest, and to subdue the hallucinations that commonly haunted canoeists at night. Then they struck out for the shore again and within an hour they had reached the right spot. Silently Tiller thanked the Greek captain. He might have been a dour bastard but his navigation had been superb.

They stayed offshore for a short while, scanning the beach and its surroundings for any movement. They saw nothing, and could only smell the fresh scent of sage wafted on the breeze. They then unlocked their double paddles, stowed the female half, and manoeuvred the cockle closer to the shore using the single paddles. This gave them a much lower profile and a completely silent approach.

They were only too aware that a sharp rock could wreck the operation, and approached the beach with great caution. When the cockle was fifty yards from it Barnesworth shipped his single paddle, leant back and extracted his legs from beneath the canvas cover. He lifted himself up carefully, straddled his cockpit, and then expertly flipped himself over and into the water before swimming to the bow and guiding it on to the beach. The craft grounded gently and Tiller extracted himself with a quick, practised movement.

Both men now worked in silent unison, for their training had made it second nature to them. They lifted the cockle, ran up the beach with it, and hid it among rocks. Tiller stripped off his paddler's suit and donned shorts, SAS beret and a service shirt with his sergeant's stripes on both sleeves. If the Germans found them the fact that they were in uniform might save them from execution, but Tiller knew all about Hitler's Commando Order and would not have put his back pay on their surviving if they were captured.

So far as intelligence knew there were no Gestapo on Rhodes, just regular Wehrmacht troops, but the orders were for all 'saboteurs' to be handed over to the Gestapo for 'questioning'. All those undertaking special operations were under no illusion that this encounter invariably meant a bullet in the back of the head. Only recently Tiller had heard that the French resistance had reported back that this had been the fate of two of the canoeists on the Gironde raid.

Barnesworth returned to the water's edge and eradicated any footmarks with a rake he had designed for the purpose. Then, as Barnesworth stripped and changed, Tiller extracted their haversacks, Stens, revolvers, rations and water bottles from the cockle before camouflaging it with netting. With a brief nod to his companion, Tiller turned inland, his pocket compass in his hand.

The ground was rocky at first but then became flat and fertile. There were plenty of olive trees and the occasional scrub but nothing that would hinder their approach to the airfield. It would take them, Tiller calculated, not much more than an hour to reach it. That would give them plenty of time to find a convenient observation point before dawn broke. A game-bird bursting from under their feet with a clatter of wings gave them an unpleasant shock, but otherwise they neither heard nor saw anything. They might as well have been on the moon. After an hour Tiller beckoned his companion.

'It's in a shallow valley under that mountain,' he said in an undertone, 'so it should be over the next brow, I reckon.'

Barnesworth nodded. Close to the crest they dropped down on all fours and wriggled forward.

The airfield was bigger than they had anticipated. It was surrounded by wire and there was a cluster of huts at the far end. At one time it must have been a civilian strip, for there were a couple of hangars and a petrol pump. At first they could not see any aircraft but as their eyes became accustomed to the dark they could see the outlines of two parked on one side of the field.

'Eyetie bombers,' Tiller whispered. He lowered his night binoculars. 'Reckon this is as good a place for a hide as any.'

They found a rock behind which they could observe the airfield, ran a small camouflage net over the dip in the ground behind it and stuck dried grass, twigs, and small branches in the netting, and then settled down in the dip. It just held the two of them and was swelteringly hot when the sun came up.

For several hours nothing much happened. They saw guards patrolling the perimeter, but no sign of any aircraft apart from the two triple-engined Savoia-Marchetti bombers. Tiller scrutinized each part of the airfield with great care while Barnesworth drew a diagram of it in his notebook, divided it into nine squares, and gave each square a letter of the alphabet. Methodically, Tiller described what he saw in each. When he got to 'G' he muttered: 'Eh, what have we here?'

It was, Tiller guessed after studying it carefully, an ammunition dump of some kind, but it was well screened by netting. He handed the binoculars to Barnesworth, who said: 'Bombs. Those are bombs. Hundreds of them. What load can those Eyetie bombers carry?'

'About 1500 kilogrammes each – no more. Perhaps less.'

'It would take them months to get rid of that lot, then.'

'So there must be others around.'

'There are,' said Barnesworth, looking skyward. 'Can't you hear them?'

Tiller listened intently, and soon caught the beat of aircraft engines. Then he saw the first. It was flying directly towards him and as it grew larger its gull-shaped wings and fixed undercarriage made its identification simple. Behind the first was another and another.

'Stukas,' he said.

'Even I recognize that bastard,' said Barnesworth softly. 'Once seen, never forgotten. Ever been bombed by one?'

Tiller shook his head. He had only seen the German Ju87 dive-bomber in action on the newsreels. Even in the cinema the scream of the aircraft as it descended on its target almost vertically had been impressive. But it was, he knew, a slow and, by now, obsolete fighting machine. If they managed to base Hurricanes on Leros the Stukas wouldn't stand a chance.

The first one swept overhead, circled behind them and came into land. It taxied to the other end of the field and up to the bomb dump, where it was soon joined by the other two. They watched as the crew clambered down from the aircraft and disappeared into one of the huts. Soon afterwards a lorry approached and disgorged what must have been the German ground crews. With them were two fuel lorries which moved along the line of aircraft and then the SBS men saw the German armourers fitting bombs to the Stukas' bomb racks under their fuselages, and then priming them. They wondered uneasily what the planes' first target was going to be.

Two hours later, as the sun was low in the sky, three more Stukas came in and the operation of fuelling and arming was repeated. Then the ground crews departed in the lorry, though some stayed behind as guards. Two had Alsatians on leashes and the two SBS men watched them release the dogs outside the perimeter wire. The animals began to quarter the ground systematically and the whistles of their handlers drifted up to the two men in their hide. Both knew that a man could pass within ten yards of them and suspect nothing, but a trained dog could pick up their scent from five times that distance. At least they had taken the elementary precaution of building their hide downwind.

The sun seemed to sink very slowly. The guards' shouts of encouragement to the dogs were wafted clearly to the two men on a breeze which stirred the dried grasses in front of their hide.

The dogs barked occasionally as they criss-crossed the ground outside the perimeter, slowly working their way towards the crest. But they were still half a mile away when darkness closed in and their handlers recalled them.

Cautiously the two men folded the netting and eradicated any sign of their presence, then withdrew from the crest. They followed the reverse compass bearing and were at the beach in just over an hour. At exactly the right time three bearded figures emerged out of the darkness, shook their hands, thrust an envelope into Tiller's hand, and vanished into the night.

They changed back into their paddle suits, launched the cockle into the calm water and an hour later reached the approximate point where the submarine had dropped them.

Barnesworth now set up the 'bongle' by lowering its rod into the water and propping the box containing the hammer on to the side of the canoe. Then he began cranking the handle – coffee-grinding, it was called – which governed the hammer hitting the rod. Tiller wondered at the ingeniousness of whoever had invented this simple device. It radiated sound waves of a recognized pitch which the submarine's hydrophones could pick up and home in on. No longer did canoeists have to try and find the submarine; instead the submarine came to the cockle.

Half an hour later the submarine rose slowly from the depths. The SBS men paddled quickly over to it and were hauled aboard by the same method as they had been launched the previous night.

The captain was in the conning tower scanning the horizon with night binoculars. 'Your little gadget is very effective,' he said with grudging approval as they passed him to go below. In the mess deck, hot cocoa was thrust into their hands. It was gratefully received for, despite their paddlers' suits, the cold had begun seeping into them as they waited for the submarine.

The effect of the benzedrine tablets they had taken before leaving the beach now began to wear off. They both slumped on to bunks and fell asleep at once, only to be woken, or so it seemed, as soon as they had closed their eyes.

'No time to go into the bay,' said the Greek captain as they joined him in the conning tower. 'You boys will have to paddle a little bit further.'

It was a lot further but they made it as the first sliver of light began to show over the mainland. Lieutenant Kosti was there to greet them with a warm handshake, and within a few minutes Larssen had joined them. Tiller turned to him wearily, handed him the envelope, and said: 'I think you'd better get everyone prepared for air raids, skipper.'

7

In the following days they did what they could to prepare for the Stukas, and warned the other islands that they might be raided. But it seemed extremely unlikely that Simi would be the Germans' target for they still did not appear to know that the SBS were on the island.

Nevertheless, as a precaution, both the caique and the MAS boat were moved out of the port. The caique was moored under a cliff, where its netting made it virtually invisible from the air, and the MAS boat was anchored in a small bay and crudely, but effectively, camouflaged. Those inhabitants with cellars were advised to turn them into shelters and those without were warned to be prepared to move into the hills.

Though Simi was not yet a target, one morning Larssen told his men that once the Germans knew the SBS were there it would be vulnerable to a landing by German troops. 'So we cannot allow the Germans to take over the outlying islands from which they might possibly launch an attack on us here. The Italian garrison on Piscopi have just radioed the castle that a German patrol has landed on the far side of the island from their headquarters. It will take some time for the Germans to get to them but they need to be reinforced. Quickly. I want you, Tiger, to take Billy and four men to Piscopi with additional arms and stores for the garrison, and make sure the Krauts are driven off.'

'Who will take us? One of the Schooner Flotilla?'

Larssen shook his head. 'It would take too long. I have spoken to Balbao. He will take you and pick you up.'

'But he still has no fuel,' Tiller objected.

'We're going up to the castle now,' Larssen replied grimly. 'No more shilly-shallying with our Italian friends. We get the fuel. Now.'

Salvini, when they arrived at Colonel Ardetti's office in the castle, blustered and prevaricated. He had, he said, still not received permission to release the fuel. When Perquesta translated this Larssen unslung his Sten and said: 'Tell Captain Salvini that if he does not produce the fuel – now – I shall take it myself.'

Salvini's expression darkened and he almost spat out his reply.

'He asks how you propose to do this,' Perquesta said. He looked distinctly uncomfortable at being the go-between.

Larssen smiled pleasantly at Salvini and said to Perquesta: 'Tell him I shoot him first. Then I shoot whoever else stops me,' and he lifted the barrel of his Sten a few inches. It was a small gesture but an unambiguous one. In the silence that followed, one of the SBS men could be heard putting the garrison through its daily exercises.

'Your pistol, please,' Larssen said, nodding at the holster strapped to Salvini's thick, glossy leather belt. Salvini's hand lingered momentarily over the holster but the butt of his pistol was covered by a leather flap which was buttoned to the holster. He would have been dead before he had even undone the flap.

Instead he shrugged, undid his belt, and dropped it and the holster on to the colonel's desk, then snapped something at Perquesta.

'Captain Salvini says that he will lay a formal complaint before the Italian Armistice Commission.'

'Fuck the Italian Armistice Commission,' said Larssen pleasantly.

'*Prego, signore?*'

'It doesn't matter. Captain Salvini and I understand one another.'

Larssen nodded to one of the SBS men. 'Take him down to the port and lock him up somewhere that's safe from the locals. I want him on the next boat out of here.'

Tiller stepped forward, undid the flap of Salvini's holster and withdrew the pistol. He slid the magazine from the butt, flicked the cartridges on to the table with his thumb, and pocketed them before returning the pistol to its holster. It would make a nice souvenir.

Larssen turned to Perquesta: 'Where do you keep your fuel?'

Perquesta took them out of the castle and up a path which led towards the hills. Around a corner they found a steel door let into the hillside which was surrounded by barbed wire and guarded by two Italians with sub-machine-guns.

Perquesta went up to them and when they shook their heads he started arguing. The guards continued to shake their heads.

'What's the matter?' Larssen said impatiently.

'They let no one in without a pass from Captain Salvini. He gave them the strictest orders.'

Larssen joined Perquesta and said: 'Tell them Salvini has been arrested. By me.'

This did not go down well with the guards, who shifted uneasily and looked at one another. One of them began to slide his weapon off his shoulder.

What Larssen did next was so quick and effortless that Tiller, standing only a few yards away, did not immediately grasp what had happened. The Dane stepped forward and in two swift movements struck one man on the side of the jaw and then rammed the same fist into the stomach of the second. As the second guard doubled up Larssen hit him accurately, though not too hard, on the back of his neck with the side of his other hand.

'Very neat, skipper,' said Tiller, surveying the two men sprawled on the ground.

'These help,' said Larssen removing the brass knuckledusters from his right hand and sliding them into his pocket. 'Not according to the Geneva Convention, Tiger. No spit and polish. Just wham, bang. You disapprove, eh? Not cricket.'

'It worked,' said Tiller. 'That's what counts.'

'Eh, Tiger, we make a pirate of you yet,' Larssen slapped him delightedly on the back.

The hands of the two unconscious guards were bound with their belts and with a short burst from his Sten Larssen smashed the lock on the gate of the compound. But the steel door was a much more formidible barrier and when they could not find the key on the guards Tiller fetched some explosive. He returned with a yellowish lump of material which had the consistency of plasticine and was the size of a large orange. He moulded it round a small metal cone, attached it with tape to the keyhole and took out a pencil fuse from a container which looked like a small cigar tin.

'Ten minutes is the shortest time delay I've got,' he said.

'We can wait,' said Larssen. 'Just don't blow up the fuel as well.'

'Come on, skipper,' said Barnesworth reprovingly. 'Tiger does this sort of thing in his sleep.'

Tiller removed the coloured safety strip from the five-inch fuse, stuck it in the plastic explosive, squeezed the fuse's soft copper tube to activate it, and retired to a safe distance.

Perquesta, who had watched Tiller prepare the charge in puzzled amazement, said as they waited: 'That is explosive? Never have I seen explosive like that.'

'It's RDX,' Tiller explained. 'Research Development Explosive. What you call T4. Mix it with beeswax or oil and it becomes malleable. Plastic explosive, we call it.'

What he didn't tell Perquesta, because the lieutenant seemed to have an excitable nature, was that the main ingredient of RDX was hexamine, an unstable combination of ammonia and formaldehyde. To stabilize it another explosive like amatol or TNT had to be mixed with it.

'But why the cone?' Perquesta asked.

'It concentrates the shock waves of the explosion into a very small area. Increases the power of the explosive by up to 15 times. Shaped charges, they're called.'

The explosion, when it came, was violent and effective. Larssen inspected the result approvingly. 'Good stuff, plastic explosive, but that wasn't ten minutes, Tiger.'

'So far the boffins haven't been able to come up with

a pencil fuse that isn't affected by the temperature,' Tiller replied. 'It's a hot day so it works quicker than it should. And vice versa. I reckon you could wait for ever at the North Pole.'

Perquesta was told to fetch the tractor, and its trailer, while Larssen investigated the fuel store. It was almost empty but there were a dozen large drums of high octane petrol in one corner and these, along with the half-conscious guards, were loaded on to the trailer.

'We'll take the fuel,' Larssen told Perquesta. 'You take the guards. Let your doctor look at them and then lock them up. They're Fascists and I've had enough of Salvini and his followers. We'll be back in an hour. I want every soldier not manning a gun position to be on parade in the castle quadrangle. I'm going to tell them exactly where they stand and what they must do.'

Balbao greeted them when they reached the quay with the drums of fuel. There was enough in them, he said, to take them to Piscopi and back and there would be plenty to spare 'just in case'.

Larssen asked him if he knew the waters around Piscopi.

Balbao shook his head. 'We take a local man. No problem.'

Tiller suggested Christophou, and Balbao agreed. The drums were left on the quay for the crew and the SBS men to take aboard, and Larssen and Tiller returned to the castle in the tractor. Perquesta had rounded up all the men not on duty and had paraded them in the quadrangle.

Larssen, when he addressed them through Perquesta, said he would not tolerate Fascists any longer. They would be locked up. Those not locked up would fight for the Allies and on Simi the Allies meant him. Perquesta, a fine officer, would lead them and he, Captain Larssen, would ensure they had help from his men and food and ammunition from the British Navy. God Save King Victor Emmanuel.

His address was received in stoic but friendly silence.

'Are you going in the diplomatic corps after the war, skipper?' Tiller asked with a grin as they returned to the port.

'No bloody fear,' retorted Larssen. 'I think big-game hunting is what I do. I shall be well trained for it, yes? I have the right instincts. Now you go and talk to our friend Christophou.'

But when Tiller went to the taverna Christophou was not there and when he told Angelika what he wanted him for she said her father would not be able to go. Tiller was puzzled.

'Why not?' he asked.

'Here we all seem friendly to you. But some of us are not. There is at least one collaborator here who serves the Italians, the fascist cause.'

'Are you sure?'

Angelika nodded. 'Since he took you the other day my father has been threatened. If he helps again his boat may be tampered with, perhaps sunk. He may even be killed.'

'So he is not prepared to help?'

Angelika hesitated and said: 'Yes, of course he will help if you ask him. But please do not ask him. He is not a young man any longer. It is too dangerous for him. Choose someone else.'

'But who?'

Angelika blushed. 'Ask me.'

Tiller's expression made her laugh. 'I know these islands like – how do you say? – the back of my hand.'

Tiller congratulated her on her English and asked where she had learnt it. 'At college. Then I worked for a tourist firm in Athens. Showing the English around the Parthenon and other places. I also speak Italian. Well? You will take me?'

'It might be risky,' Tiller protested. 'And might not collaborators threaten you?'

'If they found out, yes. But I make sure they do not find out. If anyone asks, my mother will say I am ill.'

'I think she fancies you, Tiger,' Larssen said when Tiller told him about Angelika. 'Still, we don't want to cause trouble for Christophou and there's no time to find anyone else. I don't see what else we can do.'

Larssen looked at Balbao, who shrugged and nodded reluctantly. Women were never popular aboard a ship – they were thought to bring bad luck – but he couldn't see any alternative either. 'So long as she knows her job,' Balbao said.

As soon as darkness fell Angelika, dressed in her father's clothes and cloth cap, came aboard, asked for the MAS boat's charts of the area and went below to study them. An hour later, after all the patrol's equipment, which included a swimmer's suit for Barnesworth, had been loaded, along with stores and arms for the Piscopi garrison, the MAS boat left the quay and headed out to sea.

'Get your heads down while you can, boys,' Tiller told his men. 'You might not be getting much kip for the next day or two. I'll stay on the bridge.'

To conserve fuel and prevent a tell-tale white bow wave, which could betray its presence to a German sea patrol, the MAS boat used only one of its engines. Even so Simi quickly became a thin, dark ribbon on the sea behind them. Balbao searched the horizon ahead with his night binoculars. Angelika stood near him on the open bridge, a chart in her hand. Her presence made Tiller wonder why it was some women looked even more attractive in men's clothes than they did in their own.

After an hour one of the crew brought them mugs of ersatz coffee. Tiller found it almost undrinkable but the night was chilly and it warmed his insides.

Balbao and Angelika spoke in rapid Italian and then the girl tapped Tiller lightly on the arm. 'You need to go alongside?'

Tiller nodded. 'We need to get the stores ashore quickly.'

'There is only one place. Here.' She shone a shaded torch on the chart and indicated with her forefinger a promontory to the north of the bay. 'The commander wants to go alongside the quay. It's all right for a small caique like my father's, but it is too shallow for an MAS boat.'

'It is deep enough where you want to go?'

'Yes. But it is just a flat rock which sticks out into the water. It can only be done in fine weather when the sea is calm.'

'And it will stay calm?'

Angelika nodded. 'No *meltemi* tonight.'

'What do you think, Commander?' Tiller asked Balbao.

'We see,' said Balbao enigmatically. Out of earshot of Angelika he added: 'Our pilot is pretty, Sergeant. But how can we be sure she knows what she is doing?'

Piscopi was now large on the horizon ahead. Balbao cut back the MAS boat's speed until it was only just making way through the oil-calm water. As the boat approached Livadia Bay, where the Italian garrison had its headquarters, the crew took up their action stations.

Tiller went below and woke his men but told them to stay where they were for the moment as there was very little room on deck. But he told Barnesworth to put on his surface swimmer's suit and then took him back to the bridge.

'This man's an expert swimmer,' Tiller said to Balbao. 'He can swim ashore and test the depth by the quay and the jetty. You won't even need to stop. Just make a pass close to it. While he's measuring you can look at the rock.'

'How will he measure it?' Balbao asked. Barnesworth produced his beach gradient reel from a pocket of his suit. Balbao examined it curiously.

'A fishing reel?'

'Very nearly,' said Barnesworth. 'Except the line on it is marked with split lead pellets so I can read off the depth in the dark or under water. It's designed for COPP parties to gauge beach gradients.'

'COPP?' Balbao queried.

'Combined Operations Pilotage Parties,' said Barnesworth. 'They're the lads who go ashore to recce prospective beaches before an amphibious landing. But it's easily adaptable to measure the depth of water. I just insert a crampon somewhere at water level, hook on the line and take the reel to the bottom. The lead pellets will tell me how much line has been unwound. If there's nowhere to use a crampon I just use a float. Very simple really. But if it's as shallow as our pilot says it is I won't need it.'

The explanation convinced Balbao and they crept slowly into the bay. There was no sign of life anywhere. If any of the garrison were still around they must have been fast asleep.

'Wait till you see us come back,' Tiller said to Barnesworth as he waited in the stern with him. 'Then signal us. A series of "R"s will do. But don't start swimming until I reply with a series of "O"s. You never know, there might well be some Jerry-manned MAS boats around that look like this one.'

'The captain, he say now,' said one of the crew emerging out of the dark.

'Good luck,' said Tiller.

Barnesworth lowered himself into the water from the ladder, held on for a second and then dropped. With strong powerful strokes he swam away from the MAS boat to clear its propellers, and in moments had vanished into the dark. The MAS boat increased speed slightly and turned back out to sea.

Tiller returned to the bridge with some misgivings. He did not like putting himself and his team in the hands of a former enemy and a Greek girl about whom he knew next to nothing. Still, there was nothing he could do about it now. As a precaution, he called the SBS party up from below and told them to find what cover they could on the deck. At least they would not be trapped below if something went wrong.

With Angelika giving instructions, the MAS boat turned to port. Once out of the bay Balbao turned it north and then circled slowly near the promontory that Angelika had pointed out on the chart. The large slab of rock was just where she said it would be and, with the wind blowing offshore, Balbao readily agreed it would be possible to go alongside it – provided there was enough water.

'There is,' Angelika said confidently.

They returned to the position where Barnesworth had left them and after a couple of minutes his shaded torch began flashing the agreed signal. Tiller replied and ten minutes later, like a seal surfacing for air, Barnesworth bobbed up by the counter and climbed aboard by the ladder.

'Five feet,' he said when he reached the bridge.

'Not enough,' Balbao admitted.

'Any sign of life?' Tiller asked. Barnesworth shook his head. 'I reckon the garrison have taken to the hills along with all the locals.'

The MAS boat crept back to the flat rock and everything was rapidly unloaded on to it. Balbao had to return while it was still dark and once all the stores were ashore he manoeuvred the MAS boat expertly away from the rock, and with a wave headed back to Simi. Tiller fancied that Angelika waved, too, but he could not be sure.

Two of the SBS men went ahead and scoured the buildings around Livadia Bay. To their surprise the *carabinieri* were still there, their inactivity accounted for by the number of empty Chianti bottles that lay strewn around their quarters. The SBS men brought some of them back to the rock and with their help the stores and extra arms were quickly moved into the bay.

The small garrison appeared cheered by the arrival

of the SBS. Tiller found the scruffy, balding corporal who was in charge. He looked old enough to be Tiller's father, and had that worn-down look all of the SBS had seen on the faces of Italian troops, the look of men who had been beaten and had had enough of fighting. All they wanted to do, their expressions said, was survive and go home to their families. If only life were that easy, Tiller thought grimly.

It turned out that, when pressed, the corporal spoke broken English, which, perhaps cannily, he had not revealed on the previous occasion. From him it soon became clear not only that the locals had fled into the hills when they heard the Germans were coming but that the garrison was expecting to be evacuated before they arrived. When it sunk in they might have to stay and fight they looked appalled.

Tiller and Barnesworth started by checking the Italians' equipment. They soon found that, as with all the Italian troops they had encountered so far, the garrison had inferior weapons and had little ammunition. Some of their rifles were so rusty they looked dangerous and these were replaced with the Lee Enfield rifles the SBS had brought with them – the standard British infantryman's weapon – and boxes of .303 ammunition were handed out. Tiller also made sure the Italians knew how to use the twin 6.5mm Breda light machine-guns he had brought along, and then he heated up enough tinned stew for everyone. It always helped to go into battle on a full stomach and the Italians looked half-starved.

At daylight Tiller inspected the defensive positions of the *carabinieri* and put the garrison to work to improve them. He tried to discover more about the Germans who had landed, but the corporal did not know even how many there were. He had received only one message from the lookout at Monastery Point, on the other side of the island, who had seen them land in Kamara Bay.

'He say many, many. Then the telephone not work any more.' Why it had stopped working, the corporal did not know either.

Tiller's questions were answered later that morning when the lookout arrived. On seeing the Germans land he had immediately abandoned his post, commandeered a donkey and ridden to Livadia Bay during the night. There were, he said, about twenty of them.

'They arrived on a barge which went away,' the corporal was able to add. 'It had plenty guns.'

'Sounds like a Siebel ferry,' said Barnesworth. 'Hope it doesn't turn up here.'

'How long before the Germans arrive?' Tiller said. The Italian corporal sketched the shape of the island with a twig and indicated that the patrol had gone clockwise round the island.

'Soon if they march quick.'

'The Krauts march quick,' said Barnesworth. 'You can be sure of that. Do we lay a nice little ambush for them north of here, Tiger?'

'You bet we do, Billy.'

'We leave?' the corporal asked eagerly. 'Twenty, too many Germans. Yes?'

'Twenty Germans not too many,' said Tiller, giving the Italian a friendly slap on the back. 'Not too many at all.'

'But we can do without the bleeding Luftwaffe,' said Barnesworth suddenly. 'Can you hear that, Tiger?'

It was the Blohm and Voss again. It circled once above them and then dropped a cloud of leaflets before flying off. The leaflet was in such rudimentary Italian that one of the SBS men was able to translate it without difficulty. It exhorted the Italians to support their old allies by refusing to join the British.

'Very artistic,' said Tiller, looking at the cartoon which accompanied the message. It was an ugly, slobbering bulldog which vaguely resembled Churchill and was wearing a helmet painted with the Union Jack. Its front feet were planted firmly on a valiant-looking Italian soldier shaped like Italy. Its hind feet were on the Dodecanese. The Italian was being handed a bayonet by a smiling, shining Wehrmacht soldier which the Italian was about to plunge into the bulldog's throat.

Tiller watched the Italians carefully as they studied this crude piece of propaganda. They read it impassively, but Tiller could see it had some effect. One of the Italians slowly unslung his rifle and propped it against the nearest wall.

The corporal ripped one of the sheets in two and spoke to the garrison sharply. Most of them threw the sheets away, but one slipped off his rifle and dropped it to the ground. Another folded the piece of paper carefully and put it in his pocket. Both gestures were unmistakable.

The corporal snarled and ranted. One of the soldiers reluctantly picked up his weapon, but the other refused. He was not defying authority, but every inch of him seemed to spell defeat. He'd had enough and nothing the corporal said would move him.

Then the corporal grabbed one of the sheets from the ground, dropped his trousers, and wiped his behind with it. This brought a snigger from his audience and a roar of approval when he held up the paper, smelt it, and let it drop from his thumb and forefinger with an expression of total disgust.

'Quite the little actor,' Barnesworth murmured to Tiller.

Reluctantly, the second soldier picked up his rifle and slung it back on his shoulder with an embarrassed smile. The corporal then looked at the man who had pocketed the pamphlet. The man extracted it and let it drop to the ground.

'Giovanni might have some spunk after all,' said Barnesworth. He had christened the corporal Giovanni because the Italian looked the archetypal ice-cream vendor.

'We'll soon see,' said Tiller. 'I want you to remain here, Billy, with Tranter and Simmonds and seven of these characters. The Krauts aren't going to oblige us by all of them walking into here in single file together. They're going to come from at least two directions. I'll need you to protect my back.'

Barnesworth nodded his agreement.

'I'll take the other two blokes to man the Bren. I'll also take Giovanni and one of the Bredas. He can choose which four men he wants to have with him.'

Tiller signalled the corporal to join him and sketched his plan out in the dirt. He indicated where he intended to set up the ambush to the corporal and made him understand what he intended to do. The corporal nodded. Tiller told him to choose four men and then, nodding meaningfully, put his left hand on his right bicep and flexed the muscle. Giovanni grinned. He knew exactly what Tiller meant.

He called out four names and harangued them briefly. One of them was the man who had refused to pick up his rifle.

'These good men,' he said.

To Tiller they looked no different from the others. They were unshaven, their uniforms were torn and dirty, their boots worn out. One wore plimsolls. He indicated the one who had dropped his weapon and asked if he was any good.

'My cousin,' the corporal replied.

'Christ!' said Barnesworth. 'They're worse than the bloody Mafia.'

'They probably *are* the Mafia,' Tiller said. 'Make sure he doesn't shoot you in the back, Sarge.'

'I'll keep him in front of me,' Tiller promised.

The ambush site was about a mile along the path towards the promontory. It was even better than Tiller had remembered it because the ground on either side trapped the path into a narrow defile.

Tiller placed the Bren at the start of the ambush area, knowing the two SBS men manning it would not open fire until the trap had been closed, and the less reliable Breda with its less reliable crew at the far end to seal off any escape. He then distributed the Italians along the rest of the path.

'Tell them that as they are firing from above, they must aim low,' he told the corporal, indicating his legs. In the heat of a fire-fight it was an error even the most experienced infantryman could make. Giovanni understood.

'They must not fire until I say so.' Again the Italian nodded.

The grenades, the more powerful Mills bombs, were primed and distributed, and the ambushers settled down to wait.

The Germans, when they came, could be heard a

long way off, shouting gutturally to one another and crashing through the undergrowth.

'Must think they're on a fucking Sunday picnic,' one of the SBS men muttered to Tiller as he pulled back the cocking handle on the Bren. Tiller suddenly felt the adrenalin pounding through him and he gripped the man's arm so that he looked at Tiller in astonishment.

'What is it, Sarge?' he whispered.

Tiller cursed himself under his breath. The skipper was right: he was too conventional, did not use his instincts to keep one step ahead. One day it could be the death of him – and of those with him.

'They're doing that deliberately,' he whispered.

The SBS man thought about it. He had fought against the Germans in the desert, knew they were wily adversaries. It made sense. 'They could be, at that, Sarge.'

'Take the Bren and go back to Billy,' Tiller whispered. 'Tell him most of them must be coming his way. Take all the Eyeties with you except Giovanni and his cousin, and the Breda team. Make it snappy.'

The two SBS men slipped away. Giovanni and his cousin looked too nervous to hold a gun, much less fire it straight. The shouting and the trampling was closer now. Tiller cocked his silenced Sten, gripped the thick canvas handguard around the barrel, and edged closer to the path, gesturing for the two Italians to follow him.

Suddenly three Germans appeared out of the undergrowth about a hundred yards from Tiller. He held them in his sights. He was in trouble if there were more, he thought. They were making no attempt to keep quiet, but were pushing their way through the bushes, and calling out to one another.

Tiller watched the bushes behind them. There could only be three of them, he decided. He could cope with that. He looked across at Giovanni and his cousin and indicated that he would do the shooting.

The Germans were big, blond fellows, clean, well fed and well armed, but they were very young. And much too sure of themselves.

They entered the cut without a second glance, carrying their rifles at the trail, and when they were ten yards from him Tiller stood up and fired three single shots from the Sten.

The shots made less sound than a champagne cork. The first hit the leading German in the throat before he even saw Tiller. His rifle clattered to the ground and his hands flew up to the wound as he spun round.

The second German saw Tiller just as the SBS sergeant carefully squeezed the trigger again. The bullet ripped into the soldier's chest and knocked him backwards. His legs buckled under him and he pitched forward on to the first German sprawled across the path. He was dead before he hit the ground but through some physiological quirk he retained his grip on his rifle.

Only the last German had time to do anything. He dropped down on one knee and levelled his rifle. Fleetingly, as he shot the man between his eyes, Tiller admired the speed with which the German had moved, but even with such quick reactions he had had no chance to take proper aim.

Out of the corner of his eye Tiller saw the Italians rise from cover. He waved them down impatiently and then dropped into a crouching position to listen.

A lizard crossed the path, paused enquiringly, and then scuttled into the undergrowth. The first German made a strangled gurgling sound, drummed his heels on the ground, and died. Apart from that all Tiller could hear was the buzzing of the flies which were already beginning to gather over the blood and brains seeping on to the path.

For several minutes Tiller stayed crouched by the path watching the cloud of flies. Then he rose, indicated to the Italians they were to stay where they were, went back to the two men manning the Breda, and beckoned them to follow him.

'The other Germans must have gone inland,' he said to Giovanni, indicating with his hand. 'We'll take them from behind.'

The Italians followed Tiller back down the path. As they skirted the dead Germans, Tiller was drawn to the open, staring eyes of the one he'd shot in the throat. He looked away quickly.

They headed inland. Away from the beach the ground was rocky and steep. Apart from a few stunted bushes it was almost bare of cover, but a deep gully, which carried a stream to the sea during the wet season, gave them what was needed. Even so, they had to move carefully, one at a time.

Eventually they were able to work their way round until they were directly inland from the bay. They could see the Germans now, large dots spread out across the hillside. They were moving slowly down towards the garrison's defensive positions. There was a crackle of shots and the dots dropped to ground and returned the fire. Tiller wormed his way forward until he found a good position from which the Breda could enfilade the line of advancing

Germans and he indicated it to the two Italians manning the gun.

Suddenly there was a puff of smoke from the hillside and the whoomph-crack of a mortar bomb. Shit, thought Tiller. He had not reckoned with the Germans having a mortar. They had, he knew, a reputation for using them with devastating accuracy.

'I'm going to have to take that out,' he said to Giovanni. He pointed to the German position and slit his throat with his forefinger. Giovanni nodded. 'You stay here. Fire when you know I have taken out the mortar,' he said, and he made the gesture of firing. 'Understood?' Giovanni grimaced.

Tiller worked his way up the hillside, round behind the mortar team, and then crawled forward until he was close enough to be able to throw a grenade.

There were two Germans working methodically from a small dip in the ground which made them invisible to those defending the bay. One was feeding high-explosive bombs down the mortar's barrel, from which they were ejected with a subdued crump. Tiller watched two bombs as they whirred through the air and exploded on the hillside below.

The other member of the mortar team was breaking open a wooden box full of smoke bombs and piling them beside the mortar. Tiller guessed the mortar crew was just softening up the garrison's positions before laying smoke to screen the attackers when they made their final dash forward.

Tiller crawled forward, extracted the pin from the No. 36 grenade with his teeth and lobbed it into the dip. He had primed it with an five-second fuse rather than the normal seven-second one, so it exploded with a jarring thud almost as soon as it hit the ground.

There was a terrible scream from one of the Germans; the other, holding his leg, started scrambling up the hill. Tiller lifted his Sten and fired twice; the soldier staggered and fell.

That was five of the bastards, Tiller thought. Another fifteen to go. He heard the enemy commander shouting orders in the distance and tried to pinpoint his position. He had obviously decided to attack anyway, for the patrol rose in line, from what cover they had been able to find, and began advancing on the garrison's positions.

The Germans were well beyond the range of Tiller's Sten, so he scrambled to the mortar position and snatched up one of the dead men's rifles. He thought of using the mortar, but decided it would take too long to realign it. He took careful aim at the nearest German, who was about 200 yards below him and to his right. He squeezed the rifle's trigger, and the soldier pitched forward, though whether he had been hit, or had just tripped, Tiller couldn't tell.

Then the Breda opened up below him and to his left. It was in a perfect enfilading position and three of the enemy were hit with its first burst. The figures on the hill hesitated; some went on; others dropped to the ground. A whistle blew and the German commander began shouting his orders above the firing before a brief burst from one of the garrison's Brens forced him to the ground.

It did not surprise Tiller that Barnesworth, following the adage of reinforcing success, should now mount a counter-attack on the enemy's right flank. Billy knew his stuff. What did surprise him was that Giovanni and his cousin, who must have followed him round, now rose from cover below him and charged the left end of the German line. He could hear the two men screaming what must have been Italian obscenities as they ran forward and he gave them what cover he could with his rifle until they disappeared over a ridge to his right.

Then another Bren opened up on the Germans' right flank. That was too much for the attackers and within a minute a white handkerchief appeared on the end of a rifle barrel and then another and another, and the shooting petered out.

Tiller worked his way cautiously forward. From the garrison's defensive position someone shouted, '*Hände hoch! Hände hoch!*'

Slowly, cautiously, the Germans rose from the ground, holding their hands well above their heads. Tiller watched them carefully, alert for any trick. He counted nine of them. '*Kommen Sie hier!*' the linguist shouted. '*Schnell! Schnell!*'

But the Germans were reluctant to come quickly, or indeed to come at all. They stood on the hillside as if rooted to the spot, perhaps awaiting instructions from their commander. But it was the Bren to the right of them which eventually gave them their orders, because a burst was fired from it over their heads. The closest broke into a shuffling run and the others followed suit.

Tiller worked his way back down the hillside, collected the Breda team and the two Italians – all of them now grinning from ear to ear – and made his way down to the bay. Barnesworth greeted him enthusiastically. 'Good going, Tiger. That mortar was causing us real problems. I liked the way you sent those Eyeties in as well.'

'Not my doing,' said Tiller. 'They did it on their

own initiative. Talk about Charge of the bloody Light Brigade.'

'Good Christ!' said Billy. 'Whatever next. How did you guess what the Krauts were up to?'

'I nearly didn't,' said Tiller sourly.

'Well, if you hadn't sent back that Bren and those extra men I . . .'

'If, if, if, Billy.' Tiller felt the tension snap something inside him. Barnesworth looked at his friend understandingly.

'Two Eyeties dead,' he said after a pause. 'A mortar bomb got them in their slit trench.'

Tiller, quite irrationally, felt furious. 'If they'd dug the fucking slit trench properly, with a parapet, they'd have been all right. Fucking no-hopers.'

Barnesworth paused and said gently: 'No, it landed right in the trench, Tiger. They didn't stand a chance.'

Tiller wiped his face. The fury left him as quickly as it had built up, and he said tiredly: 'You're right. Sorry, mate. Any other casualties?'

'Couple of mortar-bomb fragments, a bullet through the arm, nothing serious. One of the Eyeties was advancing in the wrong direction and got a fragment in his arse. He won't be sitting down for a while. But most of them behaved pretty well.'

'And the Krauts?'

'We found eight dead on the hill, including the mortarmen. A couple more have a hole or two in them. They'll survive if the Eyeties don't slit their throats.'

'There are three down the track,' Tiller said. He remembered the cloud of flies and added: 'We'd better bury them quick.'

The Italians were talking excitedly among themselves.

'Good, good, eh?' the corporal said enthusiastically to Tiller.

'Very good,' said Tiller. 'You're a brave man, Giovanni. All your men, brave men.' The corporal saw that Tiller meant it. His effusive gratitude at being so praised was almost embarrassing. Poor bastard, Tiller thought, the Krauts when they came would not call him brave – they'd just shoot him. If he was lucky.

Balbao arrived late at the rendezvous, having been delayed from leaving Simi when naval intelligence in Alexandria put out an alert that two Italian destroyers, now in German hands, were heading towards the islands from Crete.

He brought a sick-berth attendant with him, one of a trickle of key personnel arriving on Simi as the British effort to reinforce the islands gathered momentum. The man treated the wounded, who were then, with the prisoners and the SBS men, loaded aboard at the jetty, while more stores for the diminished garrison were brought ashore. But it was dawn before the MAS boat was ready to make its daylight dash to Simi.

Giovanni wrung Tiller's hand in farewell. 'Italians fight good, eh?'

'Very good, Giovanni, very good. Good luck, mate.'

Tiller knew he would need it. They were all going to need it.

The MAS boat's crew had just cast off when one of the crew shouted out a warning and pointed seawards.

In the exhilaration of victory Tiller had quite forgotten about the Siebel ferry and when he saw it clawing its way awkwardly around the next headland to the north he could not immediately think what it was. Balbao ordered full speed ahead and the MAS boat leapt forward as the gun crews scrambled to man their weapons.

The Siebel ferry fired first. It began pumping 105mm shells at the MAS boat as the latter picked up speed and made for the open sea. But the German gunners underestimated the astonishing acceleration of their target and the shells fell well astern. The MAS boat's twin 20mm Bredas returned the fire and Tiller could see in the half light of dawn that the arcing tracer was hitting the target.

The Siebel was well armed but it was very slow and made an easy target. The MAS boat was now making thirty knots and the German gunners had little chance of hitting it. Balbao made a run parallel with the ferry which allowed his gunners to rake it from stem to stern. Then a shell from the Bredas hit a fuel tank on the Siebel and the German vessel suddenly blew up in a sheet of flame.

Balbao slowed and manoeuvred towards the Siebel, but by the time the MAS boat arrived there was no sign of it. A large patch of oil, some of it still alight, with pieces of charred, unidentifiable wreckage floating in it, was all that remained.

8

Tiller woke with a start. There was no moon; it was still very dark. A soft breeze sighed through the caique's rigging. Occasionally it gusted more strongly for a moment, snapping a halyard against the wooden mast, making the caique's hull creak against the quayside.

The SBS had set up its headquarters in the port and a more powerful radio than the Kittyhawk in the caique had been installed there. An empty house on the quay had also been acquired as sleeping quarters, but Tiller preferred to stay on the caique, where he could keep his nightmare to himself.

He stood up and and stretched himself and Griffiths, who was on guard, called out to him: 'I'm brewing up, Sarge. Like a cuppa?'

Griffiths handed up the steaming mug and Tiller wrapped his hands around it. With autumn on the way the air had a definite nip in it. He wondered as he sipped the strong, sweet tea if Giovanni and his garrison on Piscopi would survive. The SBS had given the Italians what stores they could spare, had even left one of their precious Brens behind.

The defeat of the German patrol had certainly given the morale of the Italians a lift, he decided, not only because their former, and intensely disliked, allies, had been beaten – and had shown themselves to be beatable – but because the tiny garrison had survived its baptism of fire. The male sex was pretty basic, Tiller realized now. Only two things concerned them: that they could screw and that they weren't cowards – and they frequently needed proof of both.

Tiller had no doubt now that if the Germans returned to Piscopi the garrison would fight. Tiller had told them that if they didn't he would come back and shoot them himself. He had come to like, almost respect, those dark, scruffy men. They weren't, he knew now, as bad soldiers as their army's reputation had led him to believe. Given the right leadership, they could be tough and resilient. He remembered Giovanni's wild, whooping cries as he had charged forward on the hillside waving his gun above his head, and grinned to himself. It had been quite a sight.

'Heard you had quite a time of it on Piscopi the other day,' Griffiths said as if reading the SBS man's thoughts. 'Those Jerries you brought back with you seemed fucking fed up with life. I suppose they thought they'd just come to beat up a few Eyeties. Hadn't reckoned on you lot.'

Tiller flung the dregs of his tea into the water. 'It's just been patrols we've encountered so far,' he said. 'Reckon they'll be moving in with more fire-power soon.'

'Larssen has got the Eyeties here running around like scared rabbits,' Griffiths said cheerfully. 'When the Krauts come, we'll be ready for them.'

'Let's hope so.'

Tiller shaved, fried himself two eggs, lit a cigarette, and was watching the sun rise over the mainland when Larssen appeared on the quay.

'We've just heard from our observation post on

Stampalia that an RAF crew have been stranded there. Engine failure apparently and they had to ditch. Several of them are hurt, so they need taking off quickly. I don't want to ask Balbao as I want to conserve what fuel he has, but Andrew's back from Leros and he said he'd pick them up in the caique. But he needs one of us to go with him. Fancy a few days at sea?'

'Sure, skipper,' said Tiller, flicking his cigarette stub into the harbour. 'Better than sitting here waiting for the Krauts to come.'

'Good,' Larssen said, and then added mischievously: 'Andrew's going to need to take that girl with him, so you should have an enjoyable trip, Tiger. You know how romantic the sea can be.'

'You tell me, skipper,' said Tiller, surprised at the embarrassment he felt. 'You were in the merchant navy.'

'Ah, but only cargo ships. Never aboard liners. Too bad. Anyway, work before women, Tiger, work before women.' And with those few words of advice Larssen turned away.

'Work before women' was one of Larssen's catchphrases. It was, Tiller decided, just another way of issuing the old warning to keep your eye on the ball and not be distracted. Larssen stopped and turned round.

'Oh, Tiger?'

'Skipper?'

'I think you did a good job on Piscopi. Well done.'

'Thanks, skipper. But they almost foxed me.'

'Almost. But they didn't, did they? I begin to think I was wrong about you.'

'In what way?'

'Spit and polish, Tiger, spit and polish. A good man, I said to myself when we first met – no doubt about that. Disciplined. Well trained. All that. Just who we need if we're in a tight spot to blow something up for us. But can I make him into a pirate? I asked myself. Is he a brigand at heart. Can he think on his feet. I looked at you that first day, Tiger, with your brass belt and shiny cap badge, and I must say I had my doubts.'

Tiller glanced down at his dirt-encrusted boots and the shirt and shorts he hadn't changed for a week, and grinned. It seemed a far cry from the immaculate lines of Marines drawn up in perfect order on the parade ground at Eastney, and said so.

'I wouldn't know one end of a parade ground from another,' Larssen said. 'But you have made me think it is not a total waste of time.'

'Any news of what's happening?'

'I think it's a matter of who builds up the most forces the quickest. The boss did a good job paving the way for the army, which now has three battalions in place, one each on Kos, Samos and Leros. But it's going to be a hard job keeping them supplied. And us for that matter. Every day there seem to be more attacks by the Luftwaffe. Yesterday they sank two of our destroyers at Leros. I'd say it's touch and go at the moment. But at least they still don't seem to know we're here on Simi.'

At dusk that evening an SBS medical orderly boarded the caique with three stretchers and his medical equipment. Kristos had imposed a curfew on the port to curb the hotheads among the locals, so Angelika had no difficulty in slipping aboard unnoticed soon afterwards. Half an hour later the caique motored out of the harbour flying the Turkish ensign at the truck of her mast.

Naval intelligence at Beirut had passed on to the SBS the information that, according to the Andartes' report Tiller had brought back from Rhodes, the Germans were indeed rapidly building up reinforcements and supplies on the island, and were also increasing their air and sea patrols among the other islands. There was, therefore, an increased risk of encountering an armed schooner or caique, so the Solothurn was loaded and a spare magazine placed beside it under the foresail. Griffiths propped himself against the mast ready to man it at a moment's notice; the others had their Lanchester carbines and Stens out of sight but close at hand.

The cockle had been removed and the three stretchers had been lashed to the deck in its place under the folds of the mainsail. There was, too, extra water, drums of fuel, and ammunition. Angelika acknowledged Tiller's presence with an impassive nod and a brief smile before settling herself beside Maygan in the cockpit. They spread out a local chart on their knees to estimate the best course for the caique to take to their destination.

Stampalia was the most westerly of the Dodecanese and lay some seventy miles from Simi. To reach it, Maygan and Angelika decided the safest route was to sail north towards the finger of Turkish coastline that stuck out into the Aegean and helped to form the Gulf of Doris. Though the Germans as well as the British infringed Turkish neutral waters, it made sense to keep as close as possible to the Turkish coastline and to make as much of the open-sea crossing as possible during the hours of darkness.

As Simi and the tiny island of Nimos to the immediate north of it dropped slowly astern the Matilda engine throbbed and burbled with a smooth power that kept a little smile of satisfaction on Stoker Bryson's face. The medic cut up a watermelon and passed slices around. The short crossing of the gulf to the Turkish mainland took less than an hour, but it seemed much longer as they scanned the night horizon and listened for the sound of marine engines.

Halfway across they fancied they did hear the faint, powerful throb of what was probably an E-boat. But they saw nothing and it soon faded, and once they were well within Turkish waters, the tension lessened. Maygan altered course to motor westwards and soon afterwards entered the bay he had decided to lay up in during daylight hours.

Once they were safely moored and the camouflage netting had been erected Griffiths brewed some tea and issued corned-beef sandwiches before they settled down to wait, and to sleep if they could. Dawn came red and glowing behind the barren mountains. They waited all day and watched the sun creep around in a deep-blue sky until, by evening, it began to sink behind the volcanic island of Nisiros, and the much smaller islands of Yali and Yassi to the north of it. No garrisons, German or Italian, had been reported on Nisiros and there was no sign of life on it when, after darkness fell, they steered between the islands.

'How the hell do you find your way around at night when there aren't any lighthouses or buoys,' Tiller asked Maygan, for the young lieutenant now seemed to have perfected a method of sailing among the islands on moonless nights to drop off SBS reconnaissance patrols or supplies for those manning lookout posts.

'By silhouette,' Maygan replied. 'You start off on a certain course knowing that you'll come to a rock or an island. That's your point of departure. You then alter course until the silhouette of one mountain or island can be seen between the gap of other mountains or islands. Or the end of one island overlaps the end of another. That's your transit. You know you're on the correct course for wherever you want to go. You can only do it in fine weather, of course, and I still need someone who knows the area to pilot me into some of the harbours or creeks. The charts we're using are hopelessly out of date.'

He showed Tiller what he meant by lining up the southern tip of Nisiros with the tiny island of Kandhilousa, which lay beyond it. As long as the outline of Kandhilousa was kept on their starboard bow they were safe from the rocks that extended from Cape Lutros, the southernmost point of Nisiros. But once the cape was abeam they changed course to keep Kandhilousa on their port bow.

Once clear of the rugged coastlines and the numerous tiny islets west of Nisiros, Maygan altered course slightly to the south to bring the caique into the tiny port of Maltezana, their agreed rendezvous with the SBS men on the island, which lay towards the northern end of Stampalia.

During the night the wind increased suddenly – the beginnings of a late *meltemi*, Angelika said – and sent spray flying across the deck, and by the early morning they were all cold and wet. At dawn they could see Stampalia ahead, its twin mountain peaks making it look at first like two separate islands. With Angelika issuing directions Maygan steered the caique towards Maltezana, threading it between several rugged islands that guarded its entrance. The foreshore was surprisingly green, a pleasant contrast from the barren hills behind, and the earth was tinged with red. Once in the bay they were sheltered from the *meltemi*.

The quay was empty except for the SBS lance-corporal waiting for them. He had brought the two uninjured members of the RAF crew to the port, but reported that the other two were quite badly hurt, so he had thought it best not to move them.

The stretchers and stores were unloaded and the Solothurn was stripped and dried and thoroughly oiled before being replaced on its bipod. Then Tiller, Bryson and the medic, guided by the SBS man, set off with two stretchers for Panormos, on the other side of the island, where the lookout post had been established. They crossed the narrow isthmus and then followed the coastline until they came to a small bay.

Overlooking the bay and with a view of a great sweep of the Aegean was a small wooden hut which the SBS men had reinforced with rocks inside. Below the horizon to the south-west was German-occupied Crete; to the north-west, beyond the scattered islands of the western Aegean, was German-occupied Greece.

'Seen much?' Tiller asked the lance-corporal, Paddy Donington, while the medic attended the two injured RAF men, who lay in one corner.

'You bet. Especially during the last couple of days. Aircraft mostly, making for Rhodes, but small shipping, too. Schooners, the occasional Siebel ferry, that sort of thing. Something big's building, I reckon. Surprised you risked it.'

'Cairo want the crew back,' said Tiller laconically. 'They're far more valuable than any of us lot.'

The medic got to his feet and came over to Tiller. He looked grave. 'I've given one a shot of morphine. He's got a broken leg. He'll be all right. But the other chap's in a bad way. No good moving him. He wouldn't last the trek back to the port, far less the boat trip to Simi.'

Tiller walked across to the dying man. He was no more than a kid. 'What's the matter with him?'

'Internal injuries probably. It's difficult to say.'

Tiller glanced at his watch. There wasn't much time. They had to sail at dusk. 'How long do you reckon?'

The medic knew what he meant. 'Impossible to say. An hour, a day – who knows?'

Tiller was wondering what to do when Donington approached him and drew him aside. 'Dave's been keeping an eye on a schooner coming in this direction from the north-west. He's had it under observation for an hour or more. It's not on the usual course for Rhodes. It could be coming here.' Tiller followed Donington along a coastal path to the ruins of what must have once been a watchtower. The SBS man, Dave Shawn, crouching among the rubble, handed Tiller his binoculars and pointed out to sea. 'That's it,' he said.

Tiller focused the binoculars on the boat. It was large, with two masts, the shorter foremast identifying it as being a schooner. But it was now under power and was butting its way at about five knots through the waves being thrown up by the *meltemi*.

'Schooner,' Shawn said. 'Looks as if it's got a trehandiri rig.'

'What the fuck's that?' said Tiller.

'The sails are hoisted on a gaff that sticks out in front of the mast as well as behind. Rather like an Arab dhow. We call it a lugger rig. The Germans use them quite a bit.'

Tiller could see four men on deck; as he scrutinized them four more came up from below. Even at the distance of some miles, there was no mistaking what they were.

'You're sure it's heading here?'

'Looks like it,' said Donington. 'Shipping for Rhodes usually passes well to the north or south.'

'How long have we got before they arrive?'

'If they're making for Maltezana – which is the likeliest place they would land – at least three hours. Perhaps more.'

They returned to the hut and Donington cranked on the landline telephone to contact Maltezana to warn them to expect visitors. Tiller collected Bryson and Donington, told the medic to stay with the RAF men and Dave, and set off for Maltezana.

Maygan, when he heard that the German schooner might be making for the port, said: 'We've got the element of surprise. We'll wait for it by the next headland and blow it out of the water.'

'What with?' Tiller asked.

'The Solothurn, of course.'

Tiller looked at the curious weapon doubtfully. 'Has anyone ever fired it?' he asked.

'I have,' said Griffiths. 'It kicks like a mule.'

'I don't propose to sit here and wait for them,' said Maygan. Tiller knew Maygan was right. The only advantage they had was surprise. He hesitated nonetheless. He did not fancy putting his life in the hands of an amateur yachtsman who had, so far as he knew, no experience of battle.

Maygan misinterpreted his reluctance. 'Come on, Tiger. There's only eight of them.'

'I only *saw* eight,' Tiller corrected him and, unwillingly, took the plunge. 'You're right, of course.'

'Good. Find a spot where we'll see them before they see us and lie up there under our camouflage net. They won't know what hit them.'

It was putting all their eggs in one basket, a bad principle at the best of times.

'How about leaving Paddy ashore?' Tiller suggested. 'He could act as lookout, warn us when they're coming in case we don't hear their engine, and he could put down some useful covering fire.'

'Good idea,' said Maygan warmly. 'Griffiths will man the Solothurn, you and Jock can have the Bren, and Donington can stay ashore. He can have a Lanchester.'

'If you don't mind, I'd prefer my Lee Enfield, sir,' said the lance-corporal politely. 'It might have a slower rate of fire but it's a bloody sight more accurate when it comes to trying to hit anything over a couple of hundred yards.'

'Fine,' said Maygan. 'Now let's look at the chart and see if we can pick a good spot.'

In the heat of the moment they had forgotten Angelika. She was sitting on a rock about a hundred yards from them, gazing out to sea, her chin cupped in her hands, the chart on her lap.

'Shit,' said Maygan. 'What are we going to do with her?'

'She can't come with us,' said Tiller immediately.

'She's safer ashore,' Maygan agreed. Tiller walked over to her and asked Angelika for the chart.

'What's happening?' she asked.

When Tiller explained the situation she agreed to stay hidden ashore provided she was given a pistol. Tiller shook his head. 'You mustn't resist if anything goes wrong. They won't know you're not a local.'

She looked at him almost contemptuously. 'They'll find out if they want to. And they will want to.'

Tiller hesitated.

'I only want a pistol so that I can shoot myself,' Angelika said fiercely. 'Have you any idea what the Germans do to anyone they suspect of being an Andarte, as you call them? What do you think they would do if they caught me?'

Tiller sank down on his haunches and looked into her face.

'Look,' he said, 'I'll give you mine if you want. But I'll never forgive you if you use it.'

For a moment she looked at him in puzzlement, and then she laughed. 'You English. Such a funny sense of humour.'

'Promise me you'll hide,' said Tiller. 'If things go wrong make your way across the island to the observation hut. It's here.' He pointed to the chart. 'They'll look after you.'

He took his Colt 9mm pistol out of its holster, extracted the clip of cartridges from the butt, and then showed her how the weapon worked before handing it to her. She weighed it in her hand and then snapped the clip of cartridges back into the butt and applied the safety-catch. From the way she did it Tiller knew she had handled a pistol before, and said so. But she just looked at him and smiled thinly, and said: 'I'll hide. I promise.'

Maygan spread the chart on a rock and pointed to a small promontory just north of the port. 'That looks perfect.'

Donington looked over Maygan's shoulder. 'Looks fine to me,' he agreed. 'I'll see you there, Sarge.' He hoisted his rifle on to his shoulder, and set off.

The promontory proved an ideal hiding-place for the caique, as there was an overhanging cliff with a tiny shelving beach inland of it. They put warps ashore, shrouded the caique in the camouflage netting, and then took up their firing positions.

Griffiths swivelled the Solothurn on its bipod ready for it to fire over the starboard bow; the Bren was set up in the cockpit, where it could fire through one of the brass bushes which had been specially let into the caique's high gunwales for just such a purpose. The range, they agreed, would probably be about 300 yards if the Germans came round the headland on course for Maltezana. At that distance even the Solothurn could hardly miss.

Soon after the caique was in position Donington appeared on the beach and called out that he had found a good concealed position from which to fire and that he could see the German schooner about a mile up the coast. She seemed to be keeping close inshore. 'Perfect,' said Maygan. 'Griffiths, fire into her engine space first and then riddle her below the water-line. Tiger, I want you to take out the helmsman and then keep the deck clear of Krauts. I'll fire first.'

Tiller nodded, flipped up the rear sights of the Bren, slid the catch to automatic, and cocked the mechanism. The pistol grip, which he held in his right hand, felt slippery with sweat, but the butt, guided by his left, nuzzled comfortably into his shoulder as he squinted down the sights.

Bryson crouched next to Tiller, his Lanchester carbine to hand, and piled up some spare magazines for the Bren.

It seemed to take an age before they first heard the faint but slow, steady thump of the schooner's diesel. It became gradually louder but then began to fade, and it took Tiller a moment to realize that the sound of it was being screened by the promontory so that he saw the schooner before he heard its engine again.

The schooner was coming on the exact course they had calculated, but it was much bigger than it had looked from the observation post. It must have been at least eighty feet long, and the pronounced curve of its hull gave it a distinctly Arab appearance. Its hull was white, or had been once, and it had a high, ornate stem which protruded above the gunwale. Sheltering behind this were two Germans with a Spandau machine-gun fixed on a bipod. Three more were standing around the foremast with Schmeisser sub-machine-guns hanging from their shoulders. In the stern the helmsman was standing on a kind of platform so that he could see his way ahead. Both his hands were on the large, curved tiller.

All of the Germans were staring ahead, except one in the cockpit, who was shading his eyes and looking behind him at the headland.

Tiller watched this man carefully as he scanned in from the headland until he was looking directly at the caique. Then the man's gaze shifted beyond the caique and into the bay behind it, and Tiller marvelled at the skill of the chief camouflage officer of the 9th Army who had devised the netting and specially coloured scrim. The man was a genius.

But the caique's netting was to disguise the caique from the air, not at close quarters from the sea, and something in the strange outline under the cliff must have alerted the German, for his gaze shifted back again to it. He lifted the binoculars slung around his neck and was focusing them on the caique when Maygan shot him with his Lanchester.

Almost simultaneously Griffiths fired his first round from the semi-automatic Solothurn. The kick was so violent that the caique rolled and bounced, but this did not prevent Tiller killing the helmsman with a short, sharp burst from the Bren.

He then swivelled the light machine-gun to the other end of the schooner and fired a more prolonged burst at the Spandau crew. As he did so he heard Bryson's Lanchester bark twice, three times, and then the Solothurn fired again.

At first the schooner seemed quite unaffected and sailed serenely on, though no one was at the helm. Then gradually she began to yaw. The Solothurn fired again, shaking the caique, and the schooner's engine faltered and then stopped, and slowly she lost way.

It was difficult for Tiller to find a target now, as the Germans on the deck had thrown themselves flat and those below had obviously thought it wiser to remain there. But Donington had a better view and his rifle cracked a number of times somewhere on the headland above the caique. The schooner was drifting very slowly now and was visibly lower in the water, but Griffiths kept pumping 20mm shells into her hull.

One of the Germans, braver – or more foolish –

than the others, opened fire from behind the foremast, but the Schmeisser's bullets sang harmlessly over the caique and a burst from the Bren tumbled him into the water.

The schooner drifted to a halt and a lick of flame came out of the main cabin. Griffiths stopped firing. They watched as the schooner began settling by the stern; the sea had already started flooding into its cockpit before the two remaining Germans burst out of a forward hatch and flung themselves into the water.

Tiller watched them dog-paddling towards the caique and was wondering how they would be able to find room for two prisoners as well as the RAF crew when the schooner blew itself apart with a muffled crump that shook the caique from stem to stern. Waves created by the detonation hammered against its side and bits of debris, thrown high in the air, started cascading into the water all around them. Then there was a large gout of steam and what remained of the schooner slid quickly into the water.

'I suppose, we'd better pick up those Krauts,' Maygan said.

'No point,' replied Tiller. He knew what happened to anyone caught in the water near an underwater explosion – their vulnerable stomachs would have been split open like gutted fish. 'They'll be very dead.'

Griffiths came aft, grinning from ear to ear. 'I said it would work, Sarge,' he said elatedly to Tiller. 'Cuckoo clocks aren't the only things the Swiss make well.'

Cuckoo clocks reminded Tiller of his long-cherished opinion of naval officers. Perhaps some of them weren't so bad, he thought now. Maygan had certainly acted with cool courage throughout the whole brief fire-fight. He already had his log out and was jotting down details before he forgot them.

'Did you see the schooner's name?' he asked, but no one had.

'You sank her too quickly, sir,' said Griffiths.

'She was a trehandiri, that's all I know,' said Tiller.

'A *what*?'

'Local craft. Lugger rig. I would've thought you would've known that, sir,' Tiller said with a grin.

'I didn't know you're an expert at recognizing boats as well as aircraft, Tiger. What do you think she was carrying to make an explosion like that?'

'Mines probably.'

The SBS men received a great reception when they returned to Livadia Bay. During the caique's absence a radio message had come through telling them to withdraw the observation post from the island and everyone guessed that indeed something big was brewing.

Bryson went to fetch the medic and arrived in time to help bury one of the RAF crewmen, who had died soon after Tiller had seen him, and to bring the other down on a stretcher. By the time LS8 left Stampalia it had been dark for two hours. The caique's deck was crowded but the weather was calm. The stretcher case was wrapped in a tarpaulin, and the others huddled together around him. Angelika remained in the cockpit with Maygan and Griffiths, who took turns to steer. Bryson opened up the Matilda engine more than he should have, making the caique roll and butt its way through the glassy water.

Nisiros was sighted an hour before dawn and as the first rays of the sun broke over the horizon ahead of them the rumble of guns and then the sound of aircraft wafted across to them from Kos, which lay on the horizon to the north.

Tiller scanned the sky with his binoculars and pointed. 'There. Look.'

Stukas were bombing the island and the rumble of the explosions floated faintly across the sea like thunder. Then bigger aircraft, which Tiller identified as Ju52 transports, appeared from the north-west and suddenly parachutes began to blossom beneath them. Above the transports flew Me109 fighters. There was no sign of any British aircraft.

'Can we go any faster, Jock?' Maygan asked, but the stoker shook his head. 'I think she's almost falling to bits as it is, sir,' he replied.

They all watched the invasion of Kos in shocked silence until the Turkish coastline blocked the faint sounds of battle from their ears as well as the island from their view.

At midday Maygan made the caique's routine position report to Simi on the radio and was told to go to Kos and collect Jarrett. But Simi did not know where Jarrett exactly was on the island as the message had been garbled.

Maygan and Tiller were just discussing the dilemma this put them in – the injured RAF man needed urgent medical attention – when ahead of them they saw another caique moving along the coast towards them under sail.

Griffiths dashed forwards to man the Solothurn and Tiller brought the Bren up from the hold before watching the slow progress of the approaching caique through his binoculars. It was about the same size as LS8 and looked genuine enough.

'What do you think, Tiger?'

'It could be a local Greek one.'

He handed the binoculars to Angelika, who confirmed that it was.

'I am going to unload our passengers,' said Maygan, 'and then make for Kos.'

Tiller nodded his agreement. When the Greek caique was within hailing distance Angelika shouted across to it. At first the crew seemed reluctant to comply but when Griffiths unveiled the Solothurn from under the foresail they quickly came to a stop.

'They come from Kalimnos,' Angelika said. 'They're genuine.'

'Tell them,' said Maygan, 'we'll pay them to take a wounded man and his friends to Simi.'

Angelika shouted again and then said to Maygan: 'They don't want money. They do it anyway.'

The Greek caique came alongside LS8 and the wounded man was carefully transferred. Then the others crossed, and Maygan indicated that Angelika should join them, but she did not move.

'You know Kos?' she asked him.

Maygan shook his head and said: 'No, but it's only over there. I can hardly miss it.'

'I know Kos. I know every rock and every bay. It is not an easy island to navigate.'

Maygan glanced at Tiller, who shrugged. What the hell, he thought, if she knows how to handle a pistol it is not as if she is some sweet innocent caught up in a war she didn't understand.

For a while, they watched the Greek caique sail back along the coast before turning about themselves.

'We'll stay by the coast after rounding the point,' said Angelika. 'Then we'll cut across to the port of Kos.'

'Is there nothing nearer?' Maygan asked, looking at the chart. Angelika pointed a slim finger. 'There's Kamares Bay. It is where ships used to go in before the war to load the ore that is mined above the port. But communications with the rest of the island are bad. The port of Kos is better.'

Once they had rounded Cape Krio and began crossing the Gulf of Kos the sound of battle, faint at first, became more distinct.

'If they take Kos,' said Maygan, 'Simi will be the meat in the sandwich between Kos and Rhodes.'

'Or the thorn in their side,' said Tiller. 'If we hold Simi their flank will be exposed.'

The port of Kos was dominated by a castle built to the south of the entry to the port. As they approached its entrance they could see a tattered Union Jack flying from its highest point.

'Hoist the white ensign,' Maygan told Griffiths. 'I don't want some trigger-happy gunner putting a hole in us.'

But the gunners had other, more important, targets, for as the caique sailed past the imposing stone walls of the fortress two Stukas came screaming almost vertically out of the sky, dropped their bombs, pulled out of their dive, banked, then disappeared to the north pursued by Bofors fire from the castle.

The double boom of the bombs was followed by clouds of dust from pulverized masonry.

'Get the Bren up here,' Maygan shouted to Tiller. 'If those bastards come back we can have a go at them.'

Inland from the port they could hear the chatter of machine-gun fire and the occasional report of something heavier being fired. Perhaps, Tiller thought, the Fallschirmjäger, the paratroops, had parachuted in some light mountain guns, a daunting prospect.

The island's defenders had obviously received some warning of the attack, because the port had been almost cleared of shipping. A wrecked landing-craft lay half sunk at one end; at the other a Tribal-class destroyer was just casting off its warps from the quay. As it passed LS8 Maygan ordered Griffiths to dip the caique's white ensign. After a prolonged pause, during which they could see a naval officer on the destroyer's open bridge studying them with interest, the destroyer replied by dipping hers.

Tiller could see from the officer's three straight gold stripes on the epaulettes of his white service shirt and the 'scrambled eggs' on the peak of his cap that he was a commander in the Royal Navy. He leant over the side of the destroyer's bridge and shouted down: 'Who the hell are you?'

'Levant Schooner Flotilla, sir,' Maygan shouted back.

'Never heard of you,' the commander replied, and moved back to the centre of his bridge.

'That's fame for you,' said Maygan to the others with a grin.

They came alongside the part of the quay the destroyer had just vacated and were met by an army major and two military policemen. The major looked harassed.

'I'm the port evacuation officer,' he said. 'What exactly do you think you're up to? We happen to be in the middle of fighting off an invasion and you come motoring in here as if you were on holiday. You're bloody lucky those Stukas didn't get you. Who are you anyway?'

'Levant Schooner Flotilla, sir,' Maygan said reeling off a casual salute.

'Never heard of you,' said the major testily, returning the salute by raising his cane in the direction of his cap. Maygan caught Tiller's eye and Tiller found it hard to suppress a smile.

'Special Operations,' added Maygan by way of explanation.

The major's expression softened slightly. 'Ah, I see. And whose orders are you under and who are these men with you?'

He looked hard at Angelika, who turned quickly away.

'Special Boat Squadron, sir,' said Tiller, saluting smartly. 'Orders to contact Major Jarrett immediately. Do you happen to know where he is?'

'Jarrett, eh?'

The name worked like a password, for the major turned to the military policemen and said: 'Show them the way to Major Jarrett's HQ as soon as they're ready.'

He turned back to Maygan and added: 'Good luck. You're going to need it.'

The deserted streets were littered with rubble, as the Stukas had been giving the port their attention ever since the German invasion had been launched. Maygan and Tiller picked their way through it behind the two military policemen.

'Where have the locals gone?' Maygan asked one of them.

'Most of them took to the hills before it started,'

he replied. 'They seemed to know what was going to happen almost before we did. Some are probably hiding in their cellars – those that have got them, that is. Here you are, sir.'

Jarrett's HQ was an old stone warehouse on the outskirts of the port. A sack covered the gap where the door had been. Tiller pulled it to one side and entered, and Maygan followed him. On the left a radio operator was working on his Morse key with his headphones. Next to him Jarrett sat on a packing case reading a signal. He looked up when Tiller entered and acknowledged his salute.

'Where the hell have you been?' he asked irritably.

'We got here as quickly as we could,' said Maygan. 'We were taking back an injured man from Stampalia when we got your message. What's happening?'

Jarrett stood up and pointed to the map of Kos pinned on the wall behind him. 'They've put two battalions ashore, one at Cape Foca, here, the other further west, and at another two points. There are also about two hundred parachutists from the Brandenburgers around Antimachia airfield. Here.'

'Brandenburgers?'

'Brandenburg Regiment. Special service troops. Kraut equivalent of Commandos. I have about twenty men up there, trying to stop them from taking it, but we've now had orders to pull out.'

'Are we going to stop them here, sir?' Tiller asked.

Jarrett shrugged. 'It doesn't look like it. We tried to organize the garrison and put some heart into them. But frankly it's a shambles and the trouble is we've got no air support. The few Spits which we had here were shot up before they even got into the air and the

Beaufighters they send from Cyprus just get chased away by the Me109s.'

The radio operator handed Jarrett another signal, which he read before crumpling it up and letting it drop to the floor.

'They've taken the airfield.' He shook his head and then added wearily: 'We need as many Flotilla caiques and boats to get here as quickly as possible to take us off. How many do you think are available right now?'

Maygan thought. 'Four caiques at the last count. Unless we've lost any in the last forty-eight hours. There are a couple of MLs as well, but they're at Castelrosso. That's about it.'

'It'll have to be enough, then,' said Jarrett. 'Andrew, I want you to take my HQ staff and myself to Leros. Right away. Tiger, I want you stay here and wait for the others to arrive from Antimachia, tell them what's happening, and then make sure they know where the caiques are. I'd already given Bob Baring orders to withdraw before the airfield fell. He knows we're withdrawing to Leros. Andrew will pick you up and take you back to Simi tomorrow. Let's go.'

As dusk fell Tiller watched LS8, its decks crowded with Jarrett's HQ staff, leave Kos harbour. An hour later, two of the caiques arrived from Leros and a third, which had been at Levita, crept in at midnight. They had all been working in the more northerly of the Dodecanese, setting up SBS observation posts on the smaller islands and taking reconnaissance patrols of the Long Range Desert Group to the bigger ones. Tiller estimated how many passengers each could take, told them what was happening, and then returned to Jarrett's HQ.

Shortly afterwards the first group of men from Bob Baring's detachment arrived. By now the perimeter of troops around the port was under heavy pressure and mortar bombs were falling among the buildings. The general opinion was that the Germans would launch an attack at dawn.

Baring and Tiller divided the SBS men between the caiques, which then sailed for Portolago, the principal harbour of Leros. Tiller, guessing that the perimeter would not hold when the German attack came, went with the last caique and at Portolago met up with Maygan, who told him that Kos had fallen.

9

With Kos lost, the caiques of the Levant Schooner Flotilla worked at night between the island and Leros to rescue as many of the British garrison as they could. The SBS landed patrols to scour the island to find any soldiers who had evaded capture and had them taken by the caiques to safety on Leros. But after a week no more could be found, the operation was abandoned, and LS8 sailed for Simi.

During the first night the *meltemi* blew and its autumn chill swept over the caique as it crept southwards around the Turkish coastline. Across the strait which divided Kos from the mainland they could see that part of the port of Kos was still smouldering, and Tiller wondered how many British soldiers had been lost on the island by the dramatic collapse of its defences.

Just before dawn they found shelter in a narrow, uninhabited Turkish bay which was sheltered from the fierce and persistent wind by a small island to the north of it. The camouflage netting was erected and the day spent sleeping. At dusk they set off again under a cloudy sky which threatened rain.

Soon after rounding Cape Krio the Matilda engine gave up again and nothing Bryson did could coax it to restart. They were forced to hoist the sails, which, with the wind on the starboard quarter, gave the caique a soaring, bouncing motion that curdled their empty stomachs.

When dawn broke the sky was grey and they approached the port of Simi in a rainstorm. Then the wind dropped and they sat in the bay with rain tipping down on top of them until eventually Larssen sent out the Italian garrison's launch to tow them in.

Larssen greeted them with the news that intelligence in Cairo had just intercepted German signals which indicated that they had decided to occupy Simi. He also said that the fall of Kos had unnerved the Italian garrison to such an extent that some of them had abandoned their uniforms and weapons, and had taken to the hills in civilian clothes.

'They know what happens to them when the Krauts come here,' he said to Tiller and drew his right forefinger across his throat. Tiller noticed that Larssen said 'when' not 'if'.

In the days that followed the Blohm and Voss twice circled Simi port and once an Me109 flew straight and low down the length of the bay. Then at dawn one morning the Italian observation post at the southern end of Simi called excitedly on their landline that they could see two or three ships approaching. As the light improved they identified one of them as a large caique. It was flying the Kriegsmarine ensign and its deck was crowded with soldiers. Following it was a small landing-craft, also crowded with soldiers, and a sleek speedboat which in peacetime must have taken tourists on day trips round the smaller islands, or perhaps had been the valued property of a local tycoon.

Larssen ordered Tiller and Barnesworth to round up as many of the garrison as were left. The two SBS men searched the castle, which was now suddenly empty and deserted, and it was not until they began combing through the outbuildings that they came across about twenty men huddled together.

Tiller bawled at them to get to their feet as the Germans were on their way, a fact that the Italians, judging by the expressions on their faces, already knew. As they reluctantly began to gather their equipment, Perquesta appeared and began to harangue them in rapid Italian.

'Tell them,' Tiller told Perquesta, 'that for them the war is not over. They are going to fight the invaders of their territory and they are going to fight bravely.'

This was received in sceptical silence.

'Tell them that I shall see that they fight bravely because I shall be right behind them. Tell them that when they attack the Germans some of them may die. But if they don't attack when ordered they will die for sure. Because I shall be behind them and will shoot anyone who does not obey.'

Perquesta looked at Tiller open-mouthed. '*Signore*, you cannot do that,' he stuttered. 'The Geneva Convention . . . It does not . . .'

'Fuck the Geneva Convention,' said Tiller. '*This* is my Geneva Convention.' He tapped his Sten gun. Perquesta swallowed hard. His translation had a marked effect on the garrison.

'I think they think you mean it, Tiger,' said Barnesworth.

'I fucking do,' said Tiller and realized that in the last few weeks he had learnt a lot from Larssen. He turned to Perquesta and saluted him smartly. 'Right, sir. Let's have them outside with weapons loaded.'

Led by Perquesta, the garrison marched in silence

down to where Larssen and the other SBS men awaited them. The German patrol, Larssen told them, was coming in to Pethi Bay, just south of Simi port, according to the Italian lookout post there. 'You and Billy come with me and this mob,' he said to Tiller. 'I want Ted Warrington and the rest of the boys as a second line of defence just outside the port.'

They trudged up the barren hillside that divided the two bays and along the top of which stood a line of old windmills. Just before they reached the skyline Larssen ordered them to halt while he went forward to reconnoitre. He came back with a grin on his face.

'There's about twenty of them,' he said. 'They're only just beginning to climb the path to the port. I can't see if they've got any mortars but apart from one Spandau, they're only armed with rifles and Schmeissers. From the way they're carrying them, they don't seem to be expecting much opposition. We'll move up to the crest, rake them with fire, then charge them with fixed bayonets.'

'Bayonets?' Perquesta looked appalled.

'Yes, bayonets. Tell your men to fix bayonets, Lieutenant.'

The SBS team watched with grim amusement as the Italians drew their bayonets and clipped them on their rifles.

'If the Krauts don't die from bayonet wounds, they'll die from tetanus,' Barnesworth said. 'Some of those bayonets haven't been out of their scabbards since the war started.'

The garrison were now ordered to spread across the hillside, with Barnesworth and Tiller covering them from the more vulnerable right flank. They moved up to the crest and when Larssen gave the order they opened fire on the German patrol below them.

To the surprise of the SBS the garrison gave a good account of themselves at first and several Germans fell. But once the enemy had gone to ground and began returning fire the Italians seemed to lose heart.

It was then that Larssen leapt to his feet and ordered the garrison to charge.

Luckily the German machine-gunner was too eager and the first burst from his Spandau was too high. But it was enough to make most of the Italians scramble back over the crest. Tiller wondered if Larssen would ever even get them on their feet again. He wished he had Giovanni and his cousin with him. They would have shown this lot what to do. He wormed his way over to Larssen, who had also been forced to take cover after the abortive bayonet charge. 'Do we wait for them to come to us, skipper, or do you and I and Billy go and get them?'

Larssen rubbed the stubble on his chin. 'There's not much cover up here. If they've got a mortar it will be a blood-bath, and anyway the Eyeties will just run for it. At least they haven't done that yet. You and Billy take some of them and try and get round the Krauts' flank. Then I can charge them while you give me covering fire.'

'Worth a try, I suppose.'

Tiller collected some of the more willing Italians, and under cover of the crest began making his way cautiously to the right. After a while he moved forward to reconnoitre and saw, about 500 yards away on the next headland, the remains of an old stone building. The ground sloped away sharply in front of it down into Pethi Bay, which he could now see from where he was lying. The ground in front of him was a series of small ridges which sloped more gradually towards the bay. He could see one or two enemy soldiers moving in and out of the stone building and wondered how many more of them there were. He could also see the top of the mast of the German caique at anchor in the bay and hoped he would get a chance to sink it. In the meantime there was the German patrol to dispose of.

Tiller gestured for Barnesworth to come forward and handed him the binoculars. 'That stone building. What are they up to?'

'Bringing up stores from the ships,' Barnesworth said. 'They must think they've come to stay. How much further to go, do you reckon?'

'Another hundred yards or so. Then we should be able to enfilade the patrol.'

Tiller signalled for the Italians to follow him and when he saw the patrol scattered across the hillside below him ordered them to open fire. The Germans scattered but there was nowhere for them to go except back to the beach and when they saw Larssen charging down the hillside driving the Italians in front of him most of them turned and ran back towards the bay. They were followed by concentrated fire from Tiller's group of Italians, who were visibly excited at seeing them on the run.

'Now what, skipper?' Tiller said when he met up with Larssen.

'There are more of them than I thought,' the Dane admitted.

'There are more of us than *they* thought, skipper,' Barnesworth said.

'But most of our men won't budge,' Larssen said in

disgust. 'I think we have to try another tack. We've got the caique and the MAS boat. We attack them from the sea. If we sank their ships they'd be cut off. You keep the bastards' heads down, Billy. Any of your Eyeties still in the fight?'

'One or two,' said Barnesworth. 'They saw the Krauts running. That cheered them up.'

'I'll send Kristos up to you with any extra men he can find. Tiger, you and I will take the caique round to the bay. I want Ted and the others aboard the MAS boat. If the Kraut boats come out, all well and good. If not we'll go in and get them.'

Despite Bryson's efforts LS8's engine was still not functioning. But the weather had cleared now and a 'soldier's breeze', as Maygan called it, was blowing off the Turkish coast, the perfect direction if they had to enter Pethi Bay. An Italian Breda was added to the caique to supplement the Solothurn and Bren, and the sails were hoisted.

'When was the last time the Royal Navy fought a battle at sea under sail,' Maygan wondered aloud. 'We're making history, lads.'

'Tell me, Andrew, what's a soldier's breeze?' Larssen asked curiously.

'One that even a soldier could sail in, of course.'

Balbao was to take the MAS boat in a wide circle so as to approach Pethi Bay from the east. Hopefully this, and the fact that it was flying an Italian ensign, might confuse the invading force and perhaps even make them hesitate to open fire on it. The caique had to tack out of the bay. This took a while and the sun was low in the sky by the time they passed the headland which protected the northern end of Pethi Bay.

Occasionally the faint sound of firing drifted across the caique from the hillside.

Gradually the bay began opening up in front of them and after a while the ruined stone building on the far side of the bay came into view.

The caique was flying the Turkish ensign, which Maygan hoped might baffle the Germans temporarily. But as soon as it was spotted a warning burst was fired over it from the Spandau which had been set up in the stone building. When the caique ignored this another burst cut up the water ahead of it.

By this time those aboard LS8 could see the German caique at anchor. Beyond it the landing-craft and the speedboat had been beached.

'See to that Spandau, Griffiths,' Maygan shouted and the leading seaman whipped the cover off the Solothurn and began pumping shots at the ruined building while Tiller and Warrington opened fire on the caique.

'Hoist the white ensign,' Maygan ordered Bryson. It was already attached to its halyard and seconds later it was fluttering at the truck of the mast.

Figures began running from the stone building down towards the bay. Bullets from the Spandau kicked up the water around the caique and the caique shivered as the Solothurn fired back. Tiller could see bits flying off the German caique as the Bren and the Breda raked its decks. Beyond it he could see the heavy machine-gun aboard the landing-craft being swivelled towards them.

Tiller lifted the sights of the Breda a couple of notches and fired a short burst at the landing-craft. The man pedalling the machine-gun mounting around fell backwards but another immediately took his place.

'Put the Kraut caique between us and that machine-gun,' Larssen shouted at Maygan. Maygan nodded and altered course.

But the German caique had been cut loose from its anchor and its engine started, and it began to move slowly across the bay as it continued to be hit by the fire from LS8.

Larssen tried to drop its helmsman with a burst from the Bren but the man's position was well protected by sandbags. Slowly, inexorably, the German caique swung towards the entrance to the bay.

Tiller squeezed the trigger of the Breda, but nothing happened and he knew at once that its complicated blow-back system had jammed. Cursing everything Italian, he picked up a Lanchester just as the heavy machine-gun on the landing-craft opened up.

The first burst went high and wide, and spattered into the cliff behind the British caique. But Tiller knew – they all knew – that their old wooden hull would not be able to absorb many of the enemy gun's heavy-calibre bullets.

Maygan changed course towards the German caique in another attempt to put it between the machine-gun and themselves but the distance was too great now. The second burst from the machine-gun shredded the caique's mainsail and smashed the gaff. The heavy wooden spar crashed down on to the deck in pieces and then fell into the water, pulling the tattered remains of the mainsail with it. The wreckage slowed the caique and, powered only by its foresail, it began to lose way.

'Cut that mainsail loose!' Maygan shouted, but

Griffiths was already leaning over the side, sawing at the ropes that still held the gaff and mainsail to the mast.

Tiller waited for the next burst, which, he knew, would rip into the hull, for even in the gathering dusk the machine-gunner could not miss his target as it was now broadside on to him.

Then behind him Tiller heard the throaty roar of the MAS boat's engines and the distinctive bof-bof-bof of its twin Bredas opening up. Balbao's gunners were using tracer and Tiller could see it arcing past the caique and on to the landing-craft.

The machine-gun stopped firing and there was a dramatic whoomph of flame as the landing-craft suddenly caught fire, and the gunners on the MAS boat turned their attention to the ruined stoned building, pumping shell after shell into it.

Germans were running everywhere and Barnesworth and his men were trying to pick them off in the gathering gloom. The German caique was now motoring away as fast as possible but the MAS boat simply blew it apart with the Bredas. Bits of planking and wooden coaming flew everywhere and the crew jumped into the water. The caique's engine stopped and without anyone at the helm an inshore current caught the drifting hulk and grounded it on an outcrop of rocks below the next headland.

This only left the speedboat, but that never even got under way, for Griffiths holed it with a shot from the Solothurn and sent the men in it tumbling into the shallow water and wading for the shore.

Suddenly it was quite dark except for the area around the burning landing-craft. A red Very light curved into the sky. Gradually the shooting above the bay petered out.

Balbao came alongside. 'Are you all right?' he asked.

Maygan gave the thumbs up and said: 'Can you give us a tow back?'

'No problem,' Balbao shouted back, elated by the success of the operation. 'Always a pleasure to help the Royal Navy.'

A line snaked to the caique from the stern of the MAS boat. Griffiths caught it deftly and tied it round the bottom of the mast.

Now that the fight was over Tiller found himself in a fury with the Breda which had let him down. He picked it up and threw it overboard.

Kristos was on the quay to greet them and to tell them that the seaborne attack had resulted in the rest of the Germans being routed, for the Italians, heartened by witnessing it, had held their ground well when the Germans tried to break through their cordon. It had given way in the end but the German survivors, more intent on survival than on driving home any kind of attack on the port, had simply dispersed into the night. They were probably making for the hills, Larssen added, in the hope that they would be able to hide out there until they were rescued. If they met any local people who might be sheltering up there he doubted if they would ever come down again.

The next day Maygan sent Tiller and Griffiths in the garrison launch to see what could be salvaged from the German caique and to bring back the damaged speedboat. They found the caique hard aground on the rocks. On searching it they found nothing of more interest than two dead Germans and a bottle of schnapps. They took the schnapps, and the caique's sails and gaff, weighted the dead Germans and dropped them overboard to the accompaniment of a perfunctory burial ceremony, and then went to look for the speedboat.

Up on the hillside above the bay they could see a party of Italians with picks and shovels scouring the ground for dead Germans to bury. The speedboat was lying in shallow water. Except for the shell hole from the Solothurn, it seemed undamaged. They bailed it out, plugged the hole, and towed it back to the port.

Bryson, who had just finished repairing the caique's engine, inspected the trophy with interest. 'The Eyeties can certainly build them fast,' he said. He checked that the speedboat's engine was still in working order. 'That's an Alfa Romeo unit which can develop God-knows-what horsepower. I reckon it's probably got a top speed of fifty knots or more.' He wiped his hands on a rag and looked suitably impressed.

Larssen, however, remained quite unmoved. 'It's no bloody use to us, is it?'

Tiller looked with fascination at the sleek craft with its long, curved counter and pointed bow, and asked: 'How fast did you say, Bill?'

'I reckon fifty knots. In flat water, that is. If it went at that speed in any kind of a sea it would sink like a stone. It beats me why the Krauts brought it along.'

'For reconnoitring the island, perhaps,' said Larssen. 'Get rid of it.'

'Eh, wait a tick, skipper,' Tiller interjected. 'You never know. It might come in handy.'

Larssen shrugged. 'All right, but get it out of sight. I

suspect from now on we'll be attracting the attention of the Stukas.'

Many of the local people had vanished before the Germans had even landed. Now they began returning to the port.

'How did the locals know?' Larssen asked Angelika when he and Tiller visited the taverna.

'It was an instinct,' she answered. 'The people here have lived with the war for a long time. They have learnt what to do to avoid being killed.'

'Where did they go?'

'Into the mountains. There is water there, and some food has been stored in a safe place. It is a way of avoiding reprisals. They did it for centuries when the Turks ruled the islands. The Turks sent out search parties but they never found anyone. Nor did the Italians. How could you find anyone in those mountains? Impossible!'

'There are Andartes up there?' Larssen asked casually.

Angelika hesitated. 'Perhaps.'

'Which ones?'

The girl's face was expressionless.

'ELAS or EDES? Which ones?' said Larssen.

Angelika wiped the palms of her hands on her apron. 'Perhaps I can find out for you,' she said quietly. 'Now please excuse me. There are other customers I must serve.'

'When the Germans come again,' Larssen said, 'they will come in strength. We will need all the help we can get.'

Angelika inclined her head. 'I understand.'

'We want to know how many of them there are and whether they need arms or ammunition,' Larssen said urgently, putting his hand on the girl's sleeve. 'Above all, we need to know if they are prepared to help us. Or if they only care about who is in power after the war. Are they politicians or fighting men, Angelika?'

The girl did not attempt to pull back from him, but for a moment, when her eyes met Larssen's, Tiller felt that perhaps the Dane had met his match. Then, just as quickly, the flash of anger at Larssen touching her was gone and she dropped her gaze.

'Please. I must go,' she said quietly. 'I'll try and find out for you.'

Larssen removed his hand. She glanced at Tiller and then turned on her heel and disappeared behind the black curtain.

Larssen gave a grunt of disgust and reached for his glass. 'I sometimes wonder if your little navigator has not got other allegiances, Tiger. I see what her father meant by being stubborn. She has quite a temper, yes?'

'She's a looker,' said Barnesworth admiringly. 'I'd never really noticed her before. Bloody good navigator, though,' he added as an afterthought.

'Perhaps we didn't tackle her the right way,' said Tiller. 'You know how touchy the Greeks can be.'

Larssen grunted again. 'You better see what you can get out of her,' he said to Tiller.

'Me?' said Tiller, alarmed. 'She's like a clam with me. Doesn't even want to pass the time of day.'

'See what you can do, Tiger. It's important. I think maybe somewhere she has a soft spot for you.'

The fall of Kos drove a wedge into the British presence on the islands, isolating the garrisons of Leros and Samos. It brought an end to any Allied fighter presence and the Luftwaffe now turned its attention to softening up the British garrison on Leros and preventing supplies from reaching it. Five weeks later it fell too, isolating the last and strongest British garrison, on Samos.

German air patrols were now so effective and so frequent that it became virtually impossible for the larger British warships to pass north-westwards between Rhodes and the Turkish mainland. But coastal forces, and the Flotilla's caiques, were still managing to get through to Simi and Samos with supplies by hugging the Turkish coastline and lying up under camouflage nets during the day.

'I've just heard the boss and his team are now on Samos,' Larssen told his patrol after Leros fell. 'But he told me the situation is serious. The bigwigs are determined to hold on because they still want Rhodes. Badly. Everyone else seems to think our position is untenable. Our job is to show them that it's not. The Krauts know we're here now, but they're too busy further north to do anything much about us – except to send in Stukas occasionally. For the time being we stay here. But we may soon have to move, perhaps to the Turkish mainland.'

There was a murmur of surprise.

'There's something else,' Larssen said after a pause. 'Naval intelligence has just reported that the two destroyers which were seen making in this direction last month are in Rhodes port. They can't do much damage there but they may be planning to move to Portolago now that Leros is in German hands. At the moment they are not fully operational and Rhodes has no proper dockyard for them. Portolago, as you know, was the Italians' main base in the area. It has all the facilities the destroyers need. I don't need to tell you the serious implications it would have if two such comparatively powerful vessels were at large in the area.'

'Reckon Griffiths's Solothurn wouldn't make much impression on them,' Barnesworth remarked lugubriously. Tiller noticed he had lately taken to sucking his teeth, an irritating habit.

'You're right there, Billy,' said Maygan. 'And frankly, the navy's now got nothing in the area that could touch them, especially once they've had their boilers cleaned and are fully fuelled and armed.'

There was a moment's silence as everyone digested this. Then Larssen, in his casual way, dropped his bombshell. 'We're being asked if there is anything we can do about them.'

'Jeesus!' Tiller groaned.

'What the hell are we supposed to do, skipper?' said Barnesworth. 'Motor out in the caique and wave them down when they pass here, and ask them to let us scuttle them?'

Larssen grinned his boyish grin. 'I hope we can think of something better than that, Billy. RAF Akrotiri managed to get some air reconnaissance photographs for us of where they are lying in Rhodes port. One of their air-sea rescue launches will deliver them to us after dark tonight.'

'There's the MAS boat,' Tiller said doubtfully. 'But what chance would that have against two destroyers even if they aren't fully operational.'

'None,' Maygan confirmed. 'But I have no doubt our Italian friends would have a go if asked.'

'Our best chance is to get them when they're in

harbour,' said Larssen. 'We can't risk waiting until they arrive in Leros. Anyway, they may not even go there. We've got to try and get them before they leave.'

'Do we know when they're leaving, skipper?' Tiller asked.

'Intelligence reckons we've got a minimum of forty-eight hours, perhaps seventy-two. But no more.'

The air reconnaissance photographs arrived that night, as promised. Larssen spread them out on the table. The vertical shots clearly showed the layout of the port's three harbours. Looking from seaward Mandraki, the smallest, was the right-hand one. Behind it lay the modern town. Next was Emborikos, where the two destroyers were moored. Behind it lay the old walled city of Rhodes, with the castle in one corner. Next to Emborikos was Akandia, the commercial harbour, with its long pier. In peacetime it was used by local ferries as well as merchant ships. The deep waters of Emborikos harbour showed up clearly on the photographs in contrast to the shallows of Akandia harbour, inshore from the pier.

Larssen arranged the relevant shots of Emborikos harbour together and began scrutinizing them closely with stereoscopic magnifiers. 'Whoever took these deserves a medal,' he said. 'Just have a look at that.'

He passed the magnifiers and photographs to Maygan, who peered at them with the viewing device. Every detail of the harbour leapt out at him with amazing three-dimensional clarity.

'How the hell do you chaps do it?' he asked the flight sergeant who had brought the photographs from Cyprus.

'It's simple enough, sir. The camera is set automatically to take a succession of photographs which each have a sixty per cent overlap with the previous print. Because of the forward movement of the aircraft each photograph is taken at a slightly difficult angle from its predecessor. As you can see, if you put two successive ones together, and view the overlap through the magnifiers, a three-dimensional effect is achieved. It usually shows up the details on the photograph with great clarity.'

'It certainly does,' said Maygan.

Even objects on the decks of the two destroyers, which were tied up alongside one another at the central quay, were crystal-clear. A man on the bridge of one could be seen shading his eyes as he looked up at the passing aircraft. Half a dozen more men had been frozen by the camera as they scrambled for what must have been the destroyer's anti-aircraft armament placed either side of its after funnel.

'The oblique ones might be more useful to you, sir,' said the flight sergeant, handing Larssen another bundle.

'How the hell did the pilot get away with it?' Larssen wondered aloud as he viewed the oblique photographs. 'He must have come in at about a hundred feet to get these.'

'The Yanks have lent us a couple of photo-recce P-38s, sir. They go like the clappers.'

Lightnings, Tiller knew, lived up to their name. Even so, he thought as he viewed the entrance to the harbour through the magnifiers, the pilot must have had tremendous guts to get that low.

The obliques were even more impressive than the vertical shots, for the harbour entrance was shown more or less as it would appear to anyone approaching from the sea. The outline of the outboard destroyer was plainly visible, though only part of the bow of the inboard one could be seen. Both had their identity numbers on their bows.

Tiller read them out: 'TA-14 and TA-17.' He looked enquiringly at the flight sergeant.

'TA is the designation the Krauts have given to destroyers they have taken over from other navies,' said the flight sergeant. 'As you know, these were Italian.'

'Do we know anything about them?' Larssen asked.

The flight sergeant handed him a sheet of paper.

'It's all on there, sir.' He glanced at his watch. 'If you'll excuse me, sir, I should go now. My skipper's not too keen to be around here at daylight. He doesn't want a Kraut bomb to spoil his deck.'

'Neither of them is new,' said Larssen, scanning the sheet of paper after the flight sergeant had left. 'The smaller one is the *San Martino*, one of the Generali class. She was built in 1920. Zoelly turbines, maximum thirty-two knots, crew of 105. The other is the *Turbine*, the first of the Turbine class. Slightly bigger and more powerful. She was built in 1927. Crew of 142, maximum speed of thirty-six knots. Both of them are around 1000 tons displacement.'

These statistics were digested in silence. Then Maygan broke it. 'And their armaments?' he asked quietly.

'The main armament of the *Turbine* is four 4.7-inch guns. She also has four 37mm and two 13mm AA guns. The *San Martino* has four four-inch and two three-inch guns, and some anti-aircraft machine-guns. And they both have torpedo tubes, of course.'

Outside they could hear the growl of the air-sea rescue launch's engines as it pulled away from the quay. The group listened to them fade away before anyone spoke.

'Shit,' said Maygan half under his breath.

Larssen scanned their despondent faces and said cheerfully: 'Now we stop arseholing around. We have a proper job to do. Tiger?'

Tiller studied the photographs carefully through the stereoscopic magnifiers once more before replying: 'There are two obvious ways of approaching the targets, by sea and by land.'

'I agree,' said Larssen. 'We must consider both. Perhaps we should try both.'

'It would take longer overland, skipper,' said Tiller. 'If we landed where we did before it is about a twenty-mile trek.'

'Can't we land closer to the port?'

'Probably, but we don't know, do we? And we have no way of reconnoitring first.'

Time spent in reconnaissance is never wasted, Tiller reminded himself. If only they had known, he and Barnesworth could have recced the area when they had landed on Rhodes.

'And by sea?'

Tiller bent over the oblique photographs with the magnifiers.

'There doesn't appear to be a boom,' he said, 'but the entrance is very narrow. No more than a couple of hundred yards, I'd say. I don't see how we could get into the harbour without being spotted. Look, you can see there are observation posts on the end of the quay on the left and on the sea wall jutting out towards the quay from the right. There also seems to be quite a high wall round the harbour. It is bound to be patrolled and anyone looking down on the harbour must have a good chance of seeing anything moving. If the destroyers were berthed on the left side, or even anchored behind the sea wall, it might be worth trying. But where they are now means we would have to go right into the harbour. Virtually impossible to do it undetected, I'd say.'

He handed Larssen the photographs and the magnifiers. Larssen's fingers drummed on the table as he studied the harbour. 'So,' he said finally. 'We must go overland, and to save time we must land close by. Six of us will go, working in independent teams of two. The MAS boat can take us and we can be ferried ashore in its dinghy.'

'How will it pick us up, skipper?' Warrington asked. 'It's short of fuel, isn't it?'

Larssen grinned. 'It won't, Ted. We'll have to make our own way back.'

No one seemed to find that a particularly daunting prospect.

'But to make such an operation viable we need to know two things,' said Larssen. 'Where it is possible to land, and if there is someone who can guide us through the town and down to the port.'

'The Andartes,' said Tiller immediately.

'Exactly. But only Cairo has contact with them and there may not be time. I'll go and talk to Balbao. Tiger, you go and find our little navigator.'

Tiller nodded reluctantly. He had not seen Angelika or her father since Larssen had asked for information about the local Andartes. They had simply vanished and Tiller had to admit to himself that he had not made any effort to find out what had happened to them.

'She has to be found,' said Larssen. 'She is the only person who may help or will know anyone locally who could. Billy, you start getting the gear together. Two limpet mines and a silent Sten for each team. Swimmer's suits under fatigues for everyone. We might not sink the sods but we can blow some holes in them and make them stay in harbour. Tiger, meet me on the MAS boat in half an hour. We do not have much time.'

10

Tiller found Larssen with Balbao in the cramped ward-room of the MAS boat. Between them was a half-empty bottle of Chianti. Both were looking grim.

'Cairo is out of contact with the Andartes,' Larssen said. 'I hope you've had better luck.'

Tiller shook his head.

The locals had told Kristos that Angelika's father had taken her away, no one could say where. When pressed by Tiller for an explanation Kristos added that Christophou had apparently removed his daughter 'to safety'. Because they feared air raids? Tiller had asked. Kristos had said no. Then was it because of collaborators? But Kristos had said there were no collaborators on Simi, which came as a surprise to Tiller after what Angelika had said and he realized later that he should have left it at that. Instead he pressed Kristos to tell him the reason the locals had given. The Greeks, Kristos had explained with a laugh, always guarded their womenfolk closely, and he had given Tiller a friendly, knowing slap on the back. Tiller had got the message.

'I think her father's taken her into the mountains,' he said.

'Many think we will be bombed soon,' Balbao commented. Tiller said nothing.

'And Rhodes?'

'Kristos talked to Dimitri, the mayor. But no one knows that coast, apparently. Kristos said he might just as well have been talking about China.'

Larssen slammed down his empty glass. 'There's no way we can rely on an overland attack, then. We must attack from the sea. But how?'

Balbao pushed the Chianti bottle towards Tiller, but Tiller shook his head. He was going to need to think clearly. In the ensuing gloomy silence an idea suddenly sparked in Tiller's mind.

'The torpedoes, skipper, the MAS boat's torpedoes! They would run through the harbour entrance and Emborikos is deeper than the other two harbours. Deep enough for a torpedo to run right up to the quay.'

Why hadn't he thought of it before! He reached for the Chianti, poured himself a glass, downed it in one go, and reached for the bottle again.

'Yes, have another, Tiger,' said Larssen quietly, 'you're going to need it.'

Tiller's hand stayed on the bottle. 'Why's that, skipper?'

'I'm sorry,' said Balbao. 'But when the armistice was announced the admiral made us neutralize all offensive weapons. All our torpedoes had their propellers and gyros removed at Leros before we came here. Our guns we kept so that we could defend ourselves if necessary. But our torpedoes are no good.'

Larssen slipped the bottle from Tiller's unresisting hand and stood up. 'I think we go and tell the others that we must find another way.'

They walked back around the bay and past the

speedboat which was hidden in a small creek. Suddenly Tiller stopped and grasped Larssen's arm.

'The MAS boat's torpedoes, skipper. It's still got them?'

'Why? Nothing can be done with them, Tiger.'

'Hold it there, skipper.' Tiller returned to the MAS boat and asked Balbao if the nineteen-inch Fiume torpedoes were still in their tubes. Balbao said they were.

'And they still have their warheads?'

'Of course,' said Balbao.

'What's in them?'

'In them?' Balbao looked bewildered.

'What explosive does your navy use in its torpedoes?' Tiller asked, suppressing his impatience with difficulty.

'What you call Torpex. What else would it be?'

'How much is in each torpedo?'

'Two hundred and fifty kilograms.'

That was more than enough. 'And would you agree to have it taken out of the warheads?'

Balbao stared at Tiller. 'What are you planning, Sergeant?'

When Tiller explained his scheme, Balbao's face lit up. 'I used to be a member of the 10th Light Flotilla. They were the only part of the navy which did anything.'

'And I want the exploder mechanisms as well.'

'It can be done.'

'Torpex?' Larssen queried when Tiller explained that he had asked Balbao to extract the explosive warhead from the torpedoes.

'It's a mixture of RDX, TNT and powdered aluminium, skipper. Half as powerful again as TNT on its own.'

'So you want to make up a special charge? Aren't your limpet mines good enough?'

'I've got a better idea. This is what we're going to sink those destroyers with.' Tiller pointed down at the speedboat.

Larssen stared down at the sleek mahogany hull shrouded beneath its camouflage netting. 'But it's a plaything, Tiger, just a holiday boat.'

'But it's fast, skipper, very fast.'

He went on to explain about the work that was being carried out by the Royal Marine Boom Patrol Detachment, and how its boom patrol boat was modelled on the Italians' explosive motor boat, or EMB.

'If Jock is as good a mechanic as the lieutenant says he is we can turn this boat into a *barchino*.'

The others were waiting for them when they returned to the SBS headquarters. Larssen explained the situation and then let Tiller describe his plan. The others listened in stunned silence.

When Tiller had finished, Warrington said: 'Are you seriously telling us you intend to turn this speedboat into an EMB by packing its bows with Torpex from the MAS boat's torpedoes? And then you intend to drive it up to the harbour and let it rip, and then bale out?'

Tiller nodded.

Larssen looked at the caique's stoker. 'Jock? It's possible?'

Bryson scratched his cheek, his Scottish caution making him consider the matter carefully. 'Aye, it's possible all right. There's no problem with the explosive charge. The difficulty is making the boat run straight after Tiger's left it.'

'Sounds fucking suicidal to me,' Warrington said.

'It's been done,' Tiller reminded him.

'Where?'

'Suda Bay, April 1941. The Eyeties used EMBs to wreck the cruiser *York* and a tanker.'

'And the drivers survived?'

'They did.'

Warrington shook his head in wonderment. 'Rather you than me, Tiger.'

'You say there are three methods of detonating the explosive?' Larssen said.

'That's right. Impact, hydrostatic, and with time fuses. The last isn't an option in this case as the exact time it would take the boat to reach the target is too imprecise to calculate.'

'What did the Eyeties use at Suda Bay?'

'Hydrostatic. That's how depth-charges are detonated. When the pressure of the water reaches a certain amount per square inch it triggers the detonator mechanism. In the case of the EMB an impact fuse detaches the bow containing the explosive when the vessel hits its target. The bow sinks under the target and is then detonated by the hydrostatic fuse.'

'Very inventive, the Italians,' Barnesworth commented. 'They can't fight, but they're inventive, I'll give them that.'

'It's the most effective way of sinking a target,' Tiller said, 'but I don't have any hydrostatic fuses. It might be possible to make one, but then we'd have to fashion a method of detaching the motor boat's bows when it hits the target. We haven't got the time and it's much too complicated.'

'That leaves an impact fuse,' Larssen said.

'It's the simplest method and a torpedo's fuse

mechanism can easily be adapted to explode the charge when it strikes the target.'

'But you can only hit the outboard destroyer,' Barnesworth objected.

'But if we hit it with the explosives from two torpedoes it could take the other with it if we're lucky.'

'And how do you escape?'

'Swim to a predesignated place where Billy can pick me up in the cockle which the MAS boat will carry to the area. We can then rendezvous with the MAS boat. We'll be back here before any Kraut will have woken up to what's happening. There will be such chaos in the harbour that it will take them ages to work out what occurred.' There was a pause while everyone digested what Tiller was proposing, and then Maygan said: 'It's either the most fiendishly clever plan I've ever heard anyone come up with – or it's the daftest, as well as the quickest, method of getting a posthumous VC. I'm not sure which. I'll have to sleep on it before I make up my mind.'

'No time for that, Andrew,' retorted Larssen. 'Anyone got a better idea?'

No one had.

'Right,' said Larssen. 'What do you need, Tiger?'

'Once we've made the necessary alterations I must find out how the speedboat steers on its own with its rudder locked. I'll need the caique to help me.'

'Can't do it here,' said Maygan firmly. 'Too risky. We'll tow the boat across to the mainland tomorrow night. I know just the spot there. Totally deserted.'

Larssen stood up. 'Let's get the boat out of the water and under cover where we can work on it.'

Using a block and tackle set up on the caique's boom, they lifted the boat out of the water and on to an old wagon they had found and pushed it to a nearby warehouse, where Griffiths and Bryson could work without being disturbed or seen. While they started work Maygan and Tiller walked to the MAS boat to join Larssen and Balbao, who were poring over a chart of the waters off northern Rhodes.

'We can take the boat and the cockle quite close to the port,' the Italian said, 'and then wait for the cockle down the coast. Around here.'

He pointed to the chart.

'Provided the weather is good, there should be no problem. There might be a local current, but we'll just have to risk that.'

'How close do you need to get to the destroyers?' Larssen asked Tiller.

'The closer the better.'

'And how do you get close without being seen or heard?'

Tiller shrugged. 'That's a risk I'll have to take.'

'Jock said the speedboat's engine at low speed would be very quiet,' said Maygan. 'But that once you open its throttle it will make a hell of a racket. I think Magnus has put his finger on what is the weak link in the plan. What we need is a diversion.'

'I go along with that,' said Tiller. 'Would the RAF be willing to mount a night raid?'

'No bombers closer than Cairo,' Larssen was thinking aloud. 'They might agree to send out a couple of Beaufighters from Cyprus. But their range is limited and they wouldn't be able to stay long. It would need split-second timing for them to be over the port at just the right moment. If they arrived too soon they'd just wake up the defences; if they arrived too late we'd be risking two valuable aircraft and their crews for nothing. No, I think we're going to have to do without the RAF.'

'The navy?' Tiller suggested, but Larssen simply said: 'Why do you think we're sitting here, thinking up a crazy plan to get you killed, Tiger?'

'I could take the caique and we could shoot up Mandraki harbour with the Solothurn,' Maygan said eagerly.

'It needs something like that,' Larssen admitted. 'But I don't think the Solothurn is exactly going to cause any panic ashore.'

Tiller snapped his fingers. 'I've got it, skipper. We could put a couple of limpet mines on the garrison launch and send that towards the shore unmanned. We'll put a time fuse in it so that it goes up just as I'm ready to send the speedboat in.'

Larssen looked doubtful. 'It could just alert the defenders. There's no guarantee it will cause a diversion.'

'I could shell the harbour,' suggested Balbao, but Larssen and Maygan vetoed the idea immediately on the grounds that the MAS boat was more valuable as a means of escape than as a diversion.

In the end a compromise was reached and it was agreed that the garrison launch would be used and that the MAS boat would only open fire if something went wrong with using the launch as a diversion.

When they returned to the warehouse Griffiths had already fashioned a flutterboard which, when a catch was released, slid along rails and off the speedboat's counter. Bryson's task, of making a control for the boat's throttle which would work from the flutter-board, was more complicated, but he had no doubts that he could do it.

Tiller had to devise a means whereby the Torpex would be exploded when the boat hit its target. The simplest solution was to insert a detonator mechanism from one of the torpedoes into the bow of the boat. But Tiller soon decided that it was expecting too much for the boat to hit its target with such accuracy. It was much more likely to hit on one side of the bow or the other. So he decided to fit the same kind of bumper as he had seen on the EMB at Southsea. Any pressure on the bumper would trigger the torpedo's detonator mechanism.

The next evening the speedboat, with its deadly cargo, was put back in the water. It floated bow down, but when Tiller climbed on to the flutterboard it came back on to an even keel, though it was noticeably lower in the water.

That night Maygan towed the speedboat across to the mainland and at dawn the next day Tiller began by testing how straight the boat ran at different speeds without any manual adjustment to the steering wheel to keep it on course. In the flat water of the Turkish bay it held a straight course with very little assistance up to about twenty knots, but beyond that speed it needed an increasingly firm hand on the wheel.

Tiller then tied the wheel with the rudder amidships and let the boat rip. This time it ran smoothly and straight up to about thirty-five knots, but if he increased the speed beyond that it began to yaw.

Next he tested how far it would run in a straight line at different speeds as he had to calculate at what distance from the target he would be able to leave the boat to run on its own. The closer he got to the harbour mouth the more likely he was to be spotted, but the closer he got the more likely he was to hit his target. He had calculated from the chart that the harbour was about 200 yards long and that the pierhead on its left, which included the quay for steamers, was another hundred.

On the other side, to seaward of the sea wall, was the pierhead of Mandraki harbour. He just hoped it did not have guards patrolling it as he would have to get very close to it before baling out. This meant that altogether the boat would have to run for a minimum of 400 yards on its own, much further, he knew, than the Italians had run at Suda Bay.

Maygan marked off this distance with two buoys and after experimenting Tiller found the speed at which the boat ran rock steady for this distance was about thirty knots. So, he calculated, it would take the boat about thirty seconds to reach its target. Tiller knew the German defences would be trying to locate the speedboat and sink it immediately he opened up its engine. But it would take time to focus their searchlights and aim their weapons – not easy to do on an object travelling at thirty knots over water on a dark night.

'Looks remarkably steady,' said Maygan when Tiller returned to the caique. 'Mind you, I still think it's a crackpot idea.'

He insisted that Tiller practise controlling the speedboat from its counter and then, while Maygan was aboard, sliding into the water with the flutterboard. The speedboat's propeller was fixed forward of the counter, so Tiller found there was no danger of being hit by it as he dropped off the counter into the water. He also found that Griffiths had given him an unexpected bonus by shaping the board so that it was quite easy to propel through the water with his hands and by kicking gently with his feet.

What would have been useful would have been those swim fins for his feet which had been captured from the Italians and which Tasler had been experimenting with. Combined Operations calculated they increased both a swimmer's power and endurance by a hundred per cent. But even without these aids Tiller found he was able to progress at a reasonable speed.

Once darkness had fallen they returned to Simi. While they had been away Bryson had altered the steering of the garrison launch so that it could be clamped using the same method as Bryson had devised for the speedboat. But as accuracy was unimportant it was decided that there was no need to test it.

By noon everything had been prepared and Tiller and the others, who had been working throughout the night, got a few hours' sleep before having a meal. As soon as darkness fell they boarded the MAS boat, and the cockle and the speedboat were hoisted aboard. The launch was too big to be stowed on deck and was towed astern.

The night seemed ideal for the operation. It was overcast, very dark, and with practically no wind. The MAS boat cut its speed to ten knots both to conserve fuel and to prevent the launch from yawing too wildly on the end of its painter. Halfway across a bottle of brandy was passed round and Tiller changed into his surface-swimmer's suit and Barnesworth into his paddler's suit.

It was the first time Tiller had worn the suit since he had arrived in the region and he checked it carefully before he donned it, making sure there were no holes in the rubberized fabric and that the urination valve and the mouth-inflated rubber stole, used for buoyancy, worked properly. He carried his commando knife in a sheath attached to his belt, but was otherwise unarmed. Also hooked to the belt was a signalling torch and a small watertight flask filled with brandy. Barnesworth had the cockle fully equipped with food and water and two silent Stens.

The MAS boat arrived off Rhodes port before midnight and eased its way inshore with its engines hardly ticking over. The island was just a hump in front of them. They could hear nothing and the port was so efficiently blacked out that they could not see anything either. When they were about five miles offshore Balbao brought the MAS boat to a standstill, and the cockle, with Barnesworth aboard, and the speedboat, were lowered into the water.

Barnesworth paddled off without pausing as he needed to be in position well before the attack was launched. The cockle was quickly swallowed up in the dark and Tiller, who was watching it, was relieved that it faded out of sight so swiftly. Poor visibility was a bonus he had not expected. He clambered down into the speedboat carefully and started its engine with the MAS boat between him and the shore.

Luckily, there was a slight offshore breeze which would help carry away the sound of his engine. Alongside him Larssen was making last-minute adjustments to the launch.

'When you're in position, you flash the letter "R" and I'll release the launch,' Larssen said and then repeated his instructions. He knew that apprehension and the cold did terrible things to the memory; he always believed that operational instructions could not be repeated too often. Tiller nodded.

'When you signal I'll put a five-minute time pencil in the limpet mines,' Larssen said. 'That should give you plenty of time.'

They made sure their watches were synchronized. Then Larssen leant across and gripped Tiller's hand. 'Good luck. See you in a couple of hours.'

'Thanks, skipper.'

Larssen let go the warps holding the speedboat and Tiller slipped its engine into gear and edged it round the stationary MAS boat.

Griffiths had fixed a compass in the speedboat's cockpit and Tiller steered due south by it. He strained his eyes into the blackness, and kept the revs of the engine right down so that the speedboat crept forward with hardly any way on it.

At first he encountered a slight swell but as the boat edged towards the land the sea became quite flat. Slowly his eyesight became used to the dark and gradually, very gradually, the island began to take shape in front of him, and after about twenty minutes he could make out the outlines of the port.

Soon Tiller was inshore of Cape Zonari, the most northerly part of the island, which lay to starboard of him, and he turned and flashed an 'R' with his shaded torch out to sea. He repeated the signal twice more, noted the time on the slate he carried, and then turned his attention once more to the shore.

Almost immediately he saw the outline of the castle against the night sky and realized he was too far to the right of Emborikos harbour. That meant there was more of a lateral inshore current than Balbao had thought.

Swearing under his breath, he began edging the speedboat to port and after a few minutes saw the two piers that made the entrance to Mandraki harbour. He was now heading south-east and for a moment he slipped the engine into neutral so that he could orientate himself.

As he peered intently into the dark he could just discern the stone sea wall that jutted out into Emborikos harbour. He engaged the engine at minimum revs and slowly the mouth of the harbour began to open up.

When he calculated he was on the correct course he swung the boat around until its bow was pointing straight into the harbour. The compass was now indicating due south.

He glanced at his watch and was alarmed to see that he only had ninety seconds left before the launch was due to explode.

He made sure the speedboat was on course, locked the wheel, wriggled stomach downwards on to the flutterboard behind him, and grasped the throttle extension. By pulling the wire out to its fullest extent and winding it round a cleat, he would jam the engine at three-quarters throttle, which would give it the required speed of thirty knots.

Lying flat, Tiller thought he could just make out the outline of the outboard destroyer against the light-coloured buildings around the quay. He looked around him and saw that he was now just inshore of the right-hand pier of Mandraki harbour. There was no movement from on shore, no light of any kind. The only sound was the faint barking of a dog and the mutter of the speedboat's engine.

He glanced at his watch and swore. The pencil fuse was either not going to work or had been retarded by the cold and he began calculating how long he could wait. The speedboat was only just making headway and the offshore breeze helping to hold it back, but it was still creeping closer to the harbour.

He'd give it ten seconds and he began counting under his breath. 'Seven . . . six . . . five . . .'

There was a huge bang to the right of him as the two limpet mines ripped the launch apart and flames lit up the night sky. The sound of the explosions reverberated on to the island and back out to sea again.

Immediately, several searchlights were switched on, a klaxon cranked itself up and then began to wail, and parachute flares blossomed in the night sky. He hadn't reckoned on those.

Tiller pulled steadily on the throttle wire until it had reached its maximum extent and felt the boat leap into life under him. It was still running true. He wound the wire around the cleat, hit the catch that released the flutterboard, and felt himself sliding backwards down the speedboat's reverse sheer counter.

The flutterboard took most of the impact on to the water, but the wash from the speedboat hit him full in the face and made him splutter and gasp. Then, using both his arms in a butterfly stroke and kicking hard with his feet, he began moving the board sideways as fast as he could. He concentrated on getting a rhythm going, but the board kept jagging into the water and slowing him down, though he did not dare abandon it.

He was vaguely aware that some guns had begun firing and more than once a searchlight lit up the sea around him before moving on. But the loudest noise was the rasping sound of his breath as he strained to move the board through the water and the slap of the water on his face, and when the explosion came the water in his ears made it seem a million miles away.

It would, he knew, take the shock from the explosion about thirty seconds to reach him and he felt the primeval instinct for survival flood adrenalin through his body. With every muscle he strained to move the flutterboard faster, but when it came the shock wave merely lifted the flutterboard slightly from the surface of the water.

Tiller stopped swimming, lowered his body into the water and just hung on to the flutterboard with his hands. To his surprise he was further to the left of the harbour than he had thought possible and supposed there must be an inshore current running counter to the main one further out.

The harbour entrance was behind him now and he could not see if the speedboat had hit its target. What he could see by the beams of the searchlights sweeping across the harbour was a rising column of smoke and a lurid glow where the destroyers were moored. He felt a great elation surge through him.

Suddenly he could hear voices borne to him by the offshore breeze and a torch was flashed from the end of the pier. Instinctively, he sank lower into the water. He could see now that it was not a torch but some kind of portable searchlight, small but powerful. Its operator began scanning the water around the end of the pier while another German soldier shouted instructions at him. A third held a rifle or sub-machine-gun at the ready.

The current was slowly carrying him sideways, away from the pier, but he was still well within the range of the searchlight. He allowed the flutterboard to drift away from him, let the air out of his rubber stole, and began to swim slowly towards the left-hand pier of Akandia harbour. But he kept glancing over his shoulder and when the searchlight began sweeping towards him he would sink gently under the water.

Once the soldier in charge started shouting and the soldier with the gun opened fire. Tiller could tell from its rapid, distinctive sound that he was using a Schmeisser. He thought that perhaps they had seen his flutterboard, but he couldn't tell for sure.

The outline of the pier and the soldiers remained quite distinct because of the fire in the harbour beyond it, but after a few minutes Tiller knew he was out of range of the searchlight and concentrated on what lay ahead of him.

It looked as if he was about halfway across Akandia harbour and swimming straight for the end of the harbour's left-hand pier. On the far side of the pier Barnesworth would be lying up in the cockle.

But if the Germans were sending search parties on to the end of each pier, Tiller realized, he would either have to swim well out to sea before approaching the other side or swim right up to the pier and move round it right under the feet of the search party. He remembered Tasler saying that anyone searching for someone often failed to look under their noses, so he chose the latter option and hoped Tasler was right.

Despite the kapok lining of his suit he was starting to feel the cold. He began swimming slightly to the right so that he would reach the pier about fifty yards before the end of it. As he approached he heard a vehicle draw up and more shouting. Three or four figures began running along the pier. He trod water and once they had passed him swam strongly until he reached the pier.

It was made of stone and it took him a moment to find a good handhold. He kept his head low in the water and looked around him. The wall of the pier was about thirty feet high and rose vertically from the water. Inshore of him were wharves. Most of these were deserted except for one or two caiques. On the seaward side there was just the sheer face of the stone pier at the end of which he could just see the glass revolving top of an unlit lighthouse.

Luckily, the end of the pier seemed to have a stone lip on it which made it more difficult for anyone looking down to see what was underneath at sea level. Cautiously he began pulling himself along the stone wall with his hands, stopping every few yards to look and listen.

As he approached the end of the pier a searchlight on it began playing on the surrounding water. At first it flicked here and there, but then began to quarter the area methodically. When Tiller noticed that even when fully depressed it could not shine within a hundred feet of the pier he pressed on as quickly as he dared.

He reached the end of the pier and began alternatively swimming under water and just floating on the surface head down, propelling himself slowly forward by pushing with his hands on the stone wall beneath the surface. Once the slop of the water on the pier tore his grip from the stonework and he felt himself being drawn seawards by an undertow. It took a lot of control not to look up but instead to turn his body back towards the pier until he felt the stonework again.

He allowed his body to sink and then he turned on his back and surfaced. Staring up at the end of the pier, he saw two helmeted heads leaning over the lip of the end of the pier and looking directly down at him. He froze, his left hand grasping a piece of protruding stone below the water.

He thought for a terrible moment that his blackened face might have been washed clean and the men were wondering what the pale, oval shape below them might be.

He could not hear them, but he could see the glow of two cigarettes. Then one butt spiralled its way down towards him and fizzed out in the water next to his head. Then the other arced out and fell some yards away, and the two smokers disappeared.

He sank down again, turned over, and began to feel his way along the outside of the pier. He had agreed with Barnesworth that it would be impossible to say exactly where the cockle should lie up as they had no means of knowing what, if any, shelter there would be for it.

It looked at first as if there was none, but then he saw that a narrow wooden jetty ran alongside the wall. It was supported on the seaward side by wooden piles and was about ten feet above the water. He supposed it was for a ship waiting for a berth on the inner side of the pier. It looked an ideal hiding-place and he approached it quickly, anxious now to get out of the water, which was chilling him to the marrow.

Under the jetty he could not see anything. He thought of calling out but decided the risk was too great. He felt his way along, but he could not see the cockle, and his heart sank when he saw he had almost reached the far end of the jetty. Billy had obviously not made it. Perhaps he had been caught or, more likely, lost his way.

Tiller came to the last diagonal wooden support for the jetty floor above him and heaved himself partly out of the water so that he could lean on it and consider his options. It would be impossible to swim to the MAS boat. If exhaustion didn't get him the cold would. He could wait in the hope that Barnesworth would turn up or the MAS boat might conceivably come and search for him. Or he could try and find some sort of boat and make his escape that way.

He was just deciding that the last option seemed to be the most practicable when he felt something cold and hard pressed up against the base of his skull, and an arm snake round his throat.

'*Du bist ein Tiger, bitte?*' a voice said quietly in his ear.

'For Christ's sake, Billy,' Tiller croaked.

Barnesworth's arm relaxed from around Tiller's throat and he returned his pistol to its holster.

'Just had to make sure, Tiger,' he whispered. 'You've stirred up a fucking hornets' nest, I can tell you.'

'Did I hit the bleeders?' Tiller asked eagerly.

'How the fuck should I know?' said Barnesworth. 'I've been clinging to the arse side of this jetty for the last forty minutes. You took your time, mate. Let's go.'

He swung from one support to another and then lowered himself gently into the front cockpit of the cockle, which lay right under the stone wall. Tiller followed him in the water and climbed into the rear cockpit from the craft's stern. He reached for the flask still attached to his belt, took a good swig of brandy, and passed it to Barnesworth.

'What now?' he whispered in Barnesworth's ear. 'Do we wait for things to quieten down, or what?'

Barnesworth turned and held up his arm with his

luminous watch on his wrist turned towards his companion.

'No time,' he whispered back. 'The sky's clear now and the moon is due up in an hour. With any luck, they'll be concentrating their searches around the harbour, not in this direction. Let's go.'

Using single paddles they emerged cautiously from under the jetty and when they had ensured the coast was clear put as much water as they could between the pier and themselves by steering eastwards.

When the darkness had swallowed up the pier they stopped to turn their single paddles into doubles. Searchlights were still playing on the water outside the port and something still seemed to be on fire in Emborikos harbour. However, they did not linger, but paddled on a course of 160 degrees by the compass as fast as they could.

The cold that Tiller had felt was now replaced by a warm glow and a feeling of intense exhilaration, and he dug his paddles into the water with zest. After an hour they could see ahead of them the promontory off which the MAS boat would be waiting for them.

When they were abeam of the headland they turned due east and began signalling out to sea with the shaded torch, and after half an hour they saw the outline of the MAS boat on their starboard side. They stopped paddling and guided it to them with the torch, and minutes later eager hands were hauling them aboard.

11

'I want to put you up for the DCM,' Maygan said enthusiastically. 'If you hadn't made it back, I'd have had a crack at getting you a posthumous VC.'

'It was a damned good try, Tiger,' Larssen said.

'Thanks, skipper,' said Tiller wearily. His sleep had been continually interrupted throughout the day by the Stukas which had started systematically grinding the port into rubble. The Germans had guessed from where the raid had been mounted and were exacting what retribution they could.

He had also just heard from Larssen that the Germans, who had been taking over the smaller islands one by one, had moved nearer to Simi by overrunning Piscopi. Tiller hated to think what might have happened to Giovanni and his Mafia there.

'What do you think went wrong, skipper?'

'Wrong?' Larssen queried. 'I'd hardly call it that. You blew half the bloody quay away.'

'But missed the destroyers,' said Tiller quietly. He had always known there must have been only a small chance of success, but the disappointment he felt was sharp.

'But according to photo recce they haven't moved,' said Maygan. 'You may have stopped them from sailing. They could be damaged in some way.'

'The lads did an incredible job on that speedboat,'

said Tiller. 'Everything worked. I can't understand it. The boat was running absolutely true.'

'A bit of flotsam in the harbour probably,' said Larssen. 'The boat only needed to touch something floating in the water to make it deviate from its course. It's bad luck, but there you are.'

'What now, skipper?'

Larssen rubbed his stubble. 'Beirut's just informed us that the navy's trying to get enough ships together to take the garrison off Samos. It looks as if the Krauts are going to try and land there soon. Beirut wants to know what we're going to do because our friend the Flag Officer Levant and Eastern Mediterranean is not going to risk any more ships to rescue the garrison if there are two destroyers on the loose. The odds against them would be stacked much too high. So if we fail, 5000 troops on Samos go into the bag.'

A silence fell while this review of the situation was assimilated.

'What a fuck-up,' said Tiller eventually. 'Whose idea was this mission, anyway?'

'Ours not to reason why, Tiger,' Larssen said.

'Ours just to do and die,' Maygan finished off the famous couplet with relish.

'On the positive side Cairo has agreed to increase the number of photo-recce flights over the port of Rhodes,' said Larssen. 'The Germans have nothing that can touch the Lightning, so it can operate with impunity. Also, my guess is – and it's only a guess – that Cairo is now giving higher priority to deciphering Kriegsmarine signals between Athens and Rhodes. Certainly the time-lag between transmission and us receiving the deciphers has decreased dramatically.'

The esoteric world of signals intelligence, run from

a building in the Cairo suburb of Heliopolis, was way above the heads of anyone present. Nevertheless, enough was known by any alert officer serving in the Middle East for Maygan to suck in his breath and say: 'Jesus! If they're doing that they're pulling out all the stops.'

'I think a lot is riding on all this,' said Larssen. 'Much more than the loss of a few destroyers and 5000 men. Don't ask me what it is because I don't know. It's just an impression I get and it's getting stronger.'

Above them there was the crump of bombs exploding and dust from the cellar roof cascaded down on them. Larssen shook it off the chart that was opened in front of him and said: 'So when the destroyers sail what course will they take? Andrew?'

'If I were them I'd take the shortest course consistent with safety,' said Maygan, following his suggested route on the chart with his forefinger. 'Which means passing Simi and sailing between Piscopi and Nisiros and then passing the western end of Kos. That's about 120 miles. Even steaming at reduced speed, they could do that in a night without trouble. That's the safest and quickest route.'

Larssen nodded his agreement. 'So how close will they come to Simi?'

Maygan bent over the chart and used a pencil and parallel rulers to draw the destroyers' most likely course from Rhodes. He then stretched the two points of his compass between the course and Simi and measured off the distance from the side of the chart.

'It depends. If they head for the western end of

Kos the most direct route would take them between Simi and Seskli. Seskli is that small island off Simi's southern coast.'

'Would they do that?'

Maygan shook his head. 'Unlikely. Not at night. They'd leave Seskli to starboard, though by how much it's impossible to say. The water's deep there so they could pass close by it if they wanted to. I'd say they'd come within a few miles of Simi. Perhaps only a mile from Seskli.'

'And how long would it take them to get there from Rhodes?'

'It shouldn't take them more than a couple of hours at the outside.'

'Two hours! Is that all?'

''Fraid so. If we want to mount some kind of attack on them as they pass Seskli, we'd have to go and wait for them by the island.'

'We've got nothing to mount an attack on them with,' protested Tiller. 'The speedboat's gone, the launch has gone. We can't use the caique as we'll need that if we have to attack the destroyers at Leros.'

'There's the MAS boat,' said Maygan.

'But that's only got its twin Bredas and a machine-gun,' Larssen pointed out. 'That won't stop them. Anyway, it's hardly got any fuel left.'

'If it's going to attack them off Seskli, it won't need much, will it?' said Maygan quietly. Larssen looked at Maygan hard and drummed his fingers on the upturned wooden crate which was acting as a table. 'What you're suggesting is that . . .'

'It rams one of them,' Maygan said. 'It's not going to be any use to us without fuel. It's an outside chance but one we shouldn't miss.'

'It's a viable option?'

'Certainly,' said Maygan. 'The MAS boat could run rings round the destroyers and neither of them is particularly big. Thousand-tonners, aren't they. If you hit one of them in the right place, in the engine space, say, you'd certainly cripple it.'

'And who's going to man the MAS boat?' Kristos asked.

'We will, of course,' said Larssen briskly. 'You couldn't expect the Eyeties to do it. Why should they?'

'Balbao may not like having his command taken from him,' Maygan suggested.

Larssen stood up, buckled on his belt and pistol holster and said briskly: 'Too bad. He won't have any choice, will he? Let's go and pay him a visit.'

Balbao seemed more amused than annoyed when Larssen told him what he proposed to do. He could see that the SBS party had no alternative to using the desperate methods they were proposing, but tried to persuade them there was no way they could put them into action.

'You've handled an MAS boat?' he asked Maygan, who shook his head.

'And you, Captain?'

'In the merchant navy we handled anything and everything,' Larssen said. 'A couple of years ago I skippered a tug to tow out a German liner from a neutral port.'

'And who will man the guns?'

'Our chaps. They have been taught how to fire German weapons and Italian ones.'

'And the engines?'

'Bryson,' said Maygan immediately.

Balbao nodded. 'A good man, but the Isotta-Fraschinis in this boat are pretty temperamental. They should have been overhauled months ago.'

He paused and looked at them, and then shook his head. 'I'm sorry, gentlemen. I cannot agree.'

'You have no option, Commander.' Larssen's hand dropped casually on to the butt of his pistol.

'Oh, but I have, Captain. All my crew have been instructed how to – how do you say? – scuttle the boat if it is necessary. We have a drill, you know, on when to carry this out.'

Larssen's hand dropped away. 'And what drill is that?'

Balbao laughed. 'Come, come, Captain. You don't expect me to tell you that.'

Stalemate, Tiller thought to himself. He could see Larssen was getting very angry. Balbao leant forward. 'May I make a suggestion?'

Larssen nodded.

'I skipper the boat, you man the guns. I see if my chief engineer will come, too. He loves those engines like babies. I don't think he allows anyone else to touch them. You understand?'

Larssen looked at Maygan, who shrugged. It was a gesture of resignation more than approval, but Larssen said: 'If we accept your conditions, how do I know you'll carry out my orders?'

Balbao smiled. 'You don't.'

'It's a high-risk operation,' Larssen warned him.

Balbao brushed Larssen's comment aside with a weary wave of his hand. 'The boat has an emergency steering position in the stern. If we are going to ram one of the destroyers, we'll use that for the final run in. We'll dump the Carley floats over the stern and jump after them and the lieutenant can pick us up in the caique. You must remember I was once a member of the 10th Light Flotilla. I am used to performing such antics.'

'This will delay our move, skipper,' Tiller said as they left the MAS boat. The bombing and the fall of Piscopi had made Simi untenable as a base for the SBS and orders had come through that Larssen was to move his team to the Turkish mainland as soon as possible. A rudimentary headquarters had been set up for them aboard a schooner which had been moved by stages from Castelrosso. It was in an isolated bay which provided good cover and was rarely visited by the Turkish coastguard. And when they did come they only came to collect their bribes.

'If this op goes wrong there won't be anything left to move,' Larssen replied.

The Stukas came over again at first light and more houses in the port crumbled to dust.

At midday a high-priority signal came on the radio from Cairo, informing the SBS men that the destroyers would sail that night at an unspecified time. Their destination was Portolago, Leros.

At dusk the MAS boat and the caique emerged from their hiding-places and went alongside the quay. Tiller, Larssen, Simmonds and Warrington, all wearing shallow-diving suits to protect them from the cold when they abandoned ship, went aboard the MAS boat and the Italian crew filed ashore. Barnesworth went with Maygan in the caique. The caique would stay out of the way behind Seskli; the MAS boat would lie in wait on the island's seaward side. It wasn't much of a plan, but they agreed it was the best available.

They were in position by ten that night. When the destroyers had not appeared by midnight they began to think that they must have taken another course, or had been prevented from sailing for some reason. But ten minutes later Balbao nudged Larssen, handed him his night-glasses, and pointed southwards.

Larssen adjusted the binoculars and scanned the inky black horizon. At first he could see nothing, then slowly, gradually, two indistinct objects began to form in the lenses. He handed back the glasses to Balbao. 'That must be them,' he agreed.

Balbao ordered slow ahead and the MAS boat crept out from under the lee of the island.

'Would they have radar?' Larssen asked.

Balbao shook his head. 'Remind me to tell you the sorry story of radar and the Italian Navy some time.'

He ordered an increase in the MAS boat's speed and told Larssen that he planned to get as close as possible to the destroyers without being detected and then, and only then, open fire on them. He would run the MAS boat parallel with the two warships, swing round the stern of the second one, and then choose which one to ram.

After a few minutes it was possible to see the two shapes without the night-glasses. It was soon apparent from the changing angle of approach that they were moving at about fifteen knots, and were moving slightly away from the MAS boat.

Their speed and course made Balbao decide it would be better to approach them from behind and swing round ahead of them. The MAS boat's engines throbbed powerfully and it was less than a mile away when a shaded signalling lamp from the leading destroyer started to flick out a message to the MAS boat.

'He wants to know who we are,' chuckled Balbao. 'We'll soon let him know.'

When the signal was ignored the destroyer opened fire with a single shot from its aft four-inch gun. The shell whirred overhead and fell into the water beyond the MAS boat. Calmly, Balbao ordered full speed ahead and the MAS boat leapt forward, its hull vibrating, its engines gurgling and thrumming. A second shell fell short and when a third narrowly missed the MAS boat Balbao shouted 'fire, fire, fire,' into the intercom which connected the bridge with the twin Bredas' crew.

The 20mm tracer arced towards the second destroyer and tiny fireballs danced on its upperworks. A fourth salvo from the destroyer's stern four-inch gun went high over the MAS boat and Tiller, who was working the forward machine-gun with Larssen, realized the MAS boat was now so close to the destroyers that their gun crews could not depress the main armament sufficiently to hit it.

Then the MAS boat was running parallel with the second destroyer and its Breda was raking its deck and bridge. Larssen and Tiller opened up with the machine-gun on the destroyer's open gun position on a circular platform behind its second funnel. They could see the gun crew, who were running to close up with their weapon, scatter and fall.

Then, in a surge of speed that Tiller calculated must have exceeded forty knots, the MAS boat began drawing ahead of the destroyers. He managed to get in one final burst, at the destroyer's bridge, and saw its glass screen shatter.

'Taking target on starboard, repeat starboard, side,' Balbao shouted into the intercom and the Breda's crew began frantically peddling the guns from port to starboard as the MAS boat swerved across the path of the second destroyer and through the wake of the first.

Larssen and Tiller swung the machine-gun round and opened fire, spraying the first destroyer's super-structure with bullets. Then the twin Bredas opened up, too, and Tiller could see that the 20mm shells were causing some damage.

After a few seconds Balbao brought the MAS boat round to starboard so that it was running parallel with the target and 200 yards from it. Again they saw the sparks as the Bredas' shells smashed into the destroyer at what was virtually point-blank range.

Balbao now slowed to the speed of the leading destroyer so that the Bredas could rake it from stern to stem. Then he increased speed again and, once it was ahead of the destroyer, swung the MAS boat away to port.

A parachute flare blossomed in the sky and lit the ink-black waters with a pale glow. But the MAS boat, now streaking away at right angles from the leading destroyer, was out of the circle of light that it created before the destroyer's guns could be brought to bear on it.

'Now what?' Larssen shouted into the intercom. 'They'll be ready for us the next time. We won't get away with that again.'

Balbao shouted back: 'I shall make a run at them so that they will think we are going to use our torpedoes. That will force them to turn this way to make the smallest possible target.'

Another parachute flare lit the sky where the destroyers supposed the MAS boat to be but Balbao had already altered course again. Tiller admired the cool skill with which the Italian was handling the MAS boat and, as he had predicted, the destroyers now both swung to port.

They were now dim outlines again, about two miles distant, moving westwards at about twenty knots, while the MAS boat was moving slowly eastwards.

'I am going to turn to port to ram the nearest destroyer,' Balbao told Larssen through the intercom. 'There is not enough fuel to do anything else. I slow down. Then you abandon ship.'

The SBS men moved aft and when the MAS boat slowed the two Carley floats were thrown overboard and Tiller and the other SBS men followed them, dropping backwards into the foaming wake of the MAS boat. Larssen watched them go before he turned and climbed on to the bridge to join Balbao. He was not about to miss the most exciting part of the action.

Balbao called for full power and told his chief engineer to abandon ship. The seconds ticked away, the destroyers to port of them were approaching fast.

'Time to move to the emergency steering position,' Larssen shouted at Balbao above the sound of the engines. Balbao shouted back: 'You abandon ship. Now.'

'What about you?' Larssen shouted. 'Go aft now.'

'Go!' Balbao shouted. 'I follow you.' He drew himself up and saluted Larssen. '*Memento Audare*

Semper, Captain. Remember always to dare. Now go!'

Larssen ran aft with the chief engineer. They threw over another Carley float and followed it. The water stunned Larssen for a moment, but then he grabbed the Carley float, climbed on to it, and dragged the engineer aboard it, too.

They watched as the MAS boat converged with the approaching destroyers. Another parachute flare lit the water and the nearest destroyer's searchlights flicked on. The MAS boat was caught in a pool of light and both enemy vessels opened up simultaneously with all their armament. Tracer arced across it as it sped unerringly towards the nearest destroyer.

'For Christ's sake, why doesn't he jump?' Larssen bawled, seeing the MAS boat was about to hit its target. 'Jump, you fool, jump.'

The MAS boat was about 200 yards from the nearest destroyer when two four-inch shells hit it above the water-line and there was an ear-splitting explosion. One moment the MAS boat was there, travelling at forty knots in the middle of the pool of light created by the flare and the searchlights, and the next there was just smoke and debris.

The flare dowsed itself in the water and the searchlights swung and scanned the debris, and were then turned off, and the dark shapes of the destroyers quickly faded into the night.

Larssen looked at his wrist compass and then began signalling with his shaded torch towards the island. Half an hour later they saw the outline of the caique approaching them, and they were quickly hauled aboard. Ten minutes later they saw the signals from the other Carley floats and their occupants, too, were hauled aboard.

'What happened?' Maygan asked Larssen as they turned for Simi.

'God knows,' said Larssen tiredly, 'except it didn't work.'

'And Balbao?'

Larssen turned to the Italian engineer. 'Your commander, why didn't he use the emergency steering position?'

The engineer looked at him blankly. 'You must be mistaken, *signore*. There was no emergency steering position.'

The Stukas were back again the following morning, circling round Simi port like vultures. There was very little left for them to destroy, but their shrieking descent on it, followed by the scream of their bombs plummeting down, was slowly wearing down the psychological resistance of the defenders. It was impossible to sleep, or even rest, and the air was filled with dust.

The Italian garrison as well as the local inhabitants had mostly fled by now, and only the bravest attempted to fire on the Stukas as they swooped down out of the sky.

In the cellar of the detachment's headquarters Larssen was using the radio himself to report with an enciphered signal to Beirut that their latest operation had failed. Beirut signalled back their regrets and asked what Larssen proposed to do now. Attack the destroyers at Portolago, replied Larssen, but he had yet to finalize his plans. Keep us informed, Beirut signalled, your operation is being given the highest priority. A photo-reconnaissance flight is being mounted today on Portolago and an ML will bring you the results tonight. Good luck.

Larssen took off the headphones and slammed them down on the table in disgust. 'How like the top brass,' he said irritably. 'They give us impossible jobs to do and then just wish us luck. You'd have thought they could have got rid of the two bloody destroyers themselves. Or found another way of taking off the garrison from Samos. Jesus, are we winning this war or not?'

Above them another bomb exploded, the concussion of it shaking the cellar.

'That's your answer, skipper,' said Tiller grimly.

Larssen sat down and spread out the chart of Leros in front of him. 'What do we know about Portolago?'

'As you can see, it is the most southerly of the three bays on the western side of the island,' said Maygan, 'and is the largest. It runs north-east south-west and is about a mile long. It almost cuts the island in two. Steep hillsides run down to it on either side. Not an easy place to attack.'

'What do you think, Tiger?'

'Looks like a job for Billy and me,' Tiller said evenly, suppressing a surge of excitement. 'Provided, of course, someone can get us there and back.'

'That's not going to be easy,' said Maygan. 'Though I'm sure I could find a way of doing it.'

Larssen shook his head. 'We need you to move everyone to the mainland, Andrew, while we're away. No, we'll see how important the bigwigs really think this operation is. We'll tell them we need the ML for the operation.'

Larssen scribbled a note on a signals pad and handed it to the radio operator who had just come on duty. He enciphered it and then sent it out in Morse. He received a reply almost immediately and handed it to Larssen.

'That's quick,' said Larssen. 'They must mean business.'

The signal confirmed that Larssen could have the motor launch for the operation and that it would be with them before dawn the next morning provided the photo-reconnaissance flight was successful.

The ML arrived that same night, having had a clear run from Paphos. Its captain was a cheerful young RNVR lieutenant, a pre-war sailing friend of Maygan's who knew the Dodecanese well from cruising among them before the war. He handed over a thick brown envelope to Larssen, who sliced it open with his commando knife.

The aerial photographs were clear and detailed, and the analysis of them by the RAF interpretation unit at Akrotiri was especially detailed. The first point Tiller noticed was that a boom protected the harbour mouth. One arm of it extended from two places on the southern headland to a single point about halfway across the harbour. Inshore of this single point they could make out what must have been a boom patrol boat. The other half of the boom extended in a straight line from the northern headland to within about 200 yards of the anchored patrol boat.

'That's not going to be easy to negotiate,' Barnesworth commented.

'Balls, Billy,' Tiller said. He could already feel the adrenalin pumping through him. 'We used to skip over obstacles like that every night in the Solent.'

On the northern side of the harbour and about a thousand yards from the entrance a largish ship was anchored under the lee of the cliffs. The interpretation unit identified this as the German ammunition ship *Anita*, which had just arrived as part of a convoy from Piraeus.

At the far end of the bay was another anchored part of the convoy, identified as a supply ship called the *Carola*, and an F-lighter, a shallow-draft craft similar to a Siebel ferry which was used by the Germans for supplying their garrisons on the islands. Astern of the *Carola* were anchored a variety of small, unidentifiable craft. On the opposite side of the bay to the ammunition ship was the naval base, with a slipway, sheds, floating dock and seaplane hangars. Larssen pointed to the naval base and said: 'There they are.'

The others crowded round. The pilot had taken a series of oblique photographs of the two destroyers as they lay at anchor close to the naval base. The stereoscopic lenses showed up every detail of their superstructure, which looked undamaged despite the hail of fire from the MAS boat's Bredas. As they pored over the photographs another signal came in from Beirut saying that 'operational contingencies' required the detachment to sink the *Anita* and, if possible, *Carola* and the F-lighter, as well as the two destroyers.

'The cockle doesn't normally carry more than eight limpets,' said Tiller. 'This lot will all need three each. That's a hell of a lot of extra weight.'

'You'll be in and out in a couple of hours,' said Larssen. 'You'll just have to leave most of the equipment behind.'

'We won't be able to use the compass with that number aboard,' Tiller objected. 'We won't have time to swing it, and we only have a compass compensator for eight.'

'I'll make sure you're dropped in the right place,' said Denvers, the ML skipper, reassuringly, 'and I'll give you the dead-reckoning course to steer.'

They went through the list of equipment but decided that if the extra limpets had to be carried then everything was expendable except the water, primus and the twenty-four-hour ration packs.

'I don't know why Cairo don't tell us to recapture the island while we're at it,' grumbled Barnesworth.

'They will, Billy, they will,' Larssen said with a grin. 'Just give them time. They probably haven't even realized yet that the Krauts are in residence there. Now, Bob, we want to arrive no later than midnight. Can you do that in one run during the hours of darkness?'

Denvers shook his head. 'I'm driving an ML, remember, not an MTB. We'll have to lie up somewhere for a day along the Turkish coast. On our runs to Samos we've been using a place called Yalikavak. The *meltemi* when it blows from the west makes the anchorage a bit uncomfortable, but the *meltemi* season is over now.'

He pointed on the chart to a small headland on the Turkish mainland north of Kos. 'There's a small fishing village but the locals keep their mouths closed – provided their hands are crossed with silver, of course.'

'Good. We can sail tonight and get there before dawn?'

'No problem.'

'And where do we rendezvous afterwards, skipper?' Tiller asked. 'On Leros somewhere?'

Larssen shook his head. 'The Krauts will be combing the island for you. Kalimnos would be safer. It's only a short distance from Portolago.'

Maygan spread out a large-scale chart of the area. 'Vathi looks suitable. Do you know it, Bob?'

Denvers nodded. 'Dropped anchor there several times before the war. It's rather like a Norwegian fiord. Very deep. It's a bloody tricky area for navigation, especially if you approach it from the south, but I know every inch of it. I could certainly take the ML in far enough to get it out of sight of any Jerry air recce.'

Larssen glanced at his watch. 'We've got about four hours of darkness left. Andrew, bring the caique alongside the quay and unload the cockle. We're going to have to see how it floats with the weight of the extra limpets.'

He looked at Tiller and Barnesworth. 'Have you both got your escape kits? You may need them.' They both pulled their silk-handkerchief maps out of their pockets and held them up.

Barnesworth flourished his SAS beret. 'I've got two hacksaw blades, one on either side. Reckon I could get out of Sing-Sing if I had to.'

'I'll make sure I tack mine in before we go,' said Tiller.

'Good. And you'd better have some money just in case you need to bribe someone.' He unlocked a steel box and produced fifty gold sovereigns which he divided between the two men who put them in a money-belt hidden under their shirts and signed for them.

'I want those back,' said Larssen sternly. 'Otherwise the boss thinks I pinch them.'

The major, Tiller decided, had the measure of Larssen all right.

Half an hour later Tiller and Barnesworth began stowing the limpet mines in the floating cockle and added a half-filled can of water and two twenty-four-hour ration packs. The cockle was now floating very low in the water: they could only hope that the sea approaching Portolago was smooth.

The cockle was lifted gently out of the water and on to the deck of the ML and its crew were handed steaming cups of hot cocoa. Tiller carefully checked the cockle once more to ensure that the limpets were safely and securely stowed.

Tiller had never been aboard an ML before. It was bigger than any of the MTBs he had seen. It was, one of the crew told him, 112 feet long and was powered by two Hall-Scott Defender engines. It was also well armed for a ship of its size, having one three-pounder and several smaller-calibre dual-purpose guns.

Denvers made straight for the Turkish coast from Simi and then worked his way northwards at a steady ten knots while Tiller, Larssen and Barnesworth slept on the deck by the cockle. They reached Yalikavak just as the first glimmer of dawn was appearing behind the mainland mountains.

Tiller could see why it had been chosen as a convenient rendezvous for the Levant Schooner Flotilla and other raiding forces, for the steep cliffs overhanging the bay gave any ships anchored there excellent cover, especially from the air. He thought at first it was empty of any vessels but as the light increased he could see first one camouflaged shape and then a second. One was a caique which belonged to the Flotilla. It had been delivering supplies during the night to one of the isolated groups of men who had escaped from Leros and were now scattered across the Dodecanese. The other was an RAF rescue launch which, because of its speed, was being used as a shuttle for sending in emergency supplies to Samos from Castelrosso and evacuating critically wounded personnel from the beleaguered island.

Denvers moored between them and the ML's camouflage netting was erected. The skipper of the rescue launch, an RAF flight-lieutenant, came aboard and was met with a barrage of questions about the situation on Samos.

'The Luftwaffe's really softening the place up,' he said. 'After the bloody nose you gave the Germans on Simi, and the mauling they received on Leros, they're not going to invade Samos before they're ready. But the Stukas are pounding the place to bits and morale isn't too good. Most of the Eyetie garrison has fled into the hills to escape the bombing and there are not enough of our blokes to stop the Krauts when they do decide to land. They keep asking me when the navy's coming to pick them up. I tell them they're coming and that the navy's never let the army down yet. Remember Dunkirk, I said, and Crete. But I don't know.'

Tiller could hear the doubt in the young flight-lieutenant's voice and could see that beneath his tan his face was haggard and his eyes were bleary from lack of sleep. 'To be frank, I think the navy's chickened out. They've lost too many ships on this caper already,' the officer said with finality.

'Don't you worry, sir, the navy hasn't chickened

out,' Tiller heard himself say. 'It will find a way. It always does.'

The young man's eyes focused wearily on Tiller and a glimmer of a smile lit his face when he saw the 'Royal Marine' flash on Tiller's shoulders. 'Ah, one of His Majesty's Jollies. My brother's one of you lot. I might have known there'd be a bootneck among you pirates. But why the winged device?' He pointed to Tiller's beret. 'Where's the globe and laurel?'

'Seconded,' said Tiller.

'I made him take it off,' said Larssen. 'No blanco and brass in this unit. He's one of us now.'

The flight-lieutenant turned to Larssen and said: 'I don't know what the hell you're up to, Captain, or even who you are, and it's none of my business. But if you've got a bootneck to look after you, you'll be OK. Good luck.'

'I was surprised to hear you sticking up for the senior service, Tiger,' Larssen said mockingly after the rescue launch had creamed out of the bay. 'I didn't think you had much time for it. What was that gag you once told me about naval officers and umbrellas.'

'Yeah, well,' Tiller said awkwardly. 'I suppose, skipper, I have to stand up for the navy when I'm among you lot.' But his surge of loyalty had surprised himself as much as it had Larssen.

'And what did he call you – a Jolly? What is that, for Christ's sake?'

'"'E was scrapin' the paint from off of 'er plates an' I sez to 'im, "oo are you?"'" Tiller quoted instantly. '"Sez 'e, 'I'm a Jolly – 'er Majesty's Jolly – soldier an' sailor too!'"'

'Kipling,' said Denvers at once.

Larssen shook his head in irritation. 'You'll never quite be one of us, will you, Tiger, whatever cap badge you wear?'

Tiller grinned and said prophetically: 'No, skipper, I suppose not. But one day perhaps you lot will be with us.'

The November sun rose over the mountains and at midday its heat began to pierce the ML's camouflage netting. Under it the SBS team checked their weapons and equipment methodically before settling down for a nap and an evening meal.

As the sun was setting a German Arado sea-plane passed overhead, searching up and down the coastline for any sign of life. There was a rush for the ML's dual-purpose guns, but the sound of the Arado's engines soon faded into the distance.

At dusk the caique weighed anchor and left the bay, the crew shouting good luck to those aboard the ML. It was a fine night, but the breeze that sprang up and ruffled the waters of the bay had the chill of winter in it.

A silence settled over the ML as they waited to receive the final signal from Beirut. In the tiny wireless cabin the wireless operator – known aboard, as wireless operators were known on every ship, as 'Sparks' – crouched over the radio, which hummed and crackled. Then, three hours after darkness had fallen, the message came through in Morse from Beirut: 'Execute Sunbeam.'

Denvers ordered the ML to weigh anchor and the engines, now in their silent mode, came to life. The netting was wound up and the ML crept out from the shelter of the cliffs.

'Steer two-seven-o,' Denvers instructed the helmsman. On deck Tiller and Barnesworth began blackening each other's face.

12

The ML's silent engines propelled the ship through the water with an almost eerie quietness – very different from the dull roar of the MAS boat.

'A penny for your thoughts, Tiger,' Barnesworth whispered after a while. He was lying next to Tiller on his back, staring up at the night sky. 'Or should I say a drachma.'

'I was just thinking of that crazy Eyetie,' Tiller said. 'What did he think he was up to?'

'Balbao? I don't know. Perhaps he wanted to show how brave the Eyeties could be. Perhaps he hated the Krauts so much he'd take any opportunity to knock a few of them off. Perhaps he thought he'd get away with it. Perhaps he knew that the MAS boat was finished without any fuel and felt that he was finished without the MAS boat. Perhaps it was a bit of each. Why do people act as they do in war? Don't ask me. I just do what I'm told and keep my head down.'

It was a sensible philosophy, Tiller decided, and wished that it was one he was able to follow, but somehow he always seemed to leap in feet first.

Normally, the hours before an operation held no worries for him. He just relaxed, and though the adrenalin would start to pump through him he never got wound up as many people did. But this time he felt distinctly edgy.

'If you ask me,' said Barnesworth, 'all these Mediterranean folk are a bit melodramatic. Know what I mean? That girl, for instance . . .'

'Angelika?'

'Yeah, that's the one. I mean one minute she was all over us, couldn't do enough to help, and the next she's scarpered. Could have left us in a right hole. I thought she took rather a shine to you, Tiger, but that didn't stop her buggering off, did it?'

'She was probably acting on orders.'

'Orders? Whose orders?'

Tiller ducked the question by saying: 'The skipper and I reckon she belongs to one of the Andarte bands.' He wondered if he would ever have a chance to find out.

Barnesworth snorted. 'Fat lot of good they've been. Spend their whole time fighting each other from what I hear. We never found out if there are any on Simi anyway, did we?'

'We didn't hear any more of those Krauts that landed,' Tiller reminded him. 'They may have mopped them up.'

'Perhaps. Perhaps not. I wouldn't have liked to have been a Kraut in those hills with all the locals up there sheltering from the Stukas. The Greeks have a terrible contempt for the Eyeties, but they loathe and detest the Germans. I reckon it was them who finished the Krauts off. Assuming,' he added darkly, 'they have been finished off.'

Denvers's number one, a chubby-faced RNVR sub-lieutenant, came along the deck. 'You two ready? We're nearly there.'

They could see now the most southerly point of Leros to starboard and the larger, higher, land mass of Kalimnos to port. It was time to prime the limpet mines. The sub-lieutenant watched them with interest as they opened the box of pencil fuses and selected the ones coloured for the five-hour time delay.

'How exactly do those fuses work?' he asked.

'When the ampoule of acetone is broken it eats away at a celluloid washer which retains the firing pin,' Tiller explained. 'The thicker the washer the longer the time delay. Quite simple really.'

'But why two fuses?' he asked.

Tiller explained that the sympathetic fuse would detonate a limpet if another limpet attached to the same target went off prematurely. 'The time pencil fuses aren't always one hundred per cent accurate,' he said. 'It depends on the temperature.'

The wireless operator came out of his cramped little cabin and said to them: 'Beirut has just radioed that Leros is partially garrisoned by Brandenburgers. So if any naval guard challenges you just shout out "Brandenburger, Patrola," and they'll probably think you're one of that lot.'

'Thanks, Sparks,' said Tiller. 'We'll keep that in mind. Is there anything else they know about the place?'

'Just that it's swarming with Jerries,' the operator said cheerfully. 'Good luck.'

Denvers scanned the coastline of Leros with his night-glasses. The minutes ticked by, and then he said quietly into the voice pipe: 'Stop engines.'

The hull of the ML stopped vibrating. It lifted and dipped in the slight swell.

'Kill both engines.'

The silence enveloped them. They listened for any sound but could hear nothing except the creak of the ML as it rose and fell on the swell.

'That's it, boys. We're here.'

Helped by the ML's crew, Tiller and Barnesworth silently lowered the cockle into the water, making sure its fragile frame was not knocked against the ML's hull. Denvers watched them from the bridge. When the cockle was afloat he looked at his watch and then stepped on to the deck and said to Tiller quietly: 'You can't see it but we're four miles off the north headland of the harbour entrance. It's due east from here and is very distinctive. You should be able to pick it without difficulty.'

'Any current?' Tiller asked.

Denvers shook his head. 'Not for the next hour or so. Then it will set north-south along the coastline, but it will be less than a knot. Nothing to worry about.'

'Wind?'

'Due south, what there is of it. The forecast is for no more than six to eight knots. Perhaps you should allow a degree or so for it if it pipes up any more than that, but if you're more than two hours on the water the current will offset it.'

'I plan to be over the boom in two hours,' said Tiller. 'And the course for Kalimnos from Portolago?'

'That's trickier.'

'The compass will be working then.'

Tiller turned his back on the shore and shone his dimmed torch on to his chart case. It contained a large-scale chart of the area on which Denvers pointed out his course to him.

'When you come out of the bay steer one-three-five until you pass this headland here. It's not much more than a mile and a half once you've crossed the boom. After you've passed the headland alter course to one-one-zero. That will take you across the straits and bring you to the eastern side of the northern extremity of Kalimnos. That's about two miles.'

On the transparent cover of the chart case Tiller had marked in blue pencil the scale in sea miles and a crude compass rose with magnetic north. With a notched pencil he now measured off one and a half miles from the scale on the chart, kept his thumbnail on the notch, put the pencil against 135 degrees on the compass rose, and moved the pencil down like a parallel ruler until its tip rested against the southern headland of the harbour entrance. He then transferred his thumbnail to the Perspex cover of the chart case, which had been roughened with emery paper so that it would take the pencil's marks, and put a cross where his thumbnail was. Then he did the same again, making a new course of 110 degrees from the cross to the northern headland of Kalimnos.

Denvers, who was looking over his shoulder, nodded. 'That's as near as dammit. You'll need to lie up somewhere on the eastern side of the headland for the day. Then you follow the coast until you reach this small promontory. It's a long haul down to there but Vathi's just beyond it. We'll be waiting for you.' He stuck out his hand. 'See you tomorrow night. Good luck.'

Tiller and Barnesworth lowered themselves carefully into the cockpits of the cockle and Tiller tucked the chart case behind his backrest.

Larssen looked down at them and said quietly: 'Don't do anything I wouldn't do, boys. Remember, work before women, work before women.'

They both gave him the thumbs up.

'Right. Let's go,' said Barnesworth in Tiller's ear and they pushed the cockle away from the ML.

At sea level there was more of a sea running than had been noticeable on the ML and the extra limpets made the cockle ride lower in the water. To add to their problems the wind began to rise beyond what Denvers had predicted, and occasionally it whipped the top off a wave and drifted it into their faces. But the extra-high v-shaped wooden breakwater they had fitted to the craft's bow prevented most of the water from running across its plywood deck.

They used double paddles and soon got a rhythm going which kept them warm. Sometimes they had to turn into a wave to prevent it from swamping them. Neither spoke but each could feel the tension in the other.

After half an hour the land began to take shape ahead of them and after another twenty minutes, when they started to come under its lee, the sea was smoother and the cockle rode more easily. Soon afterwards Tiller was relieved to see the north headland of the entrance to the bay gradually beginning to emerge from the dark.

They rested and Tiller quickly checked the chart to make sure the features he could see dimly ahead were the correct ones. The exertion and tension of keeping the heavily loaded cockle going had made them sweat profusely, and both took greedy swigs of water from the can. They'd have to go easy on that, Tiller reminded himself. There was a long way to go yet and dehydration was debilitating.

He began paddling again and could hear Barnesworth's grunt of disgust behind him for not resting longer. But he wanted to get on with it. He headed directly for the northern headland which guarded the entrance to the harbour. The headland's cliffs were steep and high and in the extra darkness that they provided the two men stopped paddling and turned their double paddles into single ones.

They kept close to the land, which now sloped down to the bay, but not too close in case there were shore patrols. Once they thought they heard boots crunching on gravel and they brought the cockle to a halt and kept their profiles low. When they did not hear the sound again they moved forward, but very slowly.

Tiller knew they must be getting close to the boom but he could not see it. Suddenly he caught the faint tinkle of a warning bell. He stopped paddling, bent forward to lessen his profile, and listened intently. The cockle drifted and again he heard the bell. Was it some kind of alarm system the Germans had rigged up?

His mouth felt dry. He licked his lips and felt the salt on them. Tinkle, tinkle. What the hell was it?

Then he felt Barnesworth prod his back. 'It's only bleeding goats,' he whispered.

The boom, when they reached it, was no obstacle for the cockle, for the technique Tiller had learnt in the Solent worked perfectly. There was no sign of life on the patrol boat, which was anchored by the narrow entrance.

Their first target was the ammunition ship, which

was anchored under the cliffs about halfway along the northern shore. The lack of any tide and the direction of the wind had made her swing on her anchor so that she lay broadside on to the cockle, with her bows pointing into the harbour.

She had a straight single funnel, situated behind the central bridge superstructure, and a prominent poop and forecastle. She looked an ordinary tramp steamer which had seen better days, but was bigger than Tiller had anticipated. Each limpet contained two pounds of explosive which could blow a hole in a ship's side six feet in diameter. This one would definitely need three limpets to make sure she sank. If the ammunition was still aboard, and it was detonated by the limpets, she would certainly sink. In fact, there wouldn't be much left of her.

He turned to port so that the cockle moved right under the cliffs. There was no beach at this point so that they did not have to worry about shore patrols. Approaching the *Anita* from the stern instead of the bow was not the right technique, but it did mean they could carry straight on across the harbour once the limpets had been put in place.

They rested again when they were opposite their target. Tiller turned his head and whispered: 'One by the propellers, then one by the engine space, and the third by the bows. Port side or starboard?'

'It would help if we could see the fucking guard,' Barnesworth grumbled in his ear. 'There must be one.'

Tiller glanced at his watch. 'We can't hang about.'

Barnesworth tapped him on the shoulder. 'There he is.'

They were some 200 yards from the ship but they

both could now see the glow of the guard's cigarette as he stood on the afterdeck looking at the shore.

'Cor, lucky bugger. I could do with a draw,' Barnesworth whispered.

Tiller felt within him the first signs of irritability with his partner and strived to suppress it. Like hallucinations it was something canoeists often encountered and which had to be dealt with rationally. Still, Barnesworth's flippant asides annoyed him and he turned and put his forefinger to his lips. He heard his swimmer grunt, but whether it was with annoyance or acceptance, he could not tell.

The guard flicked his cigarette end into the water, but instead of strolling forward he moved right into the stern of the ship and peered down.

The two SBS men sagged forward on to the plywood deck of their cockle. Tiller grasped the cockle's wooden breakwater in front of him and pressed his head down until his nose was touching the compass.

He felt himself stifling his breathing, but forced himself to suck in deep gulps of air.

Nothing happened and after what seemed an age Tiller cautiously, very gradually, raised his head. The sentry was still there. He seemed to be looking straight at the cockle. He *was* looking straight at the cockle. Tiller did not dare move.

A match flared and Tiller could see the outline of the guard's face and the rifle slung across his back as he lit another cigarette. He flicked the match into the water, and then turned and walked away down the starboard side. Relief surged through Tiller and made him gasp for air.

'Port side,' Billy hissed in his ear.

Both men opened their cockpit covers, and Barnesworth pulled from under the stern a pair of limpet mines attached to their keeper plate, and the magnetic hold-fast. He passed the mines forward to Tiller and undid the line which was wound round the hold-fast.

Tiller put the pair of mines between his feet and pulled out from under the bow the hollow steel rods that made up the placing rod. He carefully connected these, and laid the completed rod, now six feet long, across the cockle's deck. Then he dipped his paddle cautiously into the water and moved the cockle forwards.

Barnesworth prodded Tiller and indicated the ship's Plimsoll line, which was almost level with the water.

'She's still fully loaded,' he breathed into Tiller's ear. Tiller nodded and again indicated that Barnesworth should shut up.

Close to, the ship appeared huge, its steel topsides towering above them. They inched the cockle slowly under the ship's counter, on which was written in large white letters 'Anita Genoa', until they reached a point where the propeller shafts extruded from the hull.

The hull here was dented and rusty. A line of encrusted barnacles and old weed above the faint white band of the Plimsoll line showed that the ship must have been frequently loaded beyond its safety limits. Tiller pointed the weed and barnacles out to Barnesworth, for flaking rust or anything non-ferrous on the steel hull could affect the magnets on the hold-fast as well as on the limpets.

Barnesworth tapped Tiller twice on the shoulder to

indicate that he understood. Tiller lifted the hold-fast and carefully attached it to the ship's side at shoulder level and hung on to the line attached to it.

The hold-fast made what seemed to them a horrendously loud clunk as the magnets connected with the steel, and both men held their breath. When nothing happened Barnesworth tightened the line and drew the cockle closer to the ship's side.

With the hold-fast steadying the cockle, Tiller got on with the delicate task of attaching the limpet mine. He had done it many times before on exercises but he always found it difficult to detach a mine from its retaining plate, so powerful were its magnets and so restricted was the space in which he had to work.

At the third attempt he managed it, but he could feel beads of sweat running down his face. He rested a moment before bringing the mine on to the deck in front of him. He hooked it on to the end of the placing rod, screwed down on the butterfly nut to break the fuse's ampoule of acid, and slowly and very carefully lowered the mine into the water. He kept it well away from the ship's side until his hand holding the rod was just under the surface. Then he moved the mine very slowly towards the ship's side.

When the magnets were close to the steel they battened on to the ship's side with a sudden jerk and another clunk. Again they waited, but when they heard nothing Tiller pushed the rod downwards to disconnect it from the mine and brought the rod back to the surface and stowed it alongside him.

Once Tiller had finished, Barnesworth pulled off the hold-fast and moved the cockle gently forward. When they reached the middle of the ship, where the engine room lay under the central superstructure, they repeated the operation. Then they allowed the cockle to drift forward again until they were near the bow. For a moment they clung to the ship's side while they tried to locate the guard. But all they could hear was the slap of water against the vessel and a wireless somewhere playing music.

Tiller placed the third limpet and then allowed the cockle to drift out beyond the ship's bows. Its stem was straighter than on a modern ship but there was enough overhang to give them some protection from anyone looking casually down from the deck above.

They drifted slowly past the rusty anchor chain, its links dripping with water.

They had assumed the prone position, but felt horribly vulnerable. The minutes ticked by. They were aware that they were gradually drifting away from the ship and when no challenge rang out across the water they cautiously began to paddle out into the middle of the harbour.

It would have been easier to continue up the northern shore to where the F-lighter and the supply ship lay, but Larssen had decided – and Tiller and Barnesworth had agreed with him – that the longer they were in the harbour the greater chance there was of their being discovered, and that the two destroyers therefore had to be dealt with as quickly as possible.

Near the middle of the harbour, which at this point was nearly a mile wide, a patrol boat with a searchlight passed well ahead of them and they stopped and crouched low in the cockle. But the beam did not sweep near them and they waited until the sound of the patrol boat's engine had faded.

It was very dark and although the distance across the harbour was hardly more than half a mile Tiller found it difficult to keep his bearings. He was still searching the horizon ahead when Barnesworth tapped him on the shoulder and whispered: 'There, slightly to starboard.'

Tiller strained his eyes and was just able to make out a long, dark shape. As they got nearer they could see it had two funnels. The forward one was much higher than the aft one.

'That's the *San Martino*,' Barnesworth hissed into his ear. 'The smaller of the two. We'd better sheer off a bit until we can find the *Turbine*.'

They turned the cockle to port and then south again and closed with the shore. But the *Turbine* was not there. They turned west and saw the sharp silhouette of the *San Martino* ahead of them. They rested and had another swig of water, and considered what to do.

The reconnaissance photograph had plainly shown the two destroyers anchored almost side by side at the northern end of the naval base.

'They must have moved her,' Barnesworth whispered.

'That's pretty fucking obvious,' Tiller murmured furiously to himself.

'What shall we do?'

Now Tiller could not restrain the irritation in his whispered reply. 'Deal with this one and then look for the other, of course.'

What did Billy think they should do: paddle home to mummy and complain? He heard Barnesworth suck his teeth and knew his partner was also keeping his temper in check with difficulty.

He indicated that he wanted two pairs of limpet mines and Barnesworth passed them forward. Tiller tugged three of them from their retaining plates and hooked one on to his placing rod.

'Bows, amidships, and on the stern,' Barnesworth whispered. 'Port side to.'

Tiller nodded his agreement and they paddled slowly forward, this time approaching from the correct direction by keeping the destroyer bows on to the cockle. There was no sign of a sentry, though they knew there must be one, if not two. They would be German sailors, too, who were trained to be observant, while the man on the *Anita* had probably been just a civilian member of the crew.

For a moment they hung on to the destroyer's anchor chain, and now they could hear the guttural sounds of a conversation somewhere above them. There was a hoarse laugh which ended in a cough, a burst of music, faint but distinct, and a shaft of light as a bulwark door on the destroyer was opened and then closed with a clang. Somewhere a dog barked.

Tiller froze. If there was a dog on board, that could mean trouble. Dogs had an uncanny way of detecting the unusual which went way beyond their sense of smell and hearing.

He held his hand vertically just above his shoulder to indicate he wanted to wait and heard Barnesworth suck his teeth again. Impatient bastard, Tiller thought.

Again the dog barked. Where was it? Sounds at night and over water were often distorted, and always deceptive.

Tiller felt the pressure of Barnesworth's hand on his shoulder and Barnesworth whispered: 'It's on shore. Forget it.'

Again, Tiller indicated with his hand that he did not want to move until he was sure.

'For fuck's sake,' Barnesworth snarled in his ear. Tiller grasped the anchor chain in case Barnesworth decided to let go of it, and listened intently.

The conversation above them was more animated now, and Tiller thought he heard the chink of glass. At least Barnesworth had chosen the correct side to place the mines, for the conversation, Tiller could tell now, was definitely coming from the starboard side somewhere.

But the dog did not bark again and after a minute of listening to Barnesworth sucking his teeth Tiller reluctantly let go the anchor chain and propelled the cockle towards the sharp bow of the destroyer.

Its sides were clean compared to that of the ammunition ship and looked as if they had been recently repainted. How like the Kraut, Tiller thought with grudging admiration, to make even an out-of-date Eyetie warship spick and span.

He felt the cold, wet steel against his hand as he steadied the cockle for Barnesworth to apply the hold-fast, which, to their relief, made less noise than it had when applied to the ammunition ship. The first and second limpets were secured without a problem, but for some reason the third refused to adhere to the destroyer's stern near the rudder. Tiller swore under his breath, but wherever he moved the placing rod the mine's magnets refused to take.

He could feel Barnesworth's mounting impatience behind him and indicated that they should try the other side. They were moving the cockle cautiously round the stern when a powerful torch was turned on above them. They froze in the lowest position, keeping close to the ship's stern. The torch played on the water, went off, came on again, and then settled directly on them.

Tiller remembered the wireless operator's tip and shouted up, '*Patrola, Brandenburger*', and dug his paddle into the water. There was an indistinct shout from the sentry holding the torch and looking back Tiller could see he was struggling to unsling his rifle from his back. His companion, his rifle already off his shoulder, was running to join him.

With half a dozen vigorous strokes Tiller knew they could put the cockle beyond the range of the torch, and the darkness would almost immediately swallow them up. But if the guards started firing the operation would have to be aborted. It was equally certain that the destroyer's hull would be scraped with a wire hawser as a precaution and all their efforts would have been in vain.

'I'm going to face the fuckers,' he said to Barnesworth and swung the cockle around and stopped.

'*Patrola, Brandenburger*,' he called out again, and waved.

The first sentry was trying to juggle the heavy torch with his rifle and Tiller could see that he now had the barrel on the guard rail aiming straight at them, but he seemed unable to bring the torch's beam on to the cockle.

When Tiller called out, the second sentry pushed the first sentry's rifle sideways along the rail. The first sentry dropped the torch on the deck and while he was bending to pick it up the second sentry called out something in German to them.

Tiller waved again and the second sentry waved back. Tiller turned the cockle away and paddled swiftly into the darkness before the first sentry could focus the beam on them again.

'Jesus H. Christ,' Barnesworth said in his ear when they stopped to rest. 'You've got a nerve. I thought he was going to put one between your eyes.'

'So did I,' whispered Tiller. He could feel he was wet with sweat. He took a gulp of water from the can and then passed it to Barnesworth.

They were now rather too close to the naval base for comfort. They could not see anyone moving among the buildings but they sheered off before paddling parallel with the shore once more. The dog, a lot nearer now, started barking again.

'I told you it was on the shore,' Barnesworth hissed in Tiller's ear. Exuberant with relief, Tiller just turned his head and whispered: 'You've just got big lugs, Billy', and felt the guardsman punch him good-naturedly on the shoulder.

They passed several lighters moored together, and a small coastal patrol vessel of some kind which lay at the end of a long wooden pier. Ahead they could see several motor launches and tugs moored around a large floating jetty. They were considerably bigger than the MAS boat and made tempting targets, but Tiller ignored them. He had a bigger fish to fry – if they could find it.

They were just beginning to despair of ever doing so when a much bigger bulk began to loom out of the darkness ahead of them on their port side.

'That's her,' Barnesworth whispered excitedly.

Even in the dark Tiller could see from the outline of the destroyer that it was the one the MAS boat had tried to ram. They edged closer and made out the lettering 'TA14' on her bow. She was moored alongside the naval base. A large crane overhung her central superstructure and Tiller wondered if the MAS boat had, after all, inflicted some damage on her.

Then, to his consternation, he saw that the destroyer was surrounded on the seaward side by a number of much smaller ships of various sizes, and one was moored right alongside her. Tiller recognized at least two of them as being *Motosiluranti*, or MS boats, the Italian equivalent of the ML. They were larger and more heavily armed than a MAS boat and must have been, Tiller supposed, taken over by the German Navy.

But there was also a large caique, a MAS boat, and one or two others he could not identify. Judging from the activity aboard these ships, it was evident that they had only recently arrived in Portolago or, more likely, were just about to depart.

The SBS men rested and let the cockle drift while they summed up the situation. It did not take long.

'We'll never get through that lot without being spotted,' Barnesworth murmured in Tiller's ear. 'Not in a month of Sundays.'

Tiller knew he was right, for even when the crews went below or ashore a sentry would be left on deck. They might slide past one or two, but even if they managed to squeeze their way past them all they would be totally exposed when they reached the destroyer's side. They had to devise another method, and quickly.

'I'm going to circle round them and come up as near as I can astern of the destroyer,' Tiller whispered. 'Then you're going to have to swim the rest of the way with a couple of limpets and put them on her stern. At least we might be able to damage her steering gear.'

The possibility of using this method of attack had been foreseen, and Barnesworth wore a swimmer's suit and had with him a long length of line. There was nothing moored directly astern of the destroyer, but to approach it the cockle had to keep close to the shore, so that it would be moving right under the noses of any patrol.

Tiller saw that the quay of the naval base jutted out slightly into the water so that they were able to manoeuvre the cockle under it and then pull themselves towards the destroyer by pushing on the wooden beams that supported the quay. It would have been possible to get right up to the destroyer in this manner except that they soon gathered there were several men on sentry duty by the destroyer's stern. They stamped their feet and swore in German and one sent a jet of urine almost into the cockle.

Tiller backed off slightly until he felt a tap on his shoulder and he knew Barnesworth was ready. He steadied the craft while his partner slid from his cockpit and into the water. Then he handed him two limpets on their retaining plate and Barnesworth clipped them to the line. He then handed one end of the line to Tiller and slid away silently into the bay.

The limpets and the line sank beneath the surface but most of their weight was supported by Tiller. Above him he could hear the scuff of the sentries' boots on the quay and the murmur of their conversation, but the destroyer was shrouded in darkness and silence.

After twenty minutes there was a tug on the line

and Tiller began slowly and carefully hauling it in. Moments later Barnesworth's head surfaced by the cockle. He gave the thumbs up and indicated that Tiller should back off down the quay while he hung on to the cockle's bow.

Once they were far enough away from the sentries, Tiller turned the cockle and Barnesworth levered himself back into it.

'A cinch,' he whispered triumphantly. 'I put one close to its depth-charge rack. It should make an almighty bang.'

'Good man,' Tiller replied. 'Let's get the hell out of here.' He glanced at his watch. They had been in the harbour exactly two hours. It seemed like two weeks.

'What about the supply ship and the F-lighter?' Barnesworth asked.

'What about them? They only said 'if possible'. If we hang around any longer the sentry on that first destroyer might find out the Brandenburgers don't have a harbour patrol.'

Barnesworth didn't argue. They dumped the remaining mines and the compass compensator overboard and once across the boom and out of the bay Tiller set a course of one-three-five on the compass grid.

13

Away from the shelter of the bay the sea and the
wind increased, and the cockle encountered short,
steep waves which threatened to swamp it. Water
cascaded over the deck and began finding its way
into the craft. It swilled about their feet, and they
took it in turns to try and bail it out.

To add to the miserable conditions it started to
drizzle and this cut visibility to such an extent that
Tiller was concerned about making the passage across
the straits between the two islands. The compass
seemed to be behaving itself, but compasses, he
knew, were never wholly reliable. After half an
hour he told Barnesworth to keep the cockle heading
into the waves while he consulted the chart with his
shaded torch. He stared into the darkness to port and
decided, from the vague shape of the land, that he
must be opposite the headland where Denvers had
told him to alter course. He moved the compass grid
to one-one-zero.

'It could be bumpy across the strait,' he shouted
over his shoulder. He heard Barnesworth grunt an
acknowledgement.

Turning the cockle even slightly side on to the wind
and waves made it dip and swing alarmingly. After
a quarter of an hour on the new compass bearing
the veil of rain lifted momentarily. Kalimnos should

now be directly ahead of them but he could not see it, could see nothing but a black void.

Tiller dug in his blades with increased fury, but he was now feeling the extreme fatigue, a reaction that always followed the elation of a mission safely accomplished. And fatigue, he knew, brought with it hallucinations, cramped lower limbs, and intense, irrational anger with the other member of the team.

'We'll rest,' he shouted back to Barnesworth.

'We'd better keep going,' Barnesworth said. 'It'll be light soon.'

'I said we'll rest,' Tiller snapped.

'Eh, take it easy, Tiger.' Tiller felt the friendly pressure of his companion's hand on his shoulder.

He glanced at his watch. He knew Billy was right and that irritated him even more. He also knew that they also had to find a safe hiding-place before the limpets exploded. Once they went off, the whole area – land, sea and air – would be saturated with search parties and if the cockle was caught in daylight in the open sea Tiller knew they would be dead meat.

After five minutes they started again. Pain began to course through Tiller's arms as he dug in his paddles. His legs and thighs started to lose any feeling, and then he felt the first tingling agony of cramp.

The rain started again, heavier than ever, but the sea as they came under the lee of the northern headland of Kalimnos became smoother and the tops of the waves, though breaking occasionally with an alarming hiss, were no longer being whipped off by the wind. But the rain was being driven straight into their faces and Tiller could see nothing but blackness ahead.

It was like the nightmare, paddling into nothingness, going nowhere.

Each stroke was agony now. He kept being aware that his eyes were shut and he forced himself to keep them open by looking at the compass. But after a while the luminous numbers began to spin before his eyes like a roulette wheel. It took a superhuman effort of concentration for him to confirm that they were still on the correct course and not paddling round in circles.

Tiller's mind wandered. He tried to quote *Barrack-Room Ballads* to himself. But its words and rhythm were a jumble and would not come out straight.

''E isn't one o' the reg'lar Line, nor 'e isn't a kind of giddy Harumfrodite – soldier an' sailor, too . . .'

He gave up and his mind wandered back to Barnesworth and why he insisted on making comments in the middle of the operation, but now, when it was safe to shout at the top of their voices, the cat seemed to have got his tongue.

Why didn't he go to the dentist?

Was that Sydney Harbour bridge ahead? Now that was a run ashore he wouldn't forget. What was her name?

He started humming the regimental march, repeating the words a line at a time with each stroke of the paddle:

> 'A Life on the Ocean Wave,
> A home on the rolling deep,
> Where the scatter'd waters rave
> And the winds their revels keep.'

But he couldn't remember any more so he kept

repeating the first four lines, hoping the next four would come into his mind. But they didn't come and the compass spun before his eyes. What was Billy saying, why did he keep interrupting?

Barnesworth hit Tiller in his back with his fist and screamed: 'For fuck's sake, Tiger. That's land ahead, you silly sod. What do you want to do, end up halfway up a cliff?'

Tiller jerked awake and struggled to refocus his mind and eyes.

Land it was, and very near, so near he could see the waves breaking at the bottom of a cliff face. But it was indistinct, too, blurred by the rain and his own utter weariness. He stopped paddling and watched the cliff get nearer. Like the nightmare there was nothing he could do.

'Back off! Move left!' Barnesworth bawled in his ear. 'Paddle, you bastard, paddle!'

Sluggishly Tiller's mind and muscles responded. He back-paddled and slowly the craft slewed away from the cliff face. A wave slopped across them and the rain hammered down. They must be in some kind of local current, Tiller thought, for something was drawing the cockle towards the shore like a magnet. Ahead he thought he saw the first glimmer of dawn in the sky and then he heard the distant boom of an explosion.

'The limpets,' he shouted exultantly. 'Did you hear the bang?'

'It's the fucking waves hitting the fucking cliffs.' Barnesworth's fury penetrated Tiller's fuddled mind. 'Keep paddling, you silly sod, or we'll hit them, too.'

Resentment welled up in Tiller that he had made

a mistake. He thought vaguely that Barnesworth was having him on, but he had no strength to start an argument. His back ached, and the cramp in his water-soaked legs was gnawing into him. With his last remaining strength he dug his paddles into the water and tried to maintain some kind of rhythm for Barnesworth to follow. His body, accustomed to years of rigorous discipline, responded automatically to what Barnesworth was now yelling in his ear. 'In, out, in, out. Count your strokes, Tiger. Keep it steady. In, out, in, out. We're nearly out of trouble. Just a dozen more strokes. In, out, in, out.'

But his mind kept wandering so that his body seemed a machine quite apart from it. He half saw, half felt the looming presence of the land above him, and the violence of the water around the cockle, and the spray in his face, and heard Barnesworth bawling: 'In, out, in, out, dig deep, you sod.'

Then quite suddenly the water was calm, the cockle upright.

'There's a beach,' Barnesworth shouted. 'We'll go for it. Turn right, Tiger. Right.' The cockle swung, tipped, went too far to the right, then was straightened by Barnesworth. Seconds later they were in shallow water and Barnesworth half fell, half scrambled out of his cockpit. He grabbed the cockle's stern and ran it gently ashore. Tiller dropped his paddle and it floated in the water secured to his wrist by a short piece of line.

Tiller tried to pull himself out of the cockpit but the pain in his legs was excruciating and had seemingly locked them tight.

'Cramp,' he said. 'Sorry. Fucking cramp.'

Barnesworth hauled the cockle's bow on to the

sand and then swung it broadside on to the beach. Then he tipped it sideways and dragged Tiller out of his cockpit. He took a bottle of salt tablets from a pocket in the craft and handed them to Tiller with the can of water. Tiller swilled them down and struggled to his feet. He banged the calves of his legs with his hands and jigged up and down.

'Come on,' said Barnesworth. 'It'll be light soon. We've got to get under cover.'

They drained the cockle of water, picked it up and carried it up the beach. On their right was the rocky cliff top which they had just managed to avoid, but ahead and to their left the land was much lower and flatter. The beach ended in a field of olive trees. They laid the cockle down and began searching for a hiding-place.

There was no shelter around the beach, but when they moved inland they found part of a stone wall which was overhung by an olive tree. They carried the cockle there, covered it with camouflage netting and then went back to the beach to obliterate their footmarks with branches from one of the trees.

It was beginning to get light now. It was a grey, windy morning, but the rain had stopped though the clouds above them were leaden with it. They unearthed the small primus, stewed some tea in the tin mugs they used for bailing, and broke open one of the two ration packs. They devoured the biscuits and then heated a tin of stew in one of the mugs. The stew didn't seem to taste of anything but it was hot and stopped their gnawing hunger. They decided to keep the bar of chocolate until later.

'Fucking cramp,' said Barnesworth sympathetically as Tiller massaged his legs. 'It's the one thing that scares me when I'm swimming. You get stomach cramp at the wrong moment, and you sink like a stone. It's happened to me once, and I tell you, mate, I wouldn't want it to happen again.'

'Dehydration, I should think,' Tiller said. He looked at his watch. 'Those limpets should be going off soon.'

'The wind's in the wrong direction,' said Barnesworth doubtfully. 'We might not hear them.'

'We'll hear them,' Tiller promised. 'Especially if that ammunition ship goes up.'

When they came the explosions were like distant thunder, the last one much louder and longer than the other two.

'She went up all right,' said Tiller.

The two men shook hands.

'Got the sods,' Tiller said. 'Now let's get some shut-eye. I'll take the first watch.'

Barnesworth grinned at him. 'You must be joking. You wouldn't last ninety seconds. You were kipping in the cockle. The Krauts aren't going to find us here. No way. Let's get our heads down while we can.'

Tiller raised himself above the wall and scanned the interior of the island. It was bare and brown and without life of any kind. Kalimnos, they had been told, did not have a garrison and the population had deserted it long ago. Only the local fishermen and the occasional German sea patrol visited it now.

'Yeah, you're right.'

They took out their pistols, took them apart, and dried and oiled them. Then they removed the backrests from the cockle to use as pillows, lay down under the lee of the wall, and pulled part of the camouflage netting over themselves.

The next thing Tiller knew was Barnesworth shaking him vigorously.

'There's a hell of a rumpus going on over there,' he said pointing eastwards across the island. Tiller levered himself up and peered over the wall. There was nothing to see but he could hear the crump of bombs exploding and the steady thump, thump, thump of a heavy automatic weapon. They both knew what was in each other's minds.

'The ML?' Barnesworth queried eventually. Tiller shook his head with a confidence he did not feel. 'More likely they found an MTB sneaking along the Turkish coast.'

The firing and bombing went on for about twenty minutes and then suddenly stopped. It was late afternoon now and the sun had come out. They opened the second ration pack and ate everything in it without bothering to heat it, and when dusk came they carried the cockle down to the water, and launched it. The weather looked as if it was going to remain fine. But it was quite cold, and Tiller was looking forward to a proper meal aboard the ML.

They rounded the north-east tip of Kalimnos without trouble and by midnight were beyond the promontory where Vathi lay. They paddled close to the land but still almost missed the entrance to the bay, so narrow was the entrance. They turned in, narrowly missed two large rocks, and passed into the inlet. Denvers had been right. Without local knowledge it was a dangerous place.

Once inside the water opened up. Along the southern edge was a beach but the rocky shore came right down to the water on the northern side. There, lurking somewhere in the shadows, they hoped the ML would be waiting for them and eventually, around a bend in the bay, they came upon her right under a shallow, overhanging cliff.

'Shit,' said Tiller quietly. The ML had received a direct hit which had broken her in two and she lay in two distinct pieces in the shallows under the cliff.

A wreath of smoke still curled up from the tangled, blackened wreckage that had been her bridge and the barrel of the three-pounder was skewed at an improbable angle as if some giant hand had seized and bent it. The only visible part of the stern section was a half-submerged mangle of twisted steel.

They moved slowly forward through the flotsam and jetsam of any marine casualty of war: life-jackets, charred bits of wood, gratings, books, mattresses, clothes, the shredded remains of the curtains from the tiny ward-room.

Unthinkingly, Tiller poked with his paddle at a floating life-jacket and the body that he suddenly saw was attached to it rolled on to its back. The scorched, unidentifiable face stared up at him out of the dark water with wide-open, reproachful eyes. Tiller withdrew his paddle and the face, with what seemed deliberate slowness, bobbed a moment before turning over and disappearing beneath the surface. The accusing eyes, even under the water, seemed fixed on his face.

'Shit.'

They paddled up to the remains of the ML. Close to, they could smell the stench of burning and heard the gentle hiss of steam escaping from a fractured pipe.

'Nobody could survive that,' said Barnesworth. 'The bomb must have detonated her fuel and spare ammunition.'

They went alongside cautiously and climbed on to the charred and warped deck. They could only recognize Denvers, who lay on the remains of his bridge, from the two intertwined stripes of gold braid on the shoulder of a strip of shirt still attached to the grotesque bundle that had once been a human being.

Under the bridge the wireless room had been crushed almost flat. One of the crew of the three-pounder lay slumped across the breech of the gun, the other two on the deck near it. There was no need to confirm that they were dead.

Larssen and the other crew members, Tiller supposed, must have been caught below or had been blown into the water as there were no other bodies visible. Only one of the .5-inch machine-guns, with its belt of ammunition folded neatly into a box, had miraculously remained untouched by the ferocious blast that had torn the vessel apart.

Tiller worked its cocking mechanism and squinted down the barrel. 'This could be useful.'

'Too heavy to take on the cockle,' Barnesworth observed. They carried it between them and got the weapon and the ammunition box ashore. Then they returned to their craft and paddled in silence to the end of the bay, where the chart had showed them was a beach and a few scattered houses.

Some yards from it the cockle collided with what later they decided must have been a piece of debris from the ML. Tiller felt the cockle lurch and slow as it skewered itself on the half-sunken wreckage, and water began gushing in.

They paddled free of the obstruction and then leapt out as the bow began to dip beneath the surface, and pulled the cockle to the beach and on to the sand.

Barnesworth began rolling it over but Tiller said: 'Leave it. There's no point in fiddling around in the dark. More important to see if there are any survivors.'

They searched the length of the beach and the deserted houses beyond. The water's edge was littered with fragments from the ML, but they found no survivors, only one body lying face down at the far end of the beach. His fingers had dug into the sand, showing that he must have been alive when he had reached the shore.

'We'd better bury him,' said Barnesworth, but Tiller said: 'We'd better not. You know how thorough the Krauts are. They're bound to send a patrol to try and find the ML's code-books. We mustn't show we've been here.'

'They won't find code-books in that wireless room,' Barnesworth said. 'They won't find anything. There's nothing left of it.'

Instead of burying him, they noted the dead man's name from the tags around his neck. Then they carried the damaged cockle under some nearby trees and fetched the machine-gun.

'They'll come by water if they come,' Barnesworth said.

'When they come,' Tiller corrected him. They set the weapon up, using a tree as a makeshift support, so that it was trained down the creek. Then they spread out the camouflage netting, divided a bar of chocolate between them, and lay down.

Tiller wondered where Larssen had died, and how. He had come to like and admire his skipper with his dreadful accent, his skill and enthusiasm for killing Germans, and his brilliant leadership.

He slept, and the submerged face bobbed up and down. Somehow it had acquired two bullet holes in its forehead.

He opened his eyes. Barnesworth was leaning over him and shaking his shoulder. 'Stop hollering, Tiger, for Christ's sake.'

Tiller blinked. The first rays of the early-morning sun were spearing through the trees.

'Who's Mac, for Christ's sake?' Barnesworth asked.

Tiller stood up and shook the sand from his clothing. 'Mac?'

'Yeah, Mac. You were shouting "Mac".'

Tiller stretched. He felt stiff and sore. Perhaps he was getting too old for this kind of lark, he thought. Perhaps he should get a cushy number somewhere as an instructor when they got back. Or perhaps he might be one of those blokes who drummed up recruits by standing up with all his gongs on his chest and saying, ever so modestly of course, how brave he had been and how worthwhile it all was. Perhaps that dreaded phrase 'strong family ties' was not the life sentence he had always thought it.

'I don't know. I used to work with a bloke called Matt. A pre-war Olympic canoeist, he was. Mad as a hatter.'

'Matt, was it? Sounded like "Mac" to me. What happened to him?'

'He's dead,' said Tiller. 'Bought it on some op. What the fuck are we going to do with this cockle, Billy?'

In the pale morning light they turned over the craft and inspected the damage. The canvas hull had been sliced neatly as if with a knife along half its length. So sharp was the object that they'd hit that it had also sliced clean through several of the cockle's ribs, cracking and splintering them. For good measure it had ripped the buoyancy bags in the bows as well.

'That's a write-off,' Tiller declared.

'There's plenty of material around,' Barnesworth said doubtfully. 'We could try and patch it up.'

'It's a write-off,' Tiller repeated. 'There's no way we can fix that. Besides, we left the fucking repair kit behind, didn't we?'

'If we hadn't been forced to carry so many limpets. They don't care, do they? Don't give a shit.'

'Who?'

'Whoever sent us on this bloody lark. Sink this, sink that, and oh, while you're at it, old boy, sink the fucking other as well.'

Barnesworth's rage visibly swelled his face and he kicked the cockle hard.

'Steady on, Billy,' Tiller said gently. 'We'll get out of this. Somehow.'

The cockle was useless but he still didn't like seeing it kicked. Billy's rage seemed to subside but his eyes remained puffy with exhaustion.

'Yeah, I suppose so,' he said, unconvinced. Suddenly there was a sound behind them. Tiller whipped out his pistol and cocked it. The sound came again, a sort of half-gasp, half-cough. Tiller gestured to Barnesworth to back away down the beach so that he could cover him.

When Barnesworth was in position Tiller moved forward. Despite what the Killer School had taught him, he had always thought a pistol was a useless weapon and now he felt naked and vulnerable and just wished he had his Sten. Something else which had been left behind.

Out of the corner of his eye he suddenly saw a slight movement under a bush ahead of him. He drew a bead on it and waited, but it did not move again. Whatever it was it was not very threatening. An animal perhaps?

He kept his pistol pointing at the object, which looked, as he neared it, like a pile of old rags. Then he could see that it must be a survivor from the ML who had managed to drag himself off the beach and under cover.

He hurried forward, and bent over the blackened figure. It was so disfigured and burnt that it took him some moments to recognize the survivor as the ML's wireless operator. Tiller's eyes travelled down the man's body and he saw that one of his legs had been blown off below the knee. Somehow he had made a tourniquet, but the sand was soaked with blood.

'Billy!' Tiller shouted at the top of his voice. 'Get the water and the first-aid kit. Quick.'

The operator opened his eyes and tried to smile. He opened his mouth to say something but nothing came out except a croak.

'You just keep quiet, mate,' Tiller said. 'You'll be all right now, but we've got to do something about your leg.'

He took off his shirt, ripped off one of its sleeves, cut it into two lengths, and replaced the blood-sodden strip of cloth the operator had used as a tourniquet.

As he worked he remembered with a curse that the first-aid kit had been left behind as well. He found two sticks and twisted the strips of shirt around them so that the tourniquet was tight but not too tight.

Barnesworth arrived with the water and Tiller

cradled the wireless operator's head and moistened his lips and tongue. The man coughed as the water reached his throat but it revived him and he opened his eyes. His lips moved and Tiller strained to hear what he was trying to say.

'You got . . . them?'

Tiller nodded. 'Yes, we got them.'

It only then occurred to him that the Germans must have searched not only for them but for the ship which would pick them up. Kalimnos was an obvious place to rendezvous. It must have been simple to have pinpointed the most likely sites. Suddenly, Tiller felt that he was personally responsible for the disaster that had overwhelmed his detachment commander, the ML and its crew, and the dying man whose head he was cradling.

What a fuck-up it all was.

'We only got away with it because of the tip you gave us. You know: "Patrola, Brandenburger". It worked.'

A spasm crossed the man's lips.

'Are the code-books aboard, mate?' Tiller asked urgently.

The operator's head moved fractionally sideways.

'You managed to ditch them in the weighted bag?'

Just a flutter of an eyelid acknowledged that the man had followed the correct procedure. He was trying to say something again, and Tiller leant forward.

'. . . message through,' the operator whispered.

'You got a message through that you were being attacked?'

The man's eyelids flickered to say that he had.

'Beirut acknowledged?'

The eyelids flickered again.

'And Beirut said they'd pass it on to Simi?'

The man's eyelids flickered for a third and final time before his eyes went blank and his head rolled sideways.

Tiller felt the man's jugular vein, lowered his head gently to the ground, and then closed the staring eyes. He made a note of his name from his tags and stood up.

'So the caique will come and fetch us?' Barnesworth asked.

'If it can find its way in,' said Tiller.

They decided to sink the cockle. They weighted it with stones, then waded out into the creek carrying it above their heads. When the water reached their necks they let the cockle slide beneath the surface. Its drab colouring blended exactly with the bottom.

They waded ashore, covered their tracks expertly, gathered the machine-gun and ammunition box, and the water can, and searched for a hiding-place among the cliffs which would also give them a good view of the creek. If the caique came it would come at night but the Germans could come at any time. The sun was high in the sky before they found the right place: a small cave near the cliff top which was reached by a narrow strip of grass.

'They deserve to find us if they come up here,' Barnesworth said.

They took turns to stay on watch, one hour on, one hour off. It was late afternoon before the Germans arrived. But they did not come by sea, as the SBS · men had expected. Instead they came again from the sky, but this time it was their old friend the Blohm and Voss.

It circled the remains of the ML and then landed in the bay. Two soldiers climbed out of the cockpit and on to the aircraft's wings. They inflated a rubber dinghy, and paddled towards the remains of the ML and out of sight of the two SBS men hiding above them. The pilot threw out an anchor and then climbed on to the wing of the Blohm and Voss, and lay down.

Barnesworth sucked his teeth. 'He's fucking confident, isn't he?'

Signs of overconfidence was something Larssen had taught them always to watch for in the enemy as well as in themselves. It was, he said, something that could always be exploited. They looked at each other and both knew that the other was thinking of Larssen and what he would have done in the same circumstances, and then they both said together: 'Sink or swim.'

Tiller chuckled. 'Great minds think alike, Billy.'

They knew exactly what they had to do and agreed on the plan with a few brief words. They kept well clear of the ML and the beach, where the soldiers would be concentrating their search, found a place inland where they could cross the creek, moved into the remains of the village and found the ruins of a house which gave them a clear view of the bay and where they could set up the machine-gun.

They could see the rubber dinghy alongside the remains of the ML, but there was no sign of the soldiers. The pilot had stripped off his shirt. The co-pilot, they could see, had chosen to stay in the cockpit with a book. Tiller wondered idly what he could be reading.

The sun had dipped below the trees behind the SBS men before the soldiers emerged from their search. They shouted something to the pilot and lowered themselves into the rubber dinghy. The pilot sat up, put his shirt back on, and waited on the wing to grab the dinghy's painter when it was thrown to him.

'The co-pilot first,' whispered Tiller. 'With any luck, we'll get their wireless at the same time. Then the rubber dinghy. Then the pilot. And make bloody sure that ammunition belt isn't twisted.'

He flicked up the rear sight of the machine-gun. 'Two hundred?'

'I reckon so. Two-fifty, maybe. Don't fucking miss. Those Krauts look well armed.'

Tiller slid the rear sight up a notch, waited until the rubber dinghy was halfway to the seaplane and put a short burst into the cockpit. The co-pilot slumped sideways so that his head was out of the open door. Then Tiller switched to the rubber dinghy and gave its occupants a sustained burst. Out of the corner of his eye he could see the pilot running along the wing towards the open cockpit door. Coolly, he made sure that no one in the rubber dinghy had survived before switching back to the flying boat.

Incongruously, the pilot was tucking in his shirt-tails as he scrambled along. Tiller felt almost sorry for him. He knew what it was like to feel exposed, to expect a bullet in the back at any moment, knowing there was nothing you could do about it – except pray. And Tiller wasn't the praying sort. He wondered, as he squeezed the trigger, if the pilot was.

When the bullets hit, the pilot's arms flailed as if he had slipped on a banana. Then he fell head first into the water with a curious elegance that made Barnesworth comment: 'He could have made a good diver with a bit more practice.'

They watched the water and the flying boat warily. Nothing moved, except for the rubber dinghy, which bobbed up and down on the water as it rapidly deflated.

'What about the flying boat?'

'Leave it,' said Tiller.

They walked back along the beach, found two lengths of timber they could use as crude spades and after taking off their identity tags buried the wireless operator and the crewman in the sand. They marked the graves by binding pieces of stick into the shape of crosses. Then they walked along the path under the cliff, past the ML, and round the bend in the creek to find a position where they would have a clear view of the caique approaching.

It arrived soon after midnight and Tiller flashed the prearranged signal with his shaded torch. They saw it swing towards them and their signal was acknowledged. It came to a stop about 100 yards from them and they could see someone climbing into a dinghy that it had in tow.

'I'm bloody amazed they got into the creek,' said Tiller as they watched the dinghy approaching. 'That entrance is fucking hairy enough in daylight.'

Barnesworth's elbow dug into Tiller's ribs. 'I'll give you just one guess who guided them in, Tiger. Just one guess.'

Epilogue

August 1953

'We've got a few minutes left. Any questions?'

The latest draft of National Service recruits to the Royal Marines at Eastney Barracks shifted uncomfortably in their chairs. They knew they were expected to ask questions on the lecture, but could not think of any.

Then one, slightly older than the rest, and wiser in the ways of distracting a lecturer from the dull subject in hand, asked, as other members of earlier classes had asked before him: 'Will you tell us what was it *really* like, sir?'

'What was what like, lad?'

'That Aegean campaign of yours, sir. When you were in the SBS.'

'No different from many other operations. A right shambles.'

'But weren't the Eyeties on our side by then, sir?' another recruit piped up.

'What of it, lad?'

'Well, weren't they' – the recruit hesitated – 'yellow?'

'No, lad, that was the Japanese.'

The recruits sniggered politely.

'You know what I mean, sir.'

So Regimental Sergeant-Major 'Tiger' Tiller, DCM MM Royal Marines, told the class – as he had been inveigled into telling other classes before them – about Balbao and the last final dash of his MAS boat. And he told them too about Giovanni and his Mafia cousin.

And when the recruit then asked, as recruits before him always had, what kind of fighters the Greeks were, Tiller simply said, as he always said: 'They're fierce. And stubborn. I should know. I'm married to one', which delighted the class because they had been told that that was exactly what he would say.

Finally they asked, as others before them always had, about Tiller's legendary detachment commander, the Dane, a man without any military training who had won two Military Crosses. And Tiller told them about Larssen, and his genius for killing Germans, and what his favourite saying was.

'"Work before women", he always said, and he was bloody right. You idle lot of loafers just remember that. Now don't waste my time any more. Get out of here and on to the parade ground. At the double. I'll give you ninety seconds to get fell in. You're in the Royal Marines, not some bleeding pussyfooting army regiment. And don't you ever forget it.'

OTHER TITLES IN SERIES FROM 22 BOOKS

Available now at newsagents and booksellers
or use the order form provided

continued overleaf . . .

All at £4.99 net

All 22 Books are available at your bookshop, or can be ordered from:

22 Books
Mail Order Department
Little, Brown and Company
Brettenham House
Lancaster Place
London WC2E 7EN

Please enclose a cheque or postal order made payable to Little, Brown and Company (UK) for the amount due, allowing for postage and packing.

UK, BFPO & EIRE CUSTOMERS: Please allow 75p per item, to a maximum of £7.50.
OVERSEAS CUSTOMERS: Please allow £1 per item.

While every effort is made to keep prices low, it is sometimes necessary to increase cover prices at short notice. 22 Books reserves the right to show new retail prices on covers which may differ from those previously advertised in the books or elsewhere.

NAME . . . .

ADDRESS . . . .

. . . .

. . . .

I enclose my remittance for £. . . . .